Valor felt a blush rise and looked down and away
from his mesmerizing gaze.

With a sweep of his hand, he dispersed his natural
faery dust into the air. It glittered and hung
suspended about them like millions of tiny stars
fallen to earth.

Wow. Talk about instant romance. And, yes, she
was a woman who could appreciate a little
romance when it presented itself.

"Impressive. You know I'm an air witch. But I *can*
do this." She swept her hands up and water
surrounded them in dotted columns, catching
Kelyn's dust and the moonlight. They stood on a
rock star's stage.

"Stunning. You win the magic portion of this
evening. But now it's my turn. And I can't think of
anything I'd rather do than this."

Kelyn coaxed her up against his chest and locked
her in his gaze once more before he bent and
kissed her.

THE WITCH'S QUEST

MICHELE HAUF

First Published in Great Britain 2017
By Mills & Boon, an imprint of HarperCollins*Publishers*
1 London Bridge Street, London, SE1 9GF

© 2017 Michele Hauf

ISBN 978-0-263-93021-4

89-1017

Our policy is to use papers that are natural, renewable and recyclable products and made from wood grown in sustainable forests. The logging and manufacturing processes conform to the legal environmental regulations of the country of origin.

Printed and bound in Spain
by CPI, Barcelona

Michele Hauf is a *USA TODAY* bestselling author who has been writing romance, action-adventure and fantasy stories for more than twenty years. France, musketeers, vampires and faeries usually populate her stories. And if Michele followed the adage "write what you know," all her stories would have snow in them. Fortunately, she steps beyond her comfort zone and writes about countries and creatures she has never seen. Find her on Facebook, Twitter and at www.michelehauf.com.

This one is for my kids, Ashley and Jesse.
My two favorite examples of nice.

Chapter 1

The gnarled oak tree behind her looked...angry.

Valor Hearst straightened her shoulders and tried to avoid turning around to cast a glance at the disgruntled tree. Because the moment she started to look closer, things could become real. Especially in an enchanted forest such as the Darkwood.

She knelt on the forest floor, carefully plucking the *Amanita muscaria* mushrooms from a thick and curly frosting of moss. Normally, she would wear gloves to remove the poisonous red-capped shrooms, but having forgotten them, she instead used an entomologist's tweezers.

Dried yet still-glossy trails from snails streaked across a head-size fieldstone, which she scraped into a plastic baggie. The powder would serve as another fine ingredient for future spells. She'd decided that since she had risked coming here, she'd take a few minutes to gather spell ingredients before settling down to do the real work: enacting a spell that would, with hope, lure love her way.

Valor had never dared enter the Darkwood, but on this day she was feeling her confidence and was pretty sure that the warnings against witches venturing into the enchanted forest were nothing more than blather. Mortals and other paranormals visited the darkly mysterious woods all the time. She was no different from any of them. Save that her air magic packed a wallop when need be.

"So take that," she said, yet still couldn't avoid a suspicious glance over her shoulder.

Had the tree's bark curved downward in chunky folds to form a craggy frown? She narrowed her gaze, which was followed by her own frown. The bark hadn't been shaped that way when she first knelt down before the mushrooms.

Maybe?

"Quit spooking yourself," she muttered. "Crazy witch."

The Darkwood was off-limits to and unsafe for witches. That was what her friend and fellow earth witch Eryss Norling had said to her last night when they closed the Decadent Dames brewery together and wandered out to the parking lot under the half-moon.

Valor happened to be attracted to most things that were off-limits and unsafe. Whether they be events, challenges or even men. Most especially men.

She tucked the red-capped mushrooms into her fishing tackle box. It was painted in olive green camo and might have a fishhook or two in it, as well—ice fishing in the wintertime? Yes, please. But she mostly used it to collect herbs and spell ingredients. A tiny jade cricket that she had disturbed from sleeping under a mushroom leaped onto the edge of the tackle box.

"You're lucky you have a heartbeat," she said to the insect. "Otherwise, I'd pulverize your wings and use the dust in a spell."

The insect chirped and hopped off to a more private leaf.

And Valor pulled out a small mason jar half-filled with angel dust to use as a marker for the ritual sigil she now intended to create. A collection of rose petals she had gathered surreptitiously from a floral shop before heading out here today would also serve in the design.

No time to back out now. She'd come here with the intent of finally serving herself what she deserved. "Here's to love."

Cupping a handful of fine angel dust and funneling it through her curled fingers, she marked out on the thick moss the pattern that she'd studied in her great-grandma Hector's grimoire. Small, smoky quartz crystals were then placed at the compass points and rose quartz along the borders of the sigil. She kissed and blessed the flower petals, then placed them on the moss.

Leaning back to inspect her work, she decided the design looked much like a voodoo *veve*. But this sacred sigil, infused with her light magic, would wield so much more power.

She didn't notice the darkening sky as she laid a crow foot, a mouse rib and a dried rat heart at the center of the sigil. Red and pink candles were tucked into the moss, and with a snap of her fingers they ignited. So she had a little fire magic to her arsenal, as well. It was just for small tasks. A witch should never risk invoking more fire than she could handle.

Now the invocation—

Valor's hand slipped on the thick moss, and her leg suddenly slid out from under her kneeling position. She hadn't made such a move. Something tugged her ankle roughly.

She slapped the moss with both palms and yelped as her body slid backward across the forest floor, dragging her hands through angel dust, petals and crystals. Twisting at the waist, she searched in the dimming light. One of the tree roots had wrapped about her ankle, clasping the leather combat boot in a painful pinch.

"What in all the goddess's bad hair days?" She kicked at the root with her free foot.

And then the frowning bark opened wide and growled at her. The tree had a merciless hold on her. And the root only grew tighter about her ankle.

Valor had heard of faery trees. And this woods was a place where the *sidhe* mingled with those from the mortal realm. Another reason she'd been warned away. Faeries who did not live in the mortal realm generally didn't like witches.

She hadn't an enchanted sword to cut her way free. But she did have witchcraft.

"Loftus!"

Her air magic whisked over the ancient tree bark with the waning effect of a whisper. And the tree actually seemed to chuckle as its trunk heaved and the bark crinkled. The root about her ankle tugged again and her boot disappeared into the soft, loamy ground at the base of the tree.

She groped for the moss, on which the candles had extinguished and the angel dust sigil had been disturbed.

It was out of her reach. So was her tackle box, in which she'd stashed her cell phone.

This was bad. On a scale of one to ten for oh-my-mercy-this-is-bad, this probably rated a seventy.

"I'm fucked."

Valor had parked on a turnoff from the gravel road that wound about three hundred yards away from a highway. It was set near a gape in the forest and not easily seen or even known about. At the time, she'd been pleased that no one would see her car. And she'd entered the forest from the opposite end of the woods where Blade Saint-Pierre lived for the specific reason she hadn't wanted anyone to think she was trespassing. That vampire did not own the forest, but he acted as a sort of portal guardian, keeping others out of the forest.

For their own good.

Witches and the Darkwood? Not cool.

Valor tugged futilely at her pinned legs. Yes, now both were being sucked slowly down into the earth beneath the tree. She'd been here two hours for sure, and no matter how she tugged she remained pinned into the mossy ground by the oak roots. And that was exactly what had happened. She'd been *pinned* by a faery tree.

What she knew about such wicked magic was that eventually she'd be sucked completely into the earth and, perhaps, even into Faery. But she wouldn't make the journey alive. And judging by how far in she'd been drawn, she suspected the process generally took less than a day. She didn't even want to calculate how much time she had left.

She'd tried speaking a releasement spell. That had only bothered the crows perched in the crooked elm boughs overhead. They stared with beady black eyes at her like vultures waiting for carrion. She'd tried apologizing to the universe for stepping on sacred faery grounds. She'd felt the earth shudder then and had quietly lain there, palms clutching at the dried leaves and undergrowth, her cheek wet with tears.

All she'd wanted to do was invoke a spell. For her. For once in her long lifetime, she'd finally thought about herself and what she wanted.

Eyes closed now, she thought the loamy scent of moss and earth were too rich for such a fool as herself. The crisp promise of crystal clear water babbled from somewhere behind her. Even the bird chirps seemed to admonish her for being an idiot.

Would her friends think it was odd she did not show up for work tonight at the brewery? Of course Eryss would wonder. Give her a call. But Valor often did not answer her phone. Eryss would shrug and figure Valor had forgotten. It was a Thursday night. Never too busy. Instead of a staff of three, the Decadent Dames could easily manage the microbrewery with two.

They might not bother to drive by her loft at the edge of town in Tangle Lake until the next day when Valor didn't show up to help carry in a delivery of grains that was expected to arrive in the afternoon.

She'd be dead by then. Even now she sensed her energy waning, seeping from her. Bleeding her life into the ground.

"Stupid tree," she muttered. "A simple lash across the face would have served me well enough."

But she knew faeries—and their trees, for they were alive and sentient—never did anything half-assed. Be it mischief or unspeakable malice, it was either all-in or all-out.

Clasping the moonstone amulet she always wore strung from a leather cord about her neck, she bowed her head to the leaves on the forest floor before her. It was time to start thinking of leaving a message for her friends. Who may eventually find her decayed corpse still pinned to this earth, perhaps one clawing hand still sticking out from the ground, surrounded by the malevolent tree roots.

"Aggh!" She had to stop thinking of how dire her end would be. That wouldn't solve anything.

Valor grabbed a thin branch and decided the moss was so thick she could probably write in it. No. It would never work. The mason jar of angel dust sat two feet out of her reach. So blood was the next option. And her parchment? A wide maple leaf.

She broke the branch in two and was holding the serrated end poised to stab at her skin when the rapid beating of hooves alerted her. She glanced up and just had time to tuck her face against the leaves as the sleek doe beat a path toward her. The deer probably hadn't expected a nonanimal to be sitting in the forest, so the beast hadn't much time to correct her trajectory. Valor sensed the deer's surprise as her front hoof nearly stepped on her hand and she leaped high and over Valor's head.

Muttering a quiet oath and a quick blessing of thanks, Valor followed the deer's path. Then it occurred to her that something might have been after it. She swiftly turned and spied the man running toward her, a blur of gold and green. When he was but twenty feet away from her, he suddenly halted, appearing to put on the brakes as a runner in an animated cartoon would, heels skidding and body lagging behind as his speed dropped from swift to stop.

"Whoa!" Valor stretched up a hand to stop him. Which she realized was ridiculous because he'd already stopped.

Tall and lithe and not wearing a shirt, he gave a shrug of one shoulder that stretched his sleek, tight muscles up and down his abdomen. His arms twitched as he looked her over. His face was angular and cut with sharp cheekbones and a prominent slash of brow line. Short blond hair, blown wild and wavy by his racing speed, settled about his ears and forehead. Hip-hugging gray jeans revealed he was barefoot. And his abs were sculpted with more muscle than Valor could imagine what to do with. On those abs were traced violet sigils that she knew were faery in nature. And there, braceleting his wrists, were more faery sigils.

But she didn't fear him. She *knew* him.

"Valor?" And he knew her.

Kelyn Saint-Pierre padded up to her with a lanky ease that spoke more of a wild animal's gait than that of a human. Of course, he wasn't human; he was faery.

He swept a hand over his forehead, pushing the hair from his face. His violet eyes took her in from tangled brown-violet hair, moss-smudged cheek and faded green T-shirt to—her combat boots were well underground right now. It was too dark now for him to see into the shadows where all the horrible pinning action had occurred.

His expression switched from surprise to concern. "What's a witch doing in the Darkwood? Don't you know this forest is dangerous to your kind?"

So state the obvious.

Kelyn lived in the area, and she knew his sister and three brothers. Daisy Blu, a faery who had once been a werewolf, was married to Beck Severo. Valor had gone to Daisy's baby shower a month ago.

Blade was the brother who lived at the edge of this forest. That guy was a vampire but sported gothic wings that would give anyone a fright. And Stryke was a pack leader in a northern suburb.

Trouble, the eldest of the Saint-Pierre siblings, was a werewolf to the bone. And Valor and Trouble were drinking buddies who got together once in a while for Netflix and pizza. Guys like Trouble were meant for fishing trips and shooting the shit, never romance.

Summoning her pride, Valor tossed her long violet-streaked hair over a shoulder and lifted her chin. She was still able to lean on an elbow, but she knew she looked pitiful all the same. "I was just out for a walk."

Kelyn crossed his arms before his chest. His haughty posture and smirk spoke his assessment of her situation much louder than words could.

"You know," she continued casually. "Collecting some ingredients for spells. Communing with nature." She patted the moss. "Doing…witch stuff." It was difficult not to wince. Witch stuff? Ugh. She was never good at the lie. But, oh, so talented with getting herself into strange fixes.

Case in point: the witch pinned by the oak tree.

"I can see that." He made a show of peering over the ground. "Looks like a spell sigil to me. Witch stuff, eh?" Tucking his hands behind his back, Kelyn leaned forward in an admonishing teacher pose and said to her, "You know that witch stuff is the worst you could manage here in the Darkwood? The mortal realm powers you possess clash terribly with the faery energies that inhabit every inch of this woods."

"I'm not working magic at the moment. Just—" A glance to the angel-dust sigil and scattered ingredients proved her guilt. "What do you want, Kelyn? Don't you have a deer to chase?"

He righted himself and laughed. "We were racing. She won."

Right. The man was faery. And Valor knew he had wings. Trouble had told her they were big and silver and violet, and that Kelyn was ever proud of them. She also knew that of all four Saint-Pierre brothers, Kelyn was the strongest and most powerful. Or so Trouble had told her during a drunken game of truth or dare one night.

To judge by Kelyn's lean, lithe appearance, Valor had to wonder about such skills and strength. Sure, he looked riveted together with a factory gun and sculpted from solid marble, but Valor always tended toward the beefier, broader sorts. With dark hair. Always. A blond? Never had an interest.

On the other hand, why was she limiting her options when the reason she'd come to the Darkwood was to cast a spell for love?

Propping her chin in a hand and twisting at the hip to look more casual, she asked, "You go running through this forest often?"

Surely, he had noticed that her legs were sucked into the ground up to her knees, but she had a difficult time asking anyone for help. She was woman. Hear her roar!

She hated coming off as the weak one. The stupid witch who'd gone to the Darkwood without telling anyone.

"I do go for a run a few times a week. This woods is special to me." He smoothed a hand absently down his abs, which drew Valor's eye to the violet sigils. They looked like intricate mandalas, and she knew they were the source of his faery magic. "You talk to Trouble lately?"

"No," she answered defensively. Not sure why, though. She had no reason to be defensive. Kelyn must have known that she and Trouble were friends. "You?"

Stupid witch. Why was she making light conversation?

"Couple days ago. He never mentions you."

"Why should he?"

Kelyn shrugged a shoulder and cast his glance to the ground, his gaze stretching behind her. She shouldn't have said that. It was the truth, though. She considered him a friend. Just that.

"You look…stuck," he said. Suddenly, his gaze went fierce and he looked over her shoulder.

"What's—"

Before she could summon a stupid excuse, Valor heard the roar. A beastly, slobbery utterance accompanied by a foul, greasy odor that filled the air as if a stink bomb had been set off.

Kelyn leaped, and in midair his wings unfurled. The gorgeous violet-and-silver appendages lifted him with a flap or two and he met the creature that had jumped high to collide with him in a crush of growls and slapping body parts. The twosome landed on the ground ten feet before Valor, the heavy weight of Kelyn's opponent denting the moss and tearing up clods of sod.

Valor dug her fingers into the leaves and whispered a protection spell that drew a white light over her body and snapped against her form. The oak tree growled at the intrusion and she felt her knees get sucked deeper into the earth. The tree seemed to feed off her witch magic. And in the next instant, the protection shattered, like plastic crinkling over her skin, and it fell away.

Never had she felt so helpless. Pray to the goddess, Kelyn could defeat the aggressor, which was five times his size and built like a bear. It was a troll of some sort. Or so she guessed. She'd never seen one but knew they existed.

Kelyn punched the creature in its barrel gut. The troll yowled and kicked Kelyn off, sending the faery flying through the air where a flap of his wings stopped him from crashing into the tree canopy. Aiming for the troll, Kelyn arrowed down and landed a kick to the thing's blocky head.

Valor slapped her hands over her head in protection, but it didn't matter. Every moment that passed, she felt her body move minutely deeper into the cold, compressing earth.

With one final punch to its spine from Kelyn's fist, the troll went down, landing on the moss in a sprawl. It shuddered like a gelatinous gray glob of Thanksgiving Jell-O, and then, with an explosion of faery dust that decorated the air, it dissipated.

And behind the glittering shimmer stood Kelyn, wiping the dust from his arms and abs as if he had only tussled with a minor annoyance.

Valor couldn't stop looking around at the scatter of dust that glinted madly. More beautiful than she would imagine coming from such an atrocious creature. It almost put the angel dust to shame.

Kelyn approached. "What was it you were saying about muscled men rescuing you?"

"I didn't…" She'd not said anything about being rescued. But really? She might have to change her tune about the leaner versions.

"You didn't what? Ask for rescue? Looks like you might be in need of just that."

"I'm cool." Why had she said that? Why the need to act as though death were not dragging her down into the earth?

Kelyn squatted before her, arms resting on his thighs. "I can't win with you, can I, Valor?"

"What do you mean? Win?"

"You're a hard woman to please, is all."

"No, I'm not. All it takes is some good dark coffee to make me happy."

"Coffee served up with muscles. Like my brother Trouble has?"

"What? What is it with you and your concern about me and Trouble? We only ever—"

He put up a hand to stop her from saying more. "Don't need the details."

"There are no details."

Okay, well, there had been that one time. But she wasn't stupid enough to fill the brother in on the salacious stuff. Trouble had probably already done that.

"I really liked you," Kelyn said, looking aside now. He'd dropped his shoulders, and the sweat and troll dust glistening on his abs drew Valor's eye. "For a while there."

"What do you mean?" She met his lift of chin and then figured it out. "You mean…?"

He shrugged. "But then you tripped into my brother's arms and that's all she wrote. I always manage to lose the girl to him. What is it about him? He's a big lunk!"

Valor smiled at that assessment. Trouble did have some lunkish qualities. Okay, a lot of lunkish qualities.

But she had no idea Kelyn had…lusted after her? "Your brother and I are not in a relationship."

"Trouble is never *in* relationships," Kelyn said sharply.

Now he eyed her legs and squinted. He bent to study behind her, and there was nothing Valor could do to stop him, because she was stuck there.

"You've been pinned!" He gripped her by the shoulders. "What the hell? Why didn't you say something? I thought you were just lying around, digging up—whatever weird stuff it is you witches dig up in forests. Did you plan on staying here the rest of the night without saying anything?"

"I don't have much of a choice. I'm stuck! And my phone is in the spell box, which got crushed by the falling troll. I was prepared to die out here until you came along. And then your abs distracted me and I forgot to ask for help."

"Really?" He gave her the most unbelieving look ever and slapped a hand over his glittery abs. "*That's* your story?"

She nodded. "And I'm sticking to it."

"You're pinned, Valor! That only ever ends in death. How did this happen?"

"I was minding my own business, plucking some mushrooms—"

"Minding your own…? You were performing a spell!"

"Maybe."

"Valor! Even if you weren't, you've taken things." He gestured to the mangled tackle box. "Nothing should ever be taken out from the Darkwood. Especially not for magics that are not faery blessed."

"You wouldn't mind offering me a blessing or two right about now, would you?" she asked sheepishly.

Kelyn laughed softly. "I haven't such power."

"Stop laughing. It's not funny. I'm going to die here. I don't know how to get unpinned. My legs… They're getting sucked deeper and deeper. Kelyn…"

Now she surrendered to the worrying reality of imminent death. She gasped and heaved in breaths quickly. Was this what a panic attack felt like?

Kelyn gripped her by the shoulders and she had to crane her neck awkwardly to meet his delving gaze. In that moment, Valor wished she'd known about his affection toward her. He was a handsome man. And a kind one, from what she knew about him. Always volunteering around town, and he helped rehabilitate injured raptors from what she remembered Trouble telling her. The complete opposite of his boisterous and cocky older brother.

Curse her attraction to the bad boys.

"I can go for help," he said.

She grabbed his forearms, keeping him there before her. If he left her alone, she'd die. Already she had been consumed up to her thighs. "Get help from who? There's no one who can help me but a faery. You're a faery. Can't you do something? Your magic works in this forest."

He sighed heavily and shook his head. "I can fly and I've strength immeasurable and can even work some cool spells with my sigils, but I am mortal-realm-born. I've not half the power of those from Faery. And if you've been pinned by a faery tree, then you are in need of serious enchantment to get free. How long have you been here?"

"A couple hours? I came here around six."

"It's almost midnight, Valor."

"Shit. I'll be dead before morning."

"I won't let that happen."

He was sweet. But if he had no faery powers to defeat this pinning, she didn't know what he could do. She'd already insulted him once. She didn't intend to go to her maker having insulted him a second time. "Thanks. Maybe… Could you try my cell phone?"

"Where is it?"

"In my box."

Picking through the crushed plastic tackle box, he found the purple phone, but with a few taps at the cracked screen, he announced, "It's dead. Technology doesn't work here in the Darkwood. Hey, Blade's place is at the other end of the forest. I can run there and make a call—"

"No." She stretched out an arm, her fingers groping desperately. Kelyn's fingers threaded with hers. It was a natural clasp, something that felt hopeless yet bolstered her courage a little. "I don't want to be alone. Just stay with me, please?"

"Of course I will." He folded his legs and sat before her, not releasing her hand from his calming clasp. "We'll think about this. We'll come up with something."

"Actually, what I want you to do is listen to the things I need you to tell my friends."

Kelyn bracketed her face fiercely. "Don't talk like that. You will not die."

"Lying about my fate isn't going to change it. I did a stupid thing. The universe renders payment for stupidity."

"You were not stupid. Just…stubborn."

"So you've heard about me?" She tried a little laugh and it actually eased the tension between her shoulder blades. Valor blew out a breath.

And in that moment, when she knew death was her only option, she decided she couldn't walk out of this world without one last thing. "Kiss me," she said suddenly.

"What?"

"You want to, don't you? I mean, if you had a thing for me?"

"I did, but…"

"Please, Kelyn? I want the last thing I remember to be a kiss from a handsome man. I want to be held in strong arms. I want to know passion—"

And he kissed her. The sudden connection seared a delicious heat onto Valor's lips. Kelyn's arm wrapped across her back as he slid down onto the moss beside her and pulled her in tightly against his hard body. His other hand clutched at her hair. Hungrily she took from him, falling into his sweet taste, his open and easy manner. He felt like something she'd always wanted but had never known to ask for.

Why had she never noticed he'd been attracted to her?

Because she'd been too busy tagging along with the bad boys. Or those men who could only ever consider her one of the guys.

When he parted from her, their eyes lingered upon each other, as if to look away would end the kiss, their connection—her life. So they held gazes in the quiet darkness, dappled by a beam of moonlight that sifted through the latent troll dust in the air about them.

The squeezing pressure about her thighs moved higher, yet all Valor could do was whisper, "Wow."

Kelyn nodded. He touched her lips and held his fingers there for the longest time. She closed her eyes to fix this moment forever. She must. She would die with the taste of his kiss on her mouth.

"Best kiss I've ever had," he said.

She nodded and closed her eyes even tighter, fighting tears. Damn right it had been the best.

"Ah, shit."

That remark sent a frozen chill up her spine. Valor could feel Kelyn's sudden tension and she knew they were not alone. *Please don't be another troll*, she thought. Slowly she opened her eyes to see the pair of red irises that loomed over the two of them.

Chapter 2

Kelyn stepped before Valor, protecting her from the demon who had appeared in the forest. It was one of the Wicked; Kelyn knew that because the creature had red eyes. The Wicked were faeries who possessed demon heritage. Demons were looked down upon in Faery, and so the Wicked were condemned and ridiculed. This one must have been ousted from Faery. Not an uncommon thing.

Seeming to blend with the shadows that angled between the thin moonbeams, the demon topped Kelyn by a head, yet its narrow shoulders, clothed in frayed black, were deceptive in that most demons were strong and quite capable of standing up to any opponent.

"We mean you no harm," Kelyn said coolly, yet maintained a sharp edge. He set back his shoulders. He would not be defeated by a demon. "I've no prejudice against any of your kind. Move along."

"Prejudices," the demon said in a slippery tone. The dark-faced entity smirked, its black lips crimping. "You ascribe to prejudice simply by mentioning it. Unwanted one."

Kelyn did not flinch at the moniker. He'd never been allowed access to Faery. His mother was a faery and his father a werewolf. Because he'd been born in the mortal realm, Faery was not open to him. Though he'd always pined to go there. To learn about his true heritage.

The demon tilted a look toward the ground, taking in Valor, pinned to the forest floor by the elder oak. "Looks like she's in a pinch."

"Nothing we can't handle," Kelyn said. "Right, Valor?"

"Uh, yep. We're good!"

"A witch and a faery," the demon said. "Pretty." He narrowed his gaze at Kelyn's neck, where he always wore two talismans on leather cords. "Interesting. You've been to Faery?"

"No," Kelyn answered.

"But that talisman." The demon tapped his own neck.

"A gift. Now, enough of this. Begone with you!"

"Very well. But you'll never get her loose. She's been pinned through to Faery."

"How do you know? What does that mean?" Valor rushed out.

"It means you must be unpinned *from* Faery," the demon explained.

Sensing the demon wasn't so much being helpful as teasing at the dreadful future that awaited Valor, Kelyn did not relent in his stance before her and only wished he'd brought along his bow and arrows this evening. But he could take this dark creature. Easily.

The demon eyed Kelyn's clenched fist. "You said you meant me no harm."

"I'll do what I must to defend her."

"Touching. The dying witch has a faery champion."

"Leave!" Kelyn said. "Take your smirk into the shadows and let us figure this out alone."

"As you wish." The demon stepped back and spread his elongated hands out before him. "But, unlike you, I have access to Faery. I can get into Faery and unpin her. If you wish it."

Valor didn't say anything, and Kelyn was thankful she hadn't rushed to beg the demon for the help.

But really? If the Wicked could get Valor unpinned, he'd be willing to do anything. Even take a few spiteful punches, if necessary. Because Valor's life was at stake. And she hadn't much time remaining. Her hips were beginning to sink into the ground.

"You tell me true?" Kelyn asked.

The demon nodded. "I am not heartless. And…you have something I want." Again the demon's eyes glanced across Kelyn's chest where the talismans hung.

Of course such assistance would not be provided without recompense. Which was fair enough, Kelyn thought. He felt Valor's hopeful breaths taint the air. She needed rescue and he would not leave this forest without her in his arms. Alive.

"What might that be?" Kelyn asked the sly demon.

The demon smiled and walked before him, turning in a half circle before coming around to face them both and saying, "Your wings."

"No!" Valor yelled from behind Kelyn.

"That's the deal. Take it or leave it," the demon said.

"We don't—"

"Valor," Kelyn said to shush her. "Be still."

"You can't give him your wings. They are what make you…you! That's a terrible thing to ask in trade for—"

"For a life?" the demon interjected. "Seems more than fair to me. But if you're not keen on breathing, witch, then so be it."

The demon's eyes glimmered vivid pink. He was preparing to flash out of the forest as swiftly and quietly as he had appeared.

"Wait!" Kelyn reacted from his heart and soul, not his better senses. "You can have them."

The demon smiled.

"Absolutely not!" Valor punched the ground with an ineffectual fist.

Kelyn turned to face her, and the spill of tears down her cheeks startled him. Wasn't she the feisty tomboy of the group of witches who owned a local brewery? The one who hung around with Sunday and fixed cars and motorbikes, and never met a greasy engine she didn't want to take apart?

Or so he'd heard. He'd made it a point to listen when Valor was spoken about. Because he had lusted after her. Had wanted to ask her out. And almost did. Until… Trouble.

But with the lingering taste of her kiss still on his lips, he couldn't deny that those feelings had not grown any lesser.

"You are not going to sacrifice your wings for me," Valor said on a desperate pleading tone. "Just go! Get out of here!"

"And allow you to die? I am a better man than that. It's not my nature to walk away when I can help."

"Help? No! Just no! I couldn't live with myself if you gave up your wings to save me."

"Well, you're going to have to."

He tugged his ankle away from her grasping, pleading hands and turned to the demon. With an inhale that shivered through his system and tweaked at his back between his shoulder blades where his wings could unfurl, he grasped decisiveness. "We have a deal. But you will promise you'll go immediately to Faery and unpin Valor."

"With your wings in hand, my entrance to Faery will be secured. The moment you hand them over to me, I will leave and unpin your tragic lover."

Kelyn almost said "She's not my lover," but semantics were less important than getting this cruel task completed. Because to sacrifice his wings would be like handing over himself. He'd become lesser. Not even the faery he was now. He would lose…

Kelyn held out his hands. The violet sigils that circled his wrists were a match for those sigils on his chest. They were his magic. His strength. As were his wings.

But to walk away from a helpless woman when he had a means to save her?

"Do it," Kelyn said firmly.

The demon thrust out his arm, and in his blackened hand materialized a gleaming sword of violet light. "Kneel, faery."

Feeling the intense *sidhe* magic that emanated from the weapon shimmer in his veins, Kelyn dropped to his knees, his side facing the demon.

"No" gasped from Valor's lips.

Lips he'd kissed, and on which he'd tasted a sweet promise. But he must never taste that promise again. He couldn't bear it.

"Do it!" he yelled.

And his wings shivered as he unfurled them and stretched them out behind him into the fresh spring air. Moonlight glamorized the sheer violet appendages, glinting in the silver support structure that held a close resemblance to dragonfly wings.

The violet blade swept the night. Ice burned through Kelyn's body as blade met wing, bone, skin and muscle, and severed each of the four wings cleanly from his back. Overwhelmed by a searing agony, Kelyn choked back the urge to scream and dropped forward onto his elbows. His fingers dug deep into the cool moss. He gritted his jaw, biting the edges of his tongue.

Behind him, Valor screamed.

He wasn't aware as the demon gripped his severed wings and, in a shimmer of malevolence, flashed out of the Darkwood.

Bile curdled up Kelyn's throat. His stomach clenched. His wingless back muscles pulsed in search of flight. Clear ichor, speckled with his innate faery dust, spilled over his shoulders and dribbled down his arms to the backs of his hands. The violet sigils about his wrists glowed and then…flashed away, leaving his skin faintly scarred where the magical markings had been since birth.

The witch muttered some sort of incantation that felt like a desperate blessing wrapped in black silk and tied too tightly for Kelyn to access.

He wanted to scream. To die. To curse the witch. To curse his own stupidity.

But what he instead did was nod and suck back the urge to vomit. The task had been done.

He would not look back.

Suddenly Valor's body lunged forward, her hands landing on his bare feet. The tree roots had spat her up, purging her from the earth. She scrambled over them alongside him. The demon had kept his word, unpinning her from the Faery side.

Good, then. His sacrifice had been worth it.

"Oh, my goddess. Your wings." Valor gasped. "I... Kelyn?"

"Go," he said tightly.

"What?"

"Leave me, witch! Get out of this forest and never return. This is not a place for you. Be thankful for your life."

"Yes, but—I'm thankful for what you've—"

"We will never speak of this again," he said forcefully. Still, he crouched over the mossy ground, unwilling and unable to twist his head and face the witch. "Please, Valor," he said softly. "Go."

If she did not leave, he would never rise. He didn't want her to see him wingless and broken. Hobbled by his necessity for kindness, to not abandon a condemned woman.

"You need someone to look after those wounds," she said. "I might be able to find a proper healing spell if you'll walk out of here with me."

"I need you to leave," he insisted sharply. "I will walk out of the Darkwood on my own. When I am able. Do you understand?"

He sensed she nodded. The witch's footsteps backed away from him. She uttered a sound, as if she would again protest, and then the soft *cush* of her boots crushing moss moved her away from him.

And Kelyn let out his breath and collapsed onto the forest floor.

Chapter 3

Two months later

Valor walked down the street, her destination was the gas station on the corner. She had a craving for something sweet and icy that at least resembled food and that would probably give her a stomachache. It was what she deserved.

When she spied the classic black Firebird cruise by, she picked up her pace and then halted on the sidewalk but a dash from the parking lot where the car had pulled in to stop before a hardware store. That was Kelyn Saint-Pierre's car. His brother Blade had fixed up the 1970s' vehicle with spare parts and a wicked talent for auto body reconstruction. She knew it was Kelyn's car because she'd been trying to speak to him for months. Ever since their harrowing encounter in the Darkwood.

When he had sacrificed his wings for her.

She wanted him to know she had not taken that sacrifice lightly. That it meant something to her. But she didn't have a clue how to tell him that. To not make it sound like a simple yet dismissive "Hey, thanks." And she'd been racking her brain for ways to repay him. But how did one offer something equal to the wings that were once his very identity?

She'd researched faeries and their wings. Wings were integral to their existence; when faeries lost them, they lost so much more. Like their innate strength and power. And sometimes even the ability to shift to small size, as the majority of faeries could do. And Kelyn could never again fly.

The man had to be devastated. And now, as she watched him get out of his car and stride toward the hardware store, Valor couldn't push herself to rush after him. But she had to. She owed him.

A tight grip about her upper arm stalled her from taking another step toward apologizing to Kelyn. Valor turned and shrugged out of Trouble Saint-Pierre's pinching hold. Built like an MMA fighter, the man exuded a wily menace that also disturbed her need to give him a hug. They had once been friends.

Had been.

"What?" She rubbed her arm. He hadn't been gentle.

"You looking to talk to my brother?"

"Yes," she said defensively.

Bravery sluiced out of her heart and trickled down to puddle in her combat boots. Trouble was the sort of man who could be imposing even when asleep. The two of them had once been drinking buddies. Now he avoided her as much as Kelyn did.

"I have to—"

"No, you don't," he interrupted with that gruff but commanding tone that warned he meant business. "You stay the hell away from my brother. You've done him enough damage."

"But I want to apologize. I know I've hurt him. Trouble!"

He shoved her aside and strode toward his brother's car, but as he stalked away, he turned and thrust an admonishing finger at her. And Valor flinched as if he'd released magic from that accusing fingertip.

She would not give up. There had to be a way to get Kelyn's wings back for him. And she wouldn't rest until she did.

Two months later

It had now been four months since that fateful night in the forest, and Kelyn had survived the loss with his head held high and his dignity intact. He could no longer shift to small size, nor could he fly. The faery sigils had disappeared from his wrists and chest, rendering his magic ineffective. But he still had his dust and—well, that was about it. His strength? Gone. When once he could beat Trouble at arm wrestling in but a blink, now his brother did his best not to win, even though Kelyn knew he was faking.

And he'd lost his connection to nature, which had once been as if his very heartbeat. Senses attuned to the world, he'd navigated his surroundings by ley lines and had listened to the wind for direction and tasted water in the stream for clues to weather and more. As a result of losing his wings, he now always felt lost.

But he wouldn't bemoan his situation or complain or

even suggest to others what a terrible life he now had. Because he was thankful for life. Such as it was.

Sitting in the corner of the local coffee shop, nursing a chai latte, he scanned the local job advertisements in the free paper he'd grabbed before walking inside. Much as the Saint-Pierre children had never needed to work, thanks to their parents' forethought to invest for each of the five of them when they were born, he now needed… something. He hadn't volunteered at The Raptor Center since losing his wings. It felt wrong to stand in the presence of such awesome nature and feel so lacking. And with the proper care, those birds could heal and then fly away. Something he could never hope to do again.

So, what could a faery who wasn't really a faery anymore do with himself? His utter uselessness weighed heavily on his shoulders. He needed to do something. To move forward, occupy his thoughts and forget about what haunted him every second of every minute of every day.

Lately, he wasn't even interested in women. Because though he never revealed he was faery to the mortal women he had dated, he still felt different. Set apart. And he couldn't get excited about going to a bar or dancing or even a hookup when that missing part of him ached.

It did ache. His back, where his wings had been severed, put out a constant dull throb. Always reminding him of the wings he once had.

Closing his eyes and tilting his head back against the café wall, he zoned out the nearby conversations and set the paper on the table. He needed a new start. But he wasn't sure what that implied or how to go about it. Two of his brothers were werewolves involved with their packs. No faeries allowed. And while his interests had tended toward the martial arts and archery, he didn't feel inspired.

When a rustle at his table alerted him, he didn't open his eyes. It was probably the barista refilling his chai. She did it at least twice on the afternoons he parked himself here in the sunny corner away from the restrooms and bustle of the order line.

But when he didn't smell the sweet spices of fresh chai infusing the air, he opened one eyelid. And sat up abruptly, gripping his empty paper cup and looking for an escape route.

"Kelyn, please, give me two minutes. Then I'll leave. Promise."

Valor Hearst sat across the small round table from him, her palms flat on a half piece of blue paper that hadn't been there before. Every hair on Kelyn's body prickled in anger and then disgust. And then…that deep part of him that had compelled him to protect her in the forest emerged and he relaxed his shoulders, allowing in a modicum of calm. And desire.

He nodded but didn't speak.

"Trust me," she said, "I've been wanting to speak to you ever since…" She looked aside, as did he. No one in the town knew what paranormal secrets the two possessed. "But I was scared. And so freaked. And then your brother told me to stay away from you. But I was determined. And now I have it."

She patted the blue paper. "I know how to get your wings back."

"First…" Valor shifted on the metal café seat, uncomfortable and nervous. The blond faery eyed her with a mix of what she guessed was anger and revulsion. Well deserved. "I'm sorry."

"Don't—" he tensed his jaw for a moment, then finished "—say that."

"But I am. Kelyn, I'm sorry for what happened in the forest. It was my fault. I am so grateful to you. And you shouldn't have done it. You should have let me die. I'm just…so, so sorry."

"It was a choice I made. You did not influence me or have a part in that decision one way or another. So stop saying sorry."

"Fine. I'll stop with the *s* word. But listen to me."

"You have approximately thirty seconds remaining of the requested two minutes."

So he was going to be a stickler? Again, his annoyance was well deserved.

"I can help you get back your wings," she said. "I found a spell to open a portal to Faery. It merely requires collecting a few necessary ingredients, and then, voilà! We're in!"

"*We're* in?" He calmly pushed aside the paper cup and leaned forward so they could speak in confidence. Valor smelled his fresh grassy scent and wondered if it was a faery thing or just innately him. Never had a man smelled so appealing to her. And generally a little auto grease or exhaust fumes was all it took for her. She was glad he hadn't stormed out of the café yet. Which he had every right to do. "Do you think I have the desire to trust you?" he asked. "To work alongside you in a fruitless quest? To…to breathe your air?"

She had expected him to hate her. So his harsh words didn't hurt. That much. Yes, they hurt. But they could never harm her as much as she had hurt him.

"I think you should do everything in your power to bring me down," she offered to his question regarding why he should care. "To expose me to humans, if that's your thing. Whatever you do, you have every right to hurt me in return."

"I don't hurt women. I don't take vengeance against one who has not moved to harm me in the first place. I don't…want to believe your silly magic can do as you say."

"My magic is not silly."

"It got you pinned in the Darkwood."

"Yes, well, state the obvious. That was my constant need to prove how stubborn I can be, not my magic. I know now to stay away from that place. By all that is sacred and the great Doctor Gregory House, I have learned my lesson." She tapped the blue paper on the table and leaned in again to speak in quieter tones. "But this spell…it's ancient. I know its source. It will work, Kelyn. Please, give me a chance to help you get back what was taken from you. I want to help you."

"I don't need your restitution, witch." He stood and grabbed the cup. Turning, with a toss, he landed it in the wastebasket eight feet away near the counter display of half-price cookies.

Valor jumped up to stand before Kelyn, blocking his exit. Yet she stood as a mere blade of grass before his powerful build and height. "That kiss you gave me when I thought I was going to die?"

He tilted his head, his eyes—violet, the color of faeries—showing no emotion.

"It changed me," Valor confessed. "I can't say how. It won't matter to you. But it did. And I haven't stopped trying to find the answer for you since then." She pressed the paper to his chest, but he didn't take it, so she tucked it lower, in the waistband of his hip-hugging gray jeans. "Read it. It's a list of ingredients required to conjure the portal spell. When you're ready to give it a try, you know where to find me."

And she turned and walked out, forcing herself not to look back. To call out to him to please make life easier for her by allowing her to try and make his life what it once was. She hadn't told him that she hadn't gone a single night without reliving that kiss before exhaustion silenced those wistful dreams. And that she wished everything had been different, that she'd never entered the Darkwood on her own personal yet fruitless quest. A quest that hadn't been accomplished, and one she'd not dared to attempt since.

When the universe spoke, she listened.

Kelyn Saint-Pierre was a remarkable man. And she might have blown her chances of ever having him trust her. So she crossed her fingers and whispered a plea to the goddess that he might want to give the spell a try. For his sake.

And, okay, for her peace of mind, as well.

The witch left a trail of sweet honey perfume in her wake. Kelyn had heard she was a beekeeper and had, more than a few times, almost gotten up the courage to visit her and ask about beekeeping. Before, that was.

Before was the only way to define his relationship with Valor now. Before he'd lost his wings, and before she'd hooked up with Trouble. Before was when he'd crushed on her and had wanted to ask her out. *Now* was, well, now everything was After. Which was a ridiculous way to go through life.

Why couldn't he put the witch out of his brain and move forward?

He knew the answer to that. And it was probably scrawled on the piece of paper that she'd tucked in his jeans. He tugged it out and crumpled it into a ball. Raising his arm to make a toss toward the wastebasket, he suddenly curled his fingers about the crunchy paper.

The answer as to why he couldn't move forward was that he wasn't done with her yet. They'd been thrown together in the Darkwood by forces beyond their control. And ever since that day, he hadn't been able to *not* think about her. He thought about that desperate kiss. A lot. It had been different from any other kiss he'd taken or had been given by a woman. Weirdly claiming. And achingly right.

He'd never felt that way about a kiss before. Of course, that was Before. Now, if he couldn't accept himself, how could he possibly accept another person into his life, no matter if it was to help him find something lost or for something so simple as another kiss?

He wanted to be brave like his brothers. To be looked up to and admired by women, also like his brothers. He wanted to know his place in this world and walk it with confidence. While all his life he'd found himself standing to the side watching his brothers, until his wings had been stripped away, he'd never felt this heavy weakness and lack that he now did.

Stryke and Trouble were strong, virile werewolves. His brother Blade was a vampire who had a touch of faery in him. Blade even had a set of dark wings. But he hadn't brought them out in Kelyn's presence since he'd lost his wings. Even his sister, Daisy Blu, possessed a strength he admired.

What was he without wings? Self-acceptance was impossible without those very necessary parts of him. They were limbs. And a man who lost a limb truly did lose a part of himself.

Walking outside the café, he uncrumpled the blue paper ball and spread it open. On the top was written in red ink *To Invoke a Portal Sidhe* and below that an ingredient list. Werewolf's claw, water from an unruly lake, a kiss from a mermaid, occipital dust from the Skull of Sidon and true love's first teardrop.

Sounded like a whole lot of bullshit to him. What, exactly, was an unruly lake? But he knew witch magic was weird and steeped in millennia of practice and tradition. And while faeries in the know could access their homeland by opening a portal in a manner to which Kelyn was not privy, there probably did exist a spell to open a portal by other means. And his mother, while she had been born in Faery, had come to this realm decades earlier and could not return, so he hadn't bothered to ask her help. No need to worry her uselessly.

But what, then? Just wander into Faery and collect his wings from the Wicked One to whom he'd freely given them? He'd made a deal: his wings for unpinning Valor. He wouldn't renege on a deal.

As he'd said to Valor, it wasn't her fault. He'd made the choice to make such a sacrifice all by himself.

Eyeing the steel mesh garbage can that stood before the café on the sidewalk, Kelyn held a corner of the blue paper. A soft wind fluttered it like…a wing.

Gulping down a swallow, he shoved the paper in a back pocket and strode toward his car.

A week later

Kelyn still hadn't contacted her. Valor set aside the tin smoking can and leaned against the cinder block wall that edged the rooftop where she kept three stacked beehives. The smoke kept the bees docile so she could check that the queens were healthy and laying eggs. This fall she would have to separate the hives because they had expanded. She'd end up with five hives, which was awesome. And while bees that lived in the city tended to create a diverse and delicious honey, she was rapidly running out of space. She needed a country home, like her beekeeping mentor, Lars Gunderson, where she could manage a larger quantity of bees.

The sun was bright and she needed to cool off, so she left the smoker on the roof and skipped down the iron stairs to her loft. It was set on the third floor of an old factory building. The lower two levels were currently being refurbished and remodeled into apartments. When she'd moved in years earlier, the place was private and vast. But with neighbors soon to occupy the lower floors and the whole neighborhood turning yuppie, her desire to start looking at country real estate increased.

Tugging the heavy corrugated steel door, which was set on a rolling track like a barn door, she shut it behind her. She pulled off the white button-up shirt she'd pulled on over her fitted gray T-shirt. Dark colors attracted bees and angered them, so she always wore white to the roof.

She whistled. Mooshi popped his head up from behind the couch, moving ever so slowly on his adventure through the wild. Cats. So independent sometimes she had to wonder who owned who.

Running her fingers through her hair, she vacillated between bending over the spell books she had to search for a possible coercion spell and calling Sunday to see if she wanted help today with modifying the '67 Corvette Stingray engine. Valor was on a two-week vacation from the brewery, which she appreciated but also always found hard to comply with.

How to get Kelyn to pay attention to her and at least give her a chance at the spell? And why couldn't she simply let this go?

"Restitution," she muttered. The word he'd used so cruelly against her.

Yes, she wanted to pay him back for the horrible thing that had happened *because of her*. No matter what kind of spin he put on it, if she had not been in that position in the Darkwood, he would never have been faced with having to sacrifice his wings.

"What should I do, Mooshi?"

A rap at her door decided for her. "That's what I'll do." She would answer the door.

Maybe it was Sunday. Her best friend, a cat shifter, had promised to stop by one day this week with some red velvet Bundt cakes from the new café in town and a whole lot of car chatter. Sunday was one of her few female friends. Most often Valor got along with men because... she was just one of the guys.

She slapped a hand to her chest. No, she wasn't going to recall that awful thing that had been said to her. The words that had sent her into the Darkwood on a desperate mission.

She was over that now. For good or for ill.

"Definitely not good," she muttered, and tugged open the sliding door.

Kelyn stood before the threshold holding the blue half sheet of paper on which she'd scrawled the spell ingredients. He raked his fingers through his messy hair and met her gaze with his piercing violet eyes. "Let's do this."

Chapter 4

Kelyn followed the witch into a familiar loft. She gestured for him to sit by the industrial steel kitchen counter that stretched a dozen feet and served as a divider between the cooking area and the rest of the vast, open space that made up half the upper floor of an old three-story business building. The businesses had vacated decades ago, and apartments were slowly taking over. Hipsters and yuppies and, apparently, witches, had moved in.

"This used to be my sister, Daisy Blu's, place," he remarked as he slid onto a wooden stool and crossed his arms. Looking over the loft, he recalled that Daisy's decorating sense had been nil, and Valor's wasn't much more evident. Though she did have a motorcycle sitting in the corner before the eight-foot-high windows that overlooked the street. A street bike. Its back fender sat beside it on the floor, and a black metal toolbox sprawled tools beside that.

"Yep. When Daisy moved in with Beck a couple years ago, I grabbed this place. Love it. And the freight elevator fits my bike."

"Nice. So you have no desire to live in Anoka, closer to the brewery?"

"Do you know that Anoka is infested with ghosts? And I have an affinity for seeing ghosts. So not cool. I prefer Tangle Lake. Just far enough away from the suburbs, but I can still get to work in half an hour."

"What is that noise?"

"I'm vacuuming. You should see it swing around soon. It's over behind the bed right now."

"One of those robotic things?"

"Yes. I am allergic to housework, so I have my cat do it."

"Uh-huh." He wasn't even sure where to start with that one, so decided to drop it for now. And a cat? Yeesh. Not his favorite domesticated animal.

Kelyn turned toward the counter to find Valor leaning on it with her elbows. If he were not mistaken, he should take that wide-eyed, dreamy gaze as somewhat smitten. But he probably was mistaken. Reading women was his forte. But reading witches? Not.

"So, this list." He shoved the wrinkled blue paper he'd kept toward her. "That's it?"

"And a few more essentials that are required for most spells. Herbs. Crystals. Rat skulls and angel dust. But I've got all that stuff."

"You have angel dust?" He knew that was a precious commodity and hard to come by.

"Sure. Got some from Zen, your brother's girlfriend. I used it for the spell in the—er…you want a beer?"

If he told the chick who worked at a brewery that beer—any kind of alcohol—wasn't to his taste, and he much preferred water, would that annoy her?

Why was he worried about annoying her? He had no stake in whether or not she liked or hated him. All that mattered was she had a plan to help him get back his wings.

"Just water, please."

She quirked a brow. Judging him. Whatever.

"Fine. I think we should collect the ingredients in the order I've written them for you." She filled a glass of water from the tap and handed it to him. "You know of any werewolves looking to donate a claw?"

"Not willingly. But Trouble does have a beef with a nasty bastard who keeps trying to mark my brother's territory as his own. I could ask him about it. And if you know Trouble…" And he knew she did.

"The guy likes a good fight."

"Always." And that was enough mention of his oldest brother. "So, once we get all these things and you invoke the spell, what, exactly, do we do in Faery?"

"Uh, find your wings?"

He stared at her for the few moments he thought it would take for her to rationalize that insane statement. But in the process, Kelyn got lost in a shimmery brown gleam. Her eyes twinkled like stars during twilight. It couldn't be real. He'd never seen such brilliant eyes before.

The witch snapped her fingers before his face, rudely bringing him up from what he realized was an open-mouthed gape. "Uh…"

"You don't want to find your wings?"

"I do, but Faery is immense. It's larger than…well, the world, I'm sure."

"It's another realm. I get that. But the reason I chose this spell over another that also opened a portal is that this one homes us in on the item we seek. If all goes well, we should walk in. See the wings. Grab them. And get the hell out of Dodge."

"Sounds too easy."

"Sounds like a fun ride on the wild side." She pulled open the fridge door and took out a beer, twisted off the cap and tossed that in a mason jar half-filled with bottle caps. The brown beer bottle sported the Decadent Dames label on the side. "So why don't you give Trouble a call?"

"Why don't you?" Kelyn asked.

Valor slammed the bottle on the counter. And he immediately regretted his accusing tone. "What do you think went on between your brother and me? Because if you think anything beyond friendship happened—"

"It doesn't matter." He cut her off because he didn't want to know. "You and I? We're just working together toward a common goal. What you do with your free time is not my business."

"You make it sound as if it bothers you. I can be friends with your family, Kelyn. I'm friends with Blade, too. And Daisy Blu. So get over yourself and don't get your wings in such a twist." She tilted back a swallow and then held the bottle to her chest. "Sorry. I shouldn't have said that."

"It's okay."

"No, it's not. You don't have any, uh…"

"Valor." Kelyn reached across the counter and

grasped her hand, which startled her so much she set down the beer. "We're good."

"How can you say that?"

"I just did. Two words. We're. Good. You don't owe me anything. You don't need to apologize. What happened was a result of a choice I made. And only I can live with that. You don't get to share that with me. And while it pretty much knocked the wind out of my sails, I'm still here. And I'm doing something about it now. So if you want to help me, then do your witchy thing and stop trying to take the credit for something you didn't do."

"I…" She exhaled heavily.

It had been difficult to say all that. Because really? Part of Kelyn did blame the witch. If she hadn't been in the Darkwood in the first place… But the wise, logical part of him knew that he'd had total control over what had happened in the forest that day four months earlier. And he was no man to put the blame on anyone else.

"Fine. I can do that. I mean, I want to do that," she said. "But please have patience with me because it's much easier to say than to do."

"I get that."

"I like you, Kelyn. You're a good guy. Faery. How are you without your wings? I need to know."

"I'm the same as ever. Except I can't fly, can't shift to small shape and I've the strength of a regular human man now. Otherwise? Peachy."

She began to frown, but he put up an admonishing finger. "Forward. For both of us. Okay?" He offered a hand for her to shake.

Valor shook it. "Deal. You call your brother. Let's go kick some werewolf ass."

"I'm cool with that—what?"

The rhythmic hum of the vacuum alerted Kelyn to the robotic disk that glided toward the kitchen. And on the back of the thing sat a plush gray cat. It cast a golden gaze up at Kelyn as it rode by, calm and regal upon its modern-day carriage.

Kelyn tugged up his leg in a protective move. "Seriously?"

"That's Mooshi," Valor said. "I told you the cat does the cleaning. He can ride that thing through the whole place. What's wrong? You don't like cats?"

"They're not my favorite critters." Kelyn again caught the cat's eye, but he read its expression as more of an I'm-bored-what-else-is-there-to-do? look than anything else. "Mooshi, master and commander of the hardwood seas. Who'da thought?"

Valor had suggested Kelyn first ask his brothers Trouble and Stryke if either wanted to donate a claw, but realized the error of her ways when the faery cast her a horrified gape. Right. That would be like cutting off a man's fingernail. But really? It *was* for a good cause. What was one fingernail when compared to a man's reason for existence?

So, instead, they decided to track down the werewolf Borse Magnuson, who was known as an all-around asshole and resident idiot. A few years ago he'd been involved in blood games, pitting starving vampires against one another in death matches. Creed Saint-Pierre, Kelyn's grandfather, had put an end to most of those illegal gaming dens. Now, lately, Borse had been trying to establish territory on Trouble's property to the north of Tangle Lake.

So their path led them to the oldest Saint-Pierre brother. And everything Valor read in Kelyn's body language as he neared his brother told her they were not right. She and Trouble, that was. Trouble told them to stop by the local gym and he met them as he was exiting the building. He wandered over to his monster Ford truck, painted in olive camo and sporting silver wolves on the mud flaps.

Valor went to bump fists with Trouble, but the man didn't oblige her. Right. Not speaking to her since Kelyn's wings had been taken. She caught Kelyn's tightened expression. What? Did the guy think she'd gotten it on with his brother? And why did that matter to him? *Oh.*

Assuming a casual stance, Valor grabbed her thick hair and, corralling it into a ponytail, swished it over her shoulder as a distraction from what she felt was a blush riding up her neck. Did Kelyn have some kind of thing for her? He'd mentioned as much in the Darkwood that dreadful night. He couldn't possibly. She was the witch who had changed his life for the worse.

And yet. There was something she had missed. And why hadn't she realized that until right now?

Bad attraction vibes, girl. So terrible at picking up on that one.

"You two are after Borse?" Trouble smacked a fist into his palm. "I want in."

"Trouble, this isn't a matter with which we need help. I just need some info on the guy. Weaknesses. Flaws. Favorite drinking holes."

"Wait, Kelyn." Much as she didn't want to pit brother against brother, Valor felt having a werewolf in the mix could help. And with Kelyn's strength waning? "Did you tell him *why* we're working together?"

Kelyn crossed his arms, lifting his chin defiantly.

When he went all serious, two frown lines appeared between his eyebrows.

No, he hadn't told his brother anything. And what kind of tension was she picking up on now? Yes, there was definitely something she had missed between herself and Kelyn.

"Can I tell him?" she asked carefully.

"Why the hell are you two even standing alongside each other?" Trouble asked. "I thought you never wanted to see her again."

"Those are words you put into my mouth, Trouble. I hold nothing against Valor."

"She was responsible for you losing your wings, man."

"It was my choice."

"I'm helping him to get his wings back." Valor rushed in before Trouble's bouncy stance turned into a one-two punch to the mean witch who had hurt his brother. The man had a tendency to react quickly and only ask the important questions after the pain had been delivered. "I have a spell that will open a portal into Faery. We need a few items for that spell. The first being a werewolf claw."

Kelyn's admonishing tilt of head was expected, but she couldn't worry about pissing off the faery any more than she already had done.

Trouble slammed his fists to his hips. "You trust her?"

"I do. And I suspect Borse will be perfectly fine with one less claw."

"You got that right. But you'll have to take it when he's shifted. He'll tear you apart, brother."

"Thanks for that vote of confidence."

"No, seriously, Kelyn. I know you are the toughest

and strongest of the Saint-Pierre boys. Or at least you were until…her."

Valor caught the werewolf's accusatory look, but she set back her shoulders and held her head high.

"You need help," Trouble said. "And if the witch can get back your wings, I'm all in for ripping Borse's claws out."

"We only need one," Valor reminded the guy, who, she had no doubt, would take off all ten of the werewolf's claws if given the opportunity. "Kelyn and I learned he's going out on the hunt tonight."

"Then we are, too," Trouble said. "But no witches allowed. This is a man's job."

"She's got magic," Kelyn said. "She's coming along."

They tracked Borse to the dive bar at the edge of Tangle Lake. It was a favorite watering hole for the Saint-Pierre brothers. The bartender knew Kelyn was always the designated driver and served him iced lemonade with a nod and a wink. Half a dozen humans lingered at the bar, a pair of them discussing the latest Twins game.

At the pool table, Borse commandeered a game to himself. He was drunk. And it generally took a lot of alcohol to get a werewolf drunk. The trio decided to wait and follow Borse out to his car before approaching him.

It felt wrong going after a drunkard. Even knowing what an asshole Borse was, Kelyn had problems using violence to get what he wanted. Completely the opposite of Trouble, who nursed a whiskey and eyed the dartboard. Kelyn had always won at darts against Trouble. He hadn't attempted a game since losing his wings. He didn't want to try now. He just didn't.

Beside him sat Valor, who'd passed on the lowbrow beer and instead had asked for a lemonade, as well. She wore a thigh strap with a blade in the holster. She'd said it was a ritual blade she used for her spells and would be best to remove the claw. She and Trouble hadn't spoken since they'd arranged to work together, and while Kelyn knew his brother had a stick up his butt about the witch after all that had happened, he was surprised he'd not picked up on any sort of weird sexual tension between the two.

Had Trouble lied about them getting it on? Valor had seemed defensive about just that, but Kelyn had cut her off, not wanting to listen to any excuses. The woman was an adult. She could have sex with whomever she wanted to.

The creaky bar door slammed and Trouble gave a short whistle to Kelyn. Borse had left, muttering something about vampires. The werewolf had parked down the street behind a chain-link fence and next to a rotting supply shed that sat at the edge of the city park. So they had the advantage of darkness and privacy.

"What the fuck?" Borse spun around at the approaching threesome. His stance wobbled, but he maintained an upright position. "Saint-Pierres, eh? That land isn't all yours, Trouble, and you know it."

Trouble punched a fist into his opposite palm and lunged for the man. The first smack of fist to jaw resounded through the park and scattered a flock of pigeons.

"Stay out of the way," Kelyn said, stepping before Valor, who had pulled out her *athame* in defense.

She didn't need to be told to avoid danger. But she didn't need to be protected, either. Especially not by the man who had once already—ah, yes. What was she thinking? Valor stepped back, giving Kelyn every bit of respect the man deserved. She had to be careful not to offend more than she already had done. A man's sense of pride was always a delicate thing.

It didn't take long for Borse and Trouble's scuffle to escalate, and as their antics moved them beneath a shadowed copse of willow, the men shifted. Shirts tore away, though they both had the sense to shift halfway. Keeping their lower halves in human shape ensured that they remained partially clothed. A necessity should an innocent wander onto the scene and a quick shift back to were form was required.

The two shifted wolves went at each other while Kelyn stalked close but did not step in to interrupt. Valor assumed they both knew what they were doing, so, holding her blade at the ready, she waited.

But would a little magic provide Trouble the advantage? Her air magic could make Trouble's punches move faster, his leaps more aggressive. If she could focus it to land only on him and not the other wolf…

"No," she admonished herself quietly. "Let the boys handle this one."

Grunts and growls accompanied the battle that seemed as if it would continue indefinitely. Valor cast Kelyn a questioning look. He returned a shrug and a nod. He got the hint.

Kelyn lunged for Borse and delivered a fist to his bloody jaw. Valor had heard the rumors about Kelyn. That one punch from him would put any man—or beast—down for the count.

Borse shook his head and smirked at Kelyn when he realized the faery was not as strong as rumor told. He grabbed Kelyn's arm even as Trouble swung a leg and took out Borse's stance. Both Borse and Kelyn went down.

And Valor clenched her fingers into her palms. She thrust out her arm, bending her fingers in preparation to release some air magic. Sucking in her lower lip, she bit, almost drawing blood. Cursing at the pain, she inhaled sharply when she saw the fighters roll to a stop. Kelyn landed on top of Borse, and Borse lay still. The thug wolf was out. But for how long?

Kelyn thrust out his hand, gesturing for her to hand the knife to him.

"Oh. Right." She rushed to him and slapped the hilt into his hand.

Trouble, in half his hulking furry glory, leaned over them. He smelled musky and hot. An animal riled. Valor didn't fear the man whose upper half resembled an über-muscled wolf, including a full wolf's head. The one she was concerned with now was Kelyn, and he—he had pressed the side of the blade to his forehead, as if in thought, and closed his eyes as he crouched over Borse.

"Kelyn," she said, "hurry! He could come to any second."

"I can't." He pushed himself up and stepped away from the fallen werewolf, walking a wide circle.

Trouble swiped a big, clawed paw for the knife, but Kelyn jerked it away from him. "Get out of here," he said to his brother. "I'm not going to do it. I can't."

"What? Do you need me to do it?" Valor asked. Her whole body shook. She was nervous and exhilarated and scared all at once.

"No, I mean I won't do this." He handed her the blade. "Who am I to harm another man for something I want? It's not a need, Valor. I *want* my wings back, but I'll survive without them. As deserving as he may be, I won't maim Borse just to make it so."

The werewolf on the ground stirred.

"Let's get out of here." Kelyn grabbed her by the upper arm and pushed her in the direction of the bar where they had parked his Firebird. "Trouble! Go!"

Trouble growled and snorted, but the werewolf took off in the opposite direction and loped through the park.

And while Valor was disappointed they'd not gotten what had been but a stroke of the blade away, she was even more impressed at Kelyn's sacrifice. Once again. And his honor.

He truly was a good man. And she was fortunate to know such a person.

They climbed into his car and watched through the chain-link fence for a while. To see if Borse would wander out in werewolf form, or perhaps man shape. And to make sure Trouble didn't return looking for the trouble he famously indulged in.

"I'm sorry," Valor said quietly.

Kelyn turned on her with a surprising rage in his eyes. "I am tired of your apologies. You did nothing wrong, witch!"

"Would you bring it down a notch? I was apologizing because I know you want your wings, and now getting them seems an impossibility. Would you let someone care about you? Seriously!" She gripped the door handle tightly. "You've more of a chip on your shoulder about letting someone in than about getting back your lost wings. What's your hang-up?"

"I don't have a hang-up, other than wondering why in Beneath I decided working with you would be a good idea."

"Because you trusted me."

"Trust had nothing to do with it. I'm here because you were my only hope."

"Sorr—" She cut off the apology. "Fine. I disappointed you."

"I was the one who refused to take the claw. It's all on me."

"Right. Do you thrive on the guilt, Kelyn?"

He cast her a condemning glare, which Valor felt at the back of her neck like an icy prickle over her skin. So maybe he wasn't as honorable as she'd surmised.

"Okay, not going to discuss that one," she said. "On to plan B. Do we have a plan B?"

"I do."

"Which is?"

Kelyn shifted into gear and the vehicle rolled over the tarmac. "There's a cabin about ten miles south from here. Belongs to a peller. My sister's husband, Beck, had a run-in with the owner a few years ago. The man…can time travel."

Valor shot him a glance, but it was too dark in the car to see his reaction to her sudden interest.

"I'm not so sure I believe in the time-travel stuff," he continued. "But he was also a wolf hunter. He hunts all sorts of species, actually. Anyway, the cabin is sometimes empty because he's gone. In another time."

"That sounds too cool, and at the same time, severely whacked."

"Yeah, but if the cabin is empty, I say we take a look around. If the guy hunts wolves, there could be…things."

"Like claws?"

She sensed Kelyn nodded. And Valor smiled. "You're in the driver's seat."

Chapter 5

Kelyn used the GPS on his phone to locate the farmhouse he'd been to twice before. And that annoyed the crap out of him. Normally, he'd navigate ley lines to find his way or simply recall the directions and turns. The ability to do so had always been innately a part of him, aligned with the sigils he'd once worn on his body.

He did not want to think any more about the skills that giving away his wings had stolen from him.

"Denton Marx is a peller," he explained as he parked the Firebird on the gravel drive before the guy's place.

"A spell breaker," Valor confirmed. "They are generally good, bad or nasty. I'm guessing Marx was the nasty sort?"

Kelyn wobbled his hand back and forth. "Depends on whose story you listen to. He did some bad things for what he thought was a good reason. My sister, Daisy

Blu, suffered because of it. But her husband, Beck, who was under a curse that was killing him, gained back his life, so they both sort of won because of Marx. I'd call him situationally convenient." He peered out the window, eyes taking in the periphery. "Doesn't look like anyone is home."

The lot did appear abandoned. Massive willow trees hung over the unmown front yard that edged a gravel road. Tall grasses disguised the ditch and frothed along the narrow drive. The rambler-style house was dark, as was the garage. The forest grew thick right up to the back of the house, though Kelyn knew there was a shed beyond it.

He'd been here a few winters earlier with his brothers. Denton had sought Daisy Blu's werewolf soul to rescue his lost love who was trapped in another time, a witch who could time travel. And Denton also time traveled. Wonders never ceased. A soul had been a requirement to work a spell to breach time. The man had failed. Thankfully.

"I don't think he's around." Kelyn opened the door and thrust out a leg, sniffing at the air. Normally his senses were dialed up to ultra. But since losing his wings? Forget about it. "I don't scent any others beyond the wildlife and floras. Let's take a look out back."

Valor followed silently, which he appreciated. If anyone were on the premises, he didn't want to alert them that they had visitors.

Pressing his wrists together to invoke magic that would heighten his senses, Kelyn cursed under his breath and swung his arms away from each other. Even after four months, he still forgot about his missing sigils. And a twinge in the center of his back, between his shoulder blades, reminded him what a fool he had been. Could a man be too damned nice?

Obviously, he could.

The grass was dry and brown here behind the house, and his footsteps crunched even as he left the gravel drive. He hadn't come armed. He didn't want to call up any more bad mojo from the universe than his actions had already done.

He didn't consider this venture breaking and entering. Just…taking a look around. Surely Denton owed the Saint-Pierre family for the pain he'd put them through with Daisy Blu and Beck.

"How do you know this guy?" Valor asked quietly as she caught up and reached his side. They wandered over some old, rotted wood boards that had been placed on the ground as a sort of walkway leading to the shed.

"He almost killed my sister and her boyfriend. Of course, that was when Beck was cursed as the ghost wolf."

"I remember that! That was a couple years ago. There was an article in the local paper about a big white wolf roaming the area."

"Beck was cursed as that white wolf."

"Wow. And you're friends with this Denton guy?"

"Not officially." He stopped before the steel door to the shed, suspecting the security would be excellent for a man who might take frequent trips away—to completely different centuries. "But if anyone has a werewolf claw, it'll be this guy. Keep watch on the house, will you?"

"Larceny. Love it." Shoving her hands in her back pockets, Valor turned to face the house.

Satisfied there were no cameras attached to the outside of the building, nor any connected on the nearby yard lightpost, Kelyn jiggled the doorknob. It was a standard knob and lock. Nothing digital. He didn't have anything to pick the lock with, so...he stepped back and gave the door a fierce kick right beside the lock mechanism. It slammed inward with a loud bang and a plume of dust.

Valor turned and gaped at him.

He smiled at her and shrugged. "Some of my talents have less finesse than others."

"So it would seem." She walked in after him. "Nothing like making an entrance. I like it."

The shed was dark, but pale moonlight strained through a dirty glass window panel set into the roof. The paned glass stretched eight feet square. It was littered with fallen leaves, yet the center of the room was lit enough to make out the dirt floor and assorted items sitting about. A mounted full-bodied buck greeted them with eerie glass eyes, its ten-point rack gleaming like ivory.

"Yikes." Valor walked up to the taxidermied creature. It stood as high as she. She studied it from head to tail, then walked back up to look into its eyes. She stroked its nose, pausing with her palm flat on its fur. Bowing her head, she said, "I'm so sorry for you."

Her empathy hit Kelyn right in the heart. Any chick who cared for nature was all right by him. "You see? The guy is an asshole."

"Duly noted. This poor creature didn't deserve such an end. I hate trophy hunters. So let's take a look around. I'll look over here and you—" He'd already begun to explore the north wall. "Yep, you know what you're doing. So, are you prepared to leave the country?"

"What?" Kelyn brushed his fingertips over an assortment of knives and tools he assumed were taxidermy items. None were clean, which made him wonder about the man's methods. Trophies would be created and tended with care and clean instruments. Magical items, on the other hand, wouldn't require such surgical cleanliness. He called over his shoulder, "Why leave the country?"

"The next item on the list is in Western Australia. Lake Hillier. The pink lake."

"Pink?"

"Yeah, I think it's algae or something that colors it literally a bubble gum pink. We need water from that lake specifically."

"Right, the unruly lake. What is an unruly lake anyway?"

"Apparently, a pink one."

"Australia is a long flight."

"That it is. And...spendy."

He caught her anxious tone. "You mean you're not going to treat me to an adventure across the globe?"

"I can pay for my own ticket. I'm just hoping you'll pay for yours?"

"I can cover us both," he offered.

"No, I can take care of myself."

"Valor. Send me the flight details and an online link and I'll take care of it. Okay?"

She nodded and picked up an old, rusted spring-loaded trap that creaked as she turned it about. "This looks dangerous and it smells."

"Probably blood on it from whatever the man last trapped."

She dropped it with a groan.

Kelyn's hand landed on a dusty glass quart jar without a cover. He could feel the vibrations wavering out from within and he bowed his head over it, placing both hands on the glass. Thankful that his senses were not currently superreceptive, he could only imagine the pain he'd sense if they had been at normal capacity.

"What is it?" Valor walked up behind him and gasped at the sight of what he held. "That's a lot of claws. And big. Sure they're not bear claws?"

"No," Kelyn said with a swallow. "These are were-wolf." It pained him to think that his brothers had gone up against Denton. Yet they had survived. Thank the gods for that. "Take one," he said quickly.

Valor reached in and pulled out a black claw that was as thick as her finger and twice as long. Then she took another. "Two to be safe." And another. "And three—"

"No." He took one of the claws and tossed it back in the jar, wincing at the horrible vibrations of pain he felt with the quick connection. "We won't be greedy. Two is more than enough."

"Fine." She shoved the claws in her jacket pocket. "Let's you, me and Doogie Howser get the hell out of Dodge."

"Doogie Howser?"

She shrugged. "TV doctors. I got a thing for them."

"I don't understand."

"You don't need to. Let's skedaddle."

They strode toward the open door. When they were but four feet away, the door suddenly slammed shut in a cloud of dust. And the door edges began to glow orange.

"The peller has an inner protection spell activated," Valor said.

She spread her hands out before her, testing the vibrations that wavered out from the door. Turning and clasping the moonstone that hung around her neck, she sensed the spell stretching along the walls and the ceiling, enclosing them completely. She didn't judge it to be anything particularly dark, more just menacing.

Kelyn spread out his hands as if to read his surroundings as she had done. She wasn't sure how much faery magic he still possessed, if any. The sigils were missing from his wrists and in their place, silvery scars served as a cruel reminder. That had to suck.

"You got some magic to get us out of here?" he asked.

"Maybe."

"I do love a decisive woman."

"Aw, you love me?" Valor flicked him a flirty wink over her shoulder. "Find me something silver, will you?"

"Okay. There's gotta be silver in a werewolf hunter's cabin." Kelyn looked around.

The shuffling Valor suddenly heard, which should have been Kelyn pushing things around on the shelves, sounded—when she thought about it—more like... hooves.

She spun around to face the stuffed deer. Which was no longer inanimate. Its eyes glowed white and its obsidian hoof pawed the dirt floor.

"Kelyn!"

"Found something that looks like a silver arrowhead. Though it's corroded." He turned and saw the same thing she did. "No kidding?"

"Toss me the arrow. Or better yet. Can you—"

"Got it!" He lunged for the buck as the beast charged Valor. The faery leaped and landed on the deer's back, one arm wrapping about its wide, strong neck.

Valor dropped and rolled across the dirt floor, out of the animal's charging path. It didn't slow, bowing its head and aiming its magnificent rack at the closed door.

Kelyn stabbed at the beast, landing the arrowhead in its chest as its antlers collided with the door. The protection spell fizzled, bursting out brilliant orange flames from around the door. The steel door blew off the shed, and the deer raced through with Kelyn riding its back.

"Can't say I've seen anything like that before," Valor muttered as she stood and brushed the dirt off her jeans. "Cool."

She wandered through the door to find Kelyn standing before a stuffed deer. He tugged the arrowhead out of its chest. The magic that had reanimated the deer had ceased the moment it left the shed.

Valor marched over and smoothed a hand over the stuffed animal's nose. "No one will believe this."

"Welcome to my world." Kelyn tossed the arrowhead in the air and caught it smartly. "Let's get out of here. Can you fit the door back into the frame?"

"Seriously? After the mess we made in there, you think replacing the door…?"

He did have a way of challenging her right in the witchcraft with his castigating, yet also kinda sexy furrowed brow.

Summoning her air magic, Valor whispered a rising spell and the door lifted and slammed back into the frame. Not at all the gentle fit-back-into-the-door-frame action she had been going for, but… "It'll do. What are we going to do about that thing?"

He smoothed a palm over the deer's back. "I like to think Marx will have a hell of a time figuring this one out when he returns."

"I like your thinking."

They wandered back to the car at the end of the drive, and after getting in the car Valor tugged out her cell phone. She perused the Delta flight schedule while Kelyn drove out and headed back to Tangle Lake. He was using the GPS on his phone and she knew it drove him buggy. Faeries were natural navigators. Poor guy. But, much as she wanted to, she wouldn't bring it up or apologize.

A ten-minute cruise down the main highway brought the Firebird to the exit for Tangle Lake. It was late, and not a lot of cars were out and about. Valor didn't live far from the exit.

"There's a flight to Australia tomorrow afternoon," she said. "You know your credit card number?"

"I do. Book the tickets."

"Sounds like a plan. Flying over an entire ocean is not going to be as fun as tonight was."

"You're not much for flying?"

"That's putting it euphemistically. Okay, give me your number."

He relayed his number to her while parking before her building. The autoconfirm promised an email soon. When Valor opened the door and stuck out a leg, he grabbed her forearm, stopping her from leaving.

"Thanks for tonight," he said. "We work well together."

"That we do. Thanks for trusting me. This spell will work, Kelyn. I promise that."

He nodded. "I'll pick you up tomorrow a couple hours before the flight."

"See you then. Thanks!"

As the Firebird rolled away, Valor had to stop herself from giving a little wave in its wake. Like *hey, yeah, that* was *fun*. Just spending time with the guy had been fun. And watching him ride the deer? She had to tell her friends about that one.

With a sigh, she wandered toward her building. The feeling that she should have leaned over and kissed him in thanks for the adventure was strong. A missed opportunity. Generally, she was a take-life-by-the-horns-and-ride-it kind of chick.

She knew why she was skittish around Kelyn. Same reason she'd given up on ever finding love. Men didn't consider her a woman. She simply wasn't...

"A real girl," she said, and followed that with another heart-clenching sigh.

Had she been able to accomplish the spell that night in the Darkwood, would she be singing a different tune now?

Could Kelyn ever see her as a woman?

Because she wanted to kiss him again. No, she *needed* to.

Chapter 6

Valor sat up on the couch, blew the tangled hair from her face and…dropped back into a dead sleep, falling forward to land her face against the hardwood arm. That woke her up again. And this time she heard the pounding and insistent knock at her door.

"Valor?"

Sounded like Kelyn's voice. Why was he at her home…she glanced toward the windows…in the middle of the night?

Her eyelids fluttered and she dropped into sleep again, this time her head falling to the side and hitting the soft leather back of the couch.

A rude meow sounded and she shook out of sleep. "No. Need to sleep. Have…flight…in morning, Mooshi."

"Valor, are you ready to go?" Kelyn called from the other side of her front door.

"Go?" She glanced toward the kitchen, seeing beyond the row of beer bottles and that one empty vodka bottle—curse her weakness for the hard stuff—where the time flashed in bright green LEDs on the stove. "Marcus Welby! It's time!"

She dragged herself off the couch and scrambled to the door, opening it. Kelyn breezed in.

"We've got to go," he said. "The flight leaves in an hour and a half, and it takes forty-five minutes to get to the airport. What the—are you not ready to go?" He reached for her head, and though Valor dodged his touch, he managed to snag his fingers in her hair. And that was possible because of the tangles. "You're wearing the same clothes as yesterday. And…you smell like a brewery."

"Yeah? Well, I do work at a brewery, smart guy."

"Not yesterday."

"Fine! I couldn't sleep," she muttered, her tongue still heavy with sleep and the remnants of a good drunk. Hell, the drunk was still with her, bless the goddess. Because it was a necessity. "I hate flying, and I'm always nervous the night before. I haven't slept. And yet…I think I must have fallen asleep, like, half an hour ago. I am so wasted."

He caught her in his arms and held her upright. "You drink to relax?"

"Beer usually calms me. Vodka seemed to take off the edge."

"Couldn't you have cast a spell or something? Valor, we've got to go. You have your bags packed?"

She gestured toward the door, where one small carry-on backpack waited. She'd had the forethought to pack after Kelyn dropped her off last night when she wasn't so nervous. Now all she wanted to do was sleep.

"The flight is long. You can sleep when we get seated." He bent and suddenly Valor found herself flung over the man's broad and reassuringly strong shoulder.

A humiliating position, and yet... Nah, she could go with it. Especially since...

Kelyn chuckled at the witch's sudden snores. He grabbed her backpack and with a glance to the cat decided Valor had to have made arrangements for its care in her absence. Probably a neighbor would stop by. He slid the door closed behind him.

What a way to begin an adventure.

Kelyn accepted an offer of ice water from the stewardess and refused another white wine for his guest. They'd been in the air four hours, and Valor could snore with the best of them. She did not do sleep deprivation well. But if she had been nervous about flying, then it was good she was sleeping now. She'd managed to lift her head once while they were waiting to board, smiled at him and then her head had hit his shoulder.

And he was enjoying it. Because right now her head lay on his shoulder, and her hand had strayed to his chest. One finger touched his skin at the base of his neck. It was weirdly intimate, and yet not. She was just a friend. And he did mark her as a sort-of friend, not an enemy. They were working toward a common goal.

But he was seriously beginning to feel the old attraction to her again. Not that it had ever gone away. Losing his wings had honestly reduced his interest in her. But the chick was not like the rest of the women he had known or lusted after. She wasn't fussy or high maintenance. He couldn't imagine any woman he'd known allowing him to carry her into the airport, hair uncombed and T-shirt wrinkled, after a sleepless night on a bender.

Valor Hearst didn't do the makeup and hair thing. Her long straight hair had a deep violet tint to it. Had to be dyed. He wasn't sure if witches could have a natural color like that. His sister, Daisy Blu's, hair was pink, but that was natural from her faery heritage.

Valor dressed as if she was ready to hop on a Harley and ride off into the sunset. Everything about her was casual confidence and gotcha smirks. One of the guys.

But the thing that had sealed his attraction to her a few years ago? It had been one night around a bonfire when a bunch of friends had gathered at a city summer festival. Beer and s'mores had been in abundance, as well as lawn darts and cheap sparklers. Valor had been pointed out to him as one of the witches who owned a local brewery. He'd thought she was pretty in that one-of-the-guys kind of way. Because she had an ease around people and wasn't always fluffing her hair or checking her cell phone for texts from girlfriends. He hadn't given her too much eye time. Until she'd laughed. It had come out as an abrupt burst of sound and ended with a snort. Ignoring what anyone thought of her and proud to be herself.

Ever since, he'd spent more time looking at her. And wanting to ask her out so he could hear that crazy, obnoxious laugh again. And wondering how she'd be as a kisser. Damn good, now that he knew. But he wished it hadn't been because she'd thought she was dying that he'd gotten that kiss.

And now he still couldn't stop looking at her and allowing his fantasies to take hold.

Valor's lips were pale pink and plump. And they were
so close to him. He wanted to touch them, but he held the
water glass in one hand and his other arm was wedged
beneath her sleeping body. So he'd take her in for as long
as he could. And enjoy this quiet moment with a woman
he wasn't sure was safe to lose anything more to. He'd
given up his wings for her.

What more did he have left, besides his heart?

Valor woke without opening her eyes. Her body took
a survey of her immediate surroundings—hard plastic
seat and walls, tight confines, stale air, compressed sensation going on in her sinuses—and she determined she
was on a plane. Not on the ground.

Mercy.

The thing about flying was that it was unnatural. Yes,
even for a witch. Witches didn't fly on broomsticks or
by their own power. Well, they could do both with the
right kind of magic. Air magic. But she'd always avoided
considering such study. And the cliché of the broomstick
was just that. She preferred her feet to remain on the
ground. And even though there had been no other option
to get where they were going—a ship would have taken
far too long—it was never easy to dispel her nerves.

Fortunately, the alcohol had worked for a while.

Now groggy but feeling rested, she came awake more
fully and curled her fingers against the hard warmth
beneath her hand. Mmm, that felt great. And her pillow
was firm but smelled nice. Like a forest after the rain.
Why was that? Weren't airplanes the least inviting and
uncomfortable conveyances in existence?

"You rest well?"

The voice vibrated against her cheek and into her very

bones, and Valor realized what exactly was up. She was lying on Kelyn, her cheek pressed against his shoulder. And that warmth under her hand? It was his hard pec. The man had to work out. Seriously.

Such a surprising but welcome bit of reality proved beyond nice. And she didn't want it to end. But really? This accidental sharing and caring between the two of them was not cool. On a scale of not-coolness, from one to ten, her current position probably topped out at an eight.

Maybe if she didn't move, he'd think she'd fallen back to sleep?

The smell of roast beef suddenly wafted through the air and Valor realized she was more hungry than embarrassed. So she slowly pushed herself up and met Kelyn's smiling violet gaze. "Morning."

"Evening, actually. At least, according to Australian time. But don't get too excited. We've still got another six hours to go."

"Ah, Meredith Gray!"

"Is she a doctor?"

"Yes, *Gray's Anatomy*. She and McDreamy—oh, never mind." She averted her eyes to the leather cords around his neck. A long, thin white spiral dangled from one of them. Looked like a seashell. On the other was a black ring of stone. She tapped it. Six more hours? Could a witch get a break? "Maybe I should go back to sleep."

"I take it you wish you could sleep through the whole flight? Maybe one more beer would have done the trick?"

She groaned. "Please don't mention beer. It was the vodka that did it for me. The beer makes me want to…"

Pee a very long time. She wouldn't say that. She and he were not that tight as bros yet.

"Aren't you hungry?" he asked. "They're serving now. Might keep your thoughts from…dire things."

"Yeah, maybe." She leaned back and slowly took her hand from his chest. "Sorry about that. Lying on you and all."

"It's all right. And you didn't drool that much."

"I—" She wiped her mouth and hoped to catch his teasing laugh, but he merely shrugged. Perfect. Not. "Really sorry about that one."

"Valor, your apologies are always superfluous. Now tell the nice stewardess what you'll have to eat."

When Valor turned to the flight attendant, she only then realized the luxurious space she sat in. It was still the inside of a tin can, but much more roomy than she'd experienced that one other time she was inside an airplane. They were in first class? Mercy, but she could never afford this ticket. And she did intend to pay the guy back.

"I'll take the roast beef," she said to the attendant, who sported a perfect blond coif and a red scarf tied about her neck. Valor refused the offer of alcohol. She'd drunk a whole growler of beer last night. Or this morning. Or whenever. Plus the bottle of vodka. Those two alcohols should not be mixed. Stupid nerves. "And some ginger ale."

Kelyn asked for the vegetarian plate and more water.

Fifteen minutes later, and after a necessary trip to the bathroom, the meal had served to relax Valor and she settled back to watch Kelyn finish his dairy-free chocolate cake. It didn't sound appetizing, but it certainly looked lush and moist. He was a vegetarian? Must have been disgusted by her shoveling in the minimal bits of roast beef she'd dug out of the gravy. He'd not said anything, though.

"Why are you so nice?" she asked.

He paused, a forkload of cake suspended before his mouth. With a shrug, he offered, "It's a Minnesota thing."

"Sure, but that's surface. And I'm from Minnesota." She pointed to her chest. "Not so nice. Mostly. People are always nice to one another, but are they *kind* nice? *Nice* is doing so because you think it's expected of you. Or because your mommy always told you 'be nice.' *Kind nice* is an innate calling to understand others and be accepting of them. That's you."

"I get that. I'll cop to kind nice eighty percent of the time. But flattery will not get you a piece of this cake. I'm eating it all myself." He forked in an appealing bite of layered chocolate frosting and cake. "See? Not so nice now, am I?"

She pouted about that. She'd wolfed down her dry cinnamon crumble so fast she hadn't even tasted it. So she enjoyed a good meal. And this first-class stuff? Not too shabby, if sparse on the meat.

"I'm no nicer than the next guy, Valor. I'm just trying to walk through this life and world respectful of all those who have as many trials and tribulations as myself."

"Yeah? What's it take to piss off a guy like you?"

"Why do you want to piss me off?"

"I don't. I'm just wondering what it takes. You can't be nice all the time. Seriously. Be honest about the remaining twenty percent. If you had one day in Trouble's shoes and could punch whoever or whatever because your temper flared as easily as his, what would it take to set you off?"

Kelyn set down the fork beside the half-eaten cake and rubbed the heel of his palm across his brow. "I guess it would have to be someone who harms another for malicious reasons."

"Like a bully?"

"Maybe."

"A murderer?"

"For sure."

"So you'd take the law into your own hands, then?"

"That's not what you asked me."

"Right." She sighed and turned toward him, nudging her shoulder into the seat. She'd already gone too far by sprawling across him while she slept. Best to be more careful about his personal space now. "Tell me what's up between you and your brother and me."

"What do you mean?"

"I know you think something about the two of us. I can sense it every time his name comes up."

"Doesn't matter."

"It does. Because every time I mention Trouble, your fingers curl into fists. See? You just did it."

He sighed and relaxed his fingers.

"Do you think me and your brother got it on?"

He didn't answer and instead shoved in another bite of cake. The force with which he stabbed the helpless dessert said all she needed to know.

"We didn't, Kelyn. I don't know what Trouble has told you, but we are just friends. Always have been, always— well, the dude has been avoiding me since…you know."

"He's protective of me. Of all his siblings. If someone does us wrong, he's going to retaliate." His attention focused on her. His irises gleamed like gemstones. Faery eyes were gorgeous. She'd never seen anything so intense and precious. "So you're telling me nothing has ever happened between the two of you? Be honest, I know you two do the Netflix-and-chill thing."

"We never chill, Kelyn. It's either pizza, beer or both. But *never* sex. I might have kissed him once. A quickie, just to, you know, test the waters. But no sex. You have to believe me. And it makes me angry that Trouble made you believe otherwise. What a jerk."

Kelyn shrugged. "Trouble is like that. Boasts about things to make himself look good."

"So he did tell you we slept together. B. J. Hunnicutt, I will so kick his ass for that."

"Maybe keep your distance from him for now. He gets an idea about a person and he goes ballistic pretty fast."

The soft light from above shadowed his eyes and emphasized his sharp bone structure. Hair raked back off his face to further expose his exquisite features, the man was beautiful in, hmm, an alien manner. Unique.

"I did believe him when he said the two of you had hooked up. And it bothered me because I like you, Valor. I've explained that. Yet I don't ever want to go after one of my brother's conquests."

"I am so not a conquest."

"I believe it."

"Thank you. So…are we good?"

He bobbed his head. "I was stupid to buy into Trouble's bragging. He does it all the time. And I know half the time it's exaggerated blustering. Idiot wolf. Will you accept my apology?"

"For what? You've done nothing but be a good brother. And if anyone needs to apologize—"

"It's neither of us. We've been through this already. Onward and with a new perspective on each other?"

"For sure."

"Great. Then to seal the deal you can have the last piece." He forked up the final chunk of chocolate cake and offered it to her.

The guy didn't have to offer twice. Valor dived for the prize. It was especially sweet, considering they'd cleared the air about something she hadn't even been aware was a problem.

So Kelyn liked her?

She could work with that.

Chapter 7

Seven hours later their feet finally touched ground. Wandering through the airport, Kelyn slung Valor's backpack across one shoulder and carried his bag on the other side. He'd had to rip the thing out of her hand. The chick was tough, but come on, let a guy do the chivalrous thing once in a while.

Now he turned to see if she still followed him—she'd gotten over her sleep deprivation just in time for midnight in Australia. Ha! He'd stolen a few winks on the flight and didn't need to sleep all that much. Despite having watched six movies and debating the merits of chemical-free lawns as opposed to spraying with an across-the-aisle passenger, he was good to go.

Valor sped up and passed him.

"I think the taxi terminal is that way," he said as she headed in the opposite direction.

"Cool, but I see an all-night buffet up ahead. And I'm starving. That tiny meal on the plane only whetted my appetite. Come on!"

Food that had actually been prepared in a real kitchen and not freeze-dried and reheated? He was in.

Kelyn picked up his pace and didn't make it to the cash register in time before Valor had confirmed she'd paid for both of them. Without waiting for his argument, she charged into the restaurant and grabbed a plate, directing him to find a table.

Let no man stand in the way of a hungry woman. Who was too darned cute as she navigated the aisles of food with a gleeful look on her face. And she was yet to notice the sprig of hair sticking straight out from the top of her head.

Ten minutes later, Kelyn sat with a plate stacked with steamed and fresh veggies, fried potatoes of various types and something called Vegemite spread on a piece of toast. And Valor had almost cleaned her first plate.

"Where do you put it all?" he asked and sipped his hot coffee.

She flexed a biceps and tapped it. "Right here. All the protein keeps me in shape for lifting the grain bags at the brewery and hefting heavy auto parts around the shop."

"That's right, you're a tool monkey."

"I prefer to call it getting my grease on, but close enough. Yeah, Daisy Blu and Beck let me and Sunday use one of the stalls at their auto body shop. We are working on a '67 Corvette Stingray. It's sweet. You like cars, Kelyn?"

"They get a guy where he needs to go. I'm more of a motorcycle man, I guess."

"Cool. I ride an old street chopper I picked up from Raven Crosse for a killer price. Fixing it up right now. But your Firebird is a classic."

"Blade fixed it up for me as a birthday present a few years ago. It was a junker I found on Craigslist for a thousand bucks. Blade can work magic with bodywork, and Beck restored the engine."

"Nice."

Reaching across the table, he patted down the tangle of hair on her head. "That's better."

She shrugged. "I'm no glamour girl. Get used to it. So, you ever hop on your motorcycle and ride up along Lake Superior? It's gorgeous in the fall with the colorful leaves. I try to go camping in the Boundary Waters at least once a year."

"Sounds like fun. But I don't own a motorcycle. I just like them. And believe it or not, I haven't been Up North. Been stuck in the Twin Cities all my freakin' life. Is this your first trip out of the country?"

"Out of the state."

"I have been lucky enough to visit Paris once. I like flying. Er...in an airplane," he felt the need to correct, because if he thought about flying with his wings... Yeah, he needed to put that heart-crushing memory aside. "You should have told me this was your first flight. I thought you'd flown before because of the, er..."

"Drunken disaster I was this morning?"

"Yeah. Seems like you had a routine established for alleviating your flight anxiety that could only have come from much experimenting."

"I've flown north to Thief River Falls to visit friends on a much smaller plane. Dude, you don't even want to know about that disaster."

He smiled at her cringing expression. To him, flight was everything. But free flight, courtesy of wings, was the ultimate. *Stop thinking about it, man.* With luck, what he'd lost would soon be regained.

"Speaking of drunken disasters…" He offered a sheepish grin. "I wasn't sure what to do, so we…left the cat behind."

"Everything's cool. My neighbor checks in on Mooshi. I thought you didn't like cats."

"I don't, but that doesn't mean I can't care about an animal's safety."

"Why the dislike? Are you allergic to cats?"

"No. I actually think it's a faery thing. Cats don't care for me, either. I'm surprised your Mooshi was so calm around me. Usually they come at me with their claws bared or else run and hide."

"Wow. Well, you are a likable guy and Mooshi is chill." She shoved in a forkload of food and looked aside.

A likable guy, eh? She liked him. But he wouldn't tease her about it. Yet. It made Kelyn feel good to know that she did. Had he a real chance to score with her now that he no longer had to worry that she and his brother had had a thing?

He sipped the weak black coffee. "So, are we headed straight to the lake tonight?"

"I'm in. The moon is almost full. We should have good light to explore."

"Is the lake accessible?"

"Sure, but I don't think it's touristy. Maybe? I didn't do a lot of research on it, but I do know it's kind of, sort of out of the way. We can head there when we're finished eating." She stood and headed for plate number two.

"Never leave a man behind." Despite his usual habit of eating small meals often throughout the day, Kelyn followed her, thinking he couldn't let a girl eat him under the table.

By the time plate number three had been cleaned, he was feeling the burn in his gut. Maybe he should concede the win on this one.

"You're kind of competitive," Valor said as she licked the whipped cream off her spoon, then stabbed it into the mush of blueberry pie. "You know that?"

"Just hungry." He pushed his plate forward on the table, thinking dessert was out of the question. Oh, that Vegemite. He shouldn't have had the third slice of toast. "Very well. I concede. You win the buffet challenge."

"I always do." She sat back, spreading her hair out across one shoulder. It was long and glossy; he imagined what it might feel like spread across his chest, tickling like sensual silk.

"You want the last piece?" She tapped the plate, on which sat a small uneaten blob of pie coated with whipped cream.

Recognizing the significance of the offer, Kelyn set aside his revulsion at all the sugar—and his full-to-the-brim stomach—and leaned across the table. She forked the pie and placed it in his mouth. It wasn't like he'd consumed a whole piece, but it was definitely the straw that broke the camel's very full stomach. He sat back with a groan.

"Poor guy. Will you be able to make this evening's adventure?" she asked, not hiding a teasing tone. "Or do you want to go snuggle up in a hotel room and recover from the food deluge?"

Snuggle up? Was she suggesting? No, she had cho-

sen the wrong word. Maybe? But as for crawling under
the covers and surrendering? Could he? *Man up, faery.*

"I'm in. How far away is the lake?"

"Not sure." She tugged out her cell phone. "I might
have to arrange transportation. This could take a bit."

Enough time to give his stomach a recovery period.

"You bring your swimsuit?" she asked as they
grabbed their luggage and filed out of the booth.

"What for? Are we going to *swim* in the lake?"

"Heck, yeah. You think I'd fly across the world to
visit a pink lake and *not* go in it?"

"I'm not much of a swimmer. Actually, I never
learned how." And please don't ask him to start now.

She shrugged. "It's cool. I think I read something
about people being extra buoyant in the water because
of the massive salt content. Dude. This is going to rock!"

Chapter 8

Witchcraft could be a handy thing when it came to enchanting a helicopter pilot and convincing him to fly over Lake Hillier. What Valor had discovered was that the lake was on Middle Island and not accessible to visitors because it was surrounded by forest. Only pre-approved visits were allowed, and such permission could take weeks to obtain.

And, indeed, the lake, when seen from overhead, was a gorgeous shade of bubble gum pink, surrounded by a white stone beach. Moonlight glistening on the waves added enough glitz that Valor commented about it being blinged out.

Why the lake was pink was still a scientific mystery, according to the chatty pilot, though the concentration of salt and bacteria did contribute to the color. The pilot said visitors were cautioned to cover any skin that would touch the water with shea butter, which Valor had purchased before they'd taken off.

It was already three in the morning, so they needed to work swiftly. With a few more magical words, Valor convinced the pilot that this was, indeed, a preapproved dropoff. And that his passengers were actually scientists on a photojournalism venture approved by the Australian tourism board. He nodded and gave them a salute as they prepared to disembark.

Valor asked the pilot to return in an hour and then they rappelled down from the helicopter, military-style. He'd managed to drop them right on the white beach outside the fragrant forest of paperbark and eucalyptus trees that hugged beach and lake. The air was heavy with the scent of air freshener, or that was what it smelled like to Valor.

Kelyn shucked off his harness and then helped Valor off with hers. He carried their only backpack, which Valor had packed with the necessary supplies. Standing on the white beach, she took things in for a moment. An uninhabited island all to themselves in the middle of a moonlit evening? *Why* had she come here?

Oh, right. This was a business trip and nothing else.

Tugging off her shirt, she tossed that on top of the backpack, then toed off her boots and pulled off her pants to reveal the bikini she wore beneath. She'd had to buy one at the airport, and much to her chagrin there hadn't been any one-pieces in her size. She hadn't swum in a pool, lake or otherwise since she was a kid, and she did not do the sunbathing thing. That was best left for real women like one of the brewery co-owners, Geneva, who probably caught her rays on the deck of a multimillion-dollar yacht, lying under the appreciative eye of her latest billionaire boyfriend. Ha!

Collecting the glass vials from the backpack, she started toward the water.

"Wow" came softly from behind her.

Kelyn pulled off his shirt and it dangled from his fingers as he looked her up and down with an assessing appreciation that would have made any woman blush proudly.

Valor shrugged and turned back to the lake. "It's just a body."

"So it is. But a nice one, at that."

Seriously? She couldn't figure what he was thinking— or looking at, for that matter. Her body was long, lean and straight. Everywhere. Small boobs and no apparent waistline because her torso plunged right into her hips and down her thighs. Valor had never considered herself a real girl when compared to the hair-fluffing, mascara-fluttering, lipstick-pouting mannequins that most men seemed to find attractive. Another point tossed to her witchy friend Geneva. Give Valor a wrench and a greasy engine, and she was one happy camper.

Kelyn caught up to her where she'd waded out about ten feet. The swim trunks fit low on his hips. The abs on the guy were nothing less than insane. More than a six-pack, for sure. But she didn't count because Valor was trying to keep from glancing at them too often and giving herself away.

Just another body, she thought of his ripped physique. She might not be a real girl, but her brain was all woman. Lusting madly for some man flesh was natural. But it was probably wiser if she did it on the sly.

"We going to put the shea butter on?" Kelyn asked

as he joined her side. The water hit them both high on the thighs.

"It's a quick pop in the lake. We can rub it in afterward and get the same effect. It'll just prevent our skin from getting dry from all the salt. You want to stay here while I go for a swim?"

"Hell, no. If the water makes us buoyant, like you said, and then you factor in that I'm a natural lightweight, I shouldn't be able to drown even if I tried."

"Is that a faery thing?"

"It is. Our bones are light and sort of honeycomb in design. For flight."

"Cool." She clasped the moonstone hanging from the cord about her neck. Nah, it wouldn't get lost if she didn't do vigorous laps. She eyed Kelyn, who assessed the water with that furrowed brow of his. "What are those?" She pointed to the charms that hung from the leather strips about his neck. "That one looks like a tiny unicorn horn."

"Close. It's a mouse alicorn."

"Seriously?"

He nodded. "And this one—" he held up the black circle that looked like a thin tourmaline ring "—has some kind of funky vibrations, but I've never been able to actually use it magically. I got them both from Faery. Never been there myself, but I know a girl who brings me back prizes from there every so often."

"Is that so? She a girlfriend?"

"Nope. But I do love her."

So he was going to be evasive about his love life? Fair enough. For as much as he claimed to like her, Valor didn't expect he'd actually want to kiss her. Again. Oh, man, remembering that kiss in the forest made her nipples harden. And she was not dressed to hide the results of those lusty thoughts. So best to avoid the discussion.

"Come on!" She dived and splashed up cool droplets. The water did taste salty as she swam a few feet and then surfaced. Sputtering out the nasty-tasting water, she flipped back her hair and stood, now waist deep. It looked less bubble gummy from this angle, but still kind of, sort of pink when it caught glimmers of moonlight. "Isn't this amazing?"

"It is a wonder." Kelyn hadn't dived, and still stood where she'd left him. The water swayed his body back and forth. "Go ahead for a swim. I can wait."

"I will. Maybe. The water tastes nasty. Let's get what we need first."

"You got something to put the water in?"

"Right here." Tugging the vials from the side of her hip where she'd tucked them in her bikini bottoms, she waved them before him. When he tried to snatch one from her, she flinched away.

"Four of them?" he challenged.

"Yep. This one is for what we need." She scooped in water and corked the vial. She tucked it back at her hip. "This one is for backup. This one is for just in case. And this one is for whatever is going to get fucked up. Because plans always get fucked. I swear it by Dana Scully."

"Valor." He closed both hands over the vials she hadn't dipped yet but didn't try to take them away from her. "We mustn't be greedy."

"Seriously? These vials will hold a few drops out of this massive lake. Hey, I only took two werewolf claws, so give me some credit for restraint. What happens if one of these breaks during our travel?"

She fluttered her lashes at him and he took the bait with a big smile and a reluctant head-bobbing yet agreeing nod.

"Fine." He crossed his arms and watched as she filled the next two vials and handed them to him. He waggled the first vial and held it up so the moon gleamed through it. "Still looks pink. This is freaky."

"You should be able to float in this lake," she offered, "for all the salt."

"Oh, yeah?" Kelyn leaned back and spread out his arms, floating away from her. "Oh, man, this is cool!"

"And look, you haven't drowned!"

"Yet!"

Filling the last vial, she tucked it at her hip alongside the other. Then, flopping backward with a splash, she joined Kelyn. It was easy to float in this water. And much better than taking another dive and tasting the horrible stuff. Her body felt as if it were floating higher than usual. Her head hadn't even gone under when she fell backward. *Cool.*

A tug at her fingertips turned her in the water and she spun in a half circle, her head floating close to Kelyn's head. He held her at arm's length. "My brothers will never believe I actually had fun in a lake."

"You're having fun?"

"Hell, yes. I've flown across the world. Jumped out of a freakin' helicopter. And now I'm floating in a pink lake. As far as life experiences go, this one tops the list."

"Seems like a faery should have had a lot of cool experiences."

"I'm like everyone else, Valor."

"Except for the wings part. But I suppose flying is like walking to you, eh?" She bumped her head against his shoulder, which set her body on a curving trajectory alongside his.

"It was," he said, and she felt his longing for what he'd once had.

Damn, she shouldn't have brought that up.

"We'll get them back for you," she encouraged. "I promise you that."

"I don't need your promise. Just the fact that you're willing to help is enough for me. So I wonder about the color of this lake. It must be algae that makes it pink."

"Probably. And just think. That algae is all over us. Getting in places we'd rather it not be."

"Sounds not so fun."

She laughed then, which always managed to come out as a chortle and a snort.

Kelyn stood abruptly and whipped his head back to disperse the water from his hair. Droplets trickled down his face. As she stood upright Valor slapped a hand over the two vials, spellbound by the moonlight that glinted in his eyes. The cool white illumination gliding along his sharp bone structure and violet eyes made them unnaturally beautiful. A true faery.

But he was staring at her with such a silly smile. And she had to wonder if she had something on her face. "What? Is it the algae? Is it pink?"

"I adore your laugh," he said.

"Ha! You're crazy. I laugh like a pig on acid."

"Maybe hallucinogenic pigs are my thing?"

"Yep, you are definitely too nice. Hand me those vials. Think we should get out and dry off before the helicopter returns?" she asked, while thinking she'd just said the stupidest thing on the planet.

Leave now, when they'd only gotten in the water and

it was like they stood on some kind of fantasy stage? She was alone with the guy. Who had expressed interest in her. Why not take advantage of it?

"Sure. But let's spend a few more minutes in the water to remember this place. And how we feel. You know… the moonlight is dancing in your eyes."

Valor felt a blush rise and looked down and away from his mesmerizing gaze.

"The water shimmers like jewels in your hair," he continued. "And there's this."

With a sweep of his hand between them, he dispersed his natural dust into the air. It glittered and hung suspended about them like millions of tiny stars fallen to earth.

Wow. Talk about instant romance. And yes, she was a woman who could appreciate a little romance when it presented itself. Which rarely happened, so…when life offered a challenge…

"You know I'm an air witch. But I can use the subtle surface winds to make this happen."

A sweep of her hand above the surface lifted up water that ascended around them in dotted columns as if caging them in. The droplets caught Kelyn's dust, and combined with the moonlight, they stood on a rock star's stage, highlighted for all to see.

"And how about this?"

Spreading out one arm and snapping her fingers shot up a spurt of water about twenty feet away. Followed by another spurt, and another, until they had become a fountain spilling diamonds beside them.

"Stunning. You win the magic portion of this evening. But now it's my turn. And I can't think of anything I'd rather do than this."

Thinking he was going to show her some of his faery magic, Valor lost all power of reasoning when he did not.

Instead, Kelyn bent and kissed her. His hand slid across her back and he coaxed her up against his chest. Her feet left the sand because the water truly was magical in making her weightless. Or maybe it was the kiss. It made her soar.

Yeah, it was the kiss.

She spread her hand up, walking her fingers over Kelyn's hard pecs as he opened her mouth and dashed his tongue with hers. Valor moaned into him, and the vibrations of her pleasure tickled in her chest. She gripped the wet ends of his hair, anchoring herself, while her knees bent and she was completely supported by his arm.

If the moon never set and the sun never rose, she would take this moment, standing in a pink lake on an unpopulated island, surrounded by faery dust and a glimmering pink water fountain, and remember it forever. Her heartbeat raced with the excitement gleaned from his touch, his taste, his intense focus on the kiss.

The last time she kissed this man, she'd thought she was going to die. Now she thought for sure she could live forever in his arms. Safe and desired. A real girl? Probably not. But she wasn't going to spoil the fantasy by thinking about it one moment longer.

Mmm, what a delicious kiss. Every part of her tingled with the giddiness. She leaned into him, hugging her hard nipples against his chest. The man moaned appreciatively. And that utterance increased her want tenfold. She dug in her nails at his shoulder, which didn't make him flinch. So much man. And all hers. For now.

And now was all that mattered.

When he pulled away, Valor whispered, "That was awesome."

"I'll say. We should kiss again—ah. Here it comes."

"What?" Something was coming? Could it be her, pretty please?

"The helicopter is back early."

"Dana Scully."

"Exactly. We'd better return to shore and pack up quickly."

Grasping her hand, he led her out of the water. As she exited, her magic ceased and the fountain dissipated. Valor pulled out the sweatshirt she'd worn here and used it to wipe off her legs and arms. They shoved pants and boots on and Kelyn flashed the LED beacon that would mark their position to the pilot.

As they stood waiting for the ride, he clasped her hand and she squeezed it. "Why did you do that?" she asked in quiet wonder.

"Kiss you? I thought you said it was awesome."

"It was. But I...I don't know. I didn't think we'd have a chance."

"Really? You've always had a chance with me, Valor."

"Until your brother."

"Which we've solved. Do you purposely argue about issues you've already won just to be annoying?"

She released their grasp and punched him on the biceps. None too gently.

"Annoying it is," he said, and rushed over to grab the rappel rope and gear that had dropped down from the helicopter.

Chapter 9

For some reason, Kelyn had paid for two first-class tickets across the world, a helicopter, rappel gear rental and a private limo. But he'd only put out for one hotel room with a king-size bed.

Valor wasn't averse to sharing a bed with a male friend. She'd done it before. Well, she'd shared the couch with Trouble because they'd both fallen asleep full of pizza and watching Bruce Willis. Yippee-ki-yay!

Setting her backpack on the end of the bed, she reasoned with herself. Sex wasn't always on the table for situations like this. She was a grown-up and the men she hung with were grown-ups, as well. They could share a bed without getting all squicky about it.

Except.

She felt a little weird about sleeping next to the guy she was kind of, sort of, starting to have feelings for. But she didn't want to tell him that. And she didn't expect he felt the same way. Only, okay, he had confessed to liking her until he'd thought she and Trouble had gotten it on. Which they had not.

And he had kissed her. Like, *totally* kissed her in the pink lake. That had been one for the books.

And now? Kelyn walked around the room, stripping off his shirt and announcing he was going to take a shower first, if she didn't mind. Despite the sensation of dried algae having worked its way into strange places on her body, Valor eagerly nodded and gestured for him to go for it.

Now that the bathroom door was closed, she collapsed onto the chair and put her bare feet up on the end of the bed. Then she took them down. There was something on her big toe. Dried algae? Beach sand? Some kind of crustacean from the pink lake? She didn't want to know. She needed a shower and to crash. It had been a long day and night, and the flight from the United States and her anxiety had only compounded her exhaustion. She could almost allow herself to fall asleep right here on the chair—not in the same bed as Kelyn—but she'd noticed a distinct smell in her hair and knew she wouldn't rest until she was clean.

The four vials of lake water sat on the table, looking barely pink under the awful yellow lamplight.

On to the next ingredient. Which, according to the research Valor had done during the cab ride to this hotel, could only be located in Wales. And Kelyn probably wasn't going to like that adventure. She'd tell him about it when it was too late to back out. And if she had to, she'd seduce him with another kiss.

She could totally work the seduction when she put her mind to it.

Smiling to herself, she tilted her head back, but sat upright when the bathroom door opened and out strolled a steaming man with slicked-back hair and abs that glistened with water droplets.

Of all the television doctors' names she had ever spoken in oath, she could not remember a single name now.

"All yours," he said, one hand propped casually over the twist in the towel at his hip. The towel rode low, exposing the cut muscles that V'd toward—oh, so many fantasies visited Valor's lusty thoughts. Most of them involved licking the water droplets from Kelyn's skin and…

"Yep." Despite her waning energy, she hopped up and slipped past him to quickly close the bathroom door. Only when she stood alone in the steamy little room did she dare to let out a breath and shake her head. "Man, those abs. Whoever thought faeries were scrawny, delicate creatures?"

How she'd managed not to drag her fingers across those spectacular ridged abs was beyond her. Would she survive this trip if they continued to share a room? Because she wasn't beyond having sex with a friend for the sake of it. To feed a desire. To get off. To have some fun.

But, for some reason, it felt dangerous to consider having sex with Kelyn. Emotionally risky. And maybe even like a commitment.

Valor shook her head. "Don't be a fool."

She'd never been one for long-term relationships. Until recently.

Because now? She craved something more than the

flirtations or few short months she'd shared with men most of her life.

But she hadn't had that in her life because she simply wasn't the kind of woman men considered for relationships. She knew that for a fact. Someone had told her so. In the most abrupt and heart-wrenching manner possible.

And besides, Kelyn would never see her as a woman who could satisfy his lust for the sexy and sensual. That man needed a real woman and not one who could only fake it when at her best.

She drew a sigil in the steam on the mirror. It was the same one she'd drawn in the moss with the angel dust that night in the Darkwood.

"You missed your chance to be loved, witch."

Kelyn pulled on a pair of clean jeans and grimaced. He normally slept naked. But that wouldn't work with Valor lying on the bed next to him. Well, it could.

He considered it a few seconds, then shook his head and zipped up the fly. "Nope."

He wasn't sure where he stood with her, and he didn't want to freak her out or press any issue for which she might not be on board. Such as the two of them getting close and…yes, sex was definitely on the table for him. But she didn't feel the same way about him as he did her. She couldn't. Why had he confessed his infatuation to her? She must think him some kind of crazy after all they'd been through.

And yet he'd gone for it at the lake. That kiss had been some kind of all right. He'd thought it was a signal between them that he was okay to move forward with whatever might happen between the two of them. But she hadn't given him that same signal, so he would have to mark the kiss off as a one-time thing.

Two times, actually. He'd not forgotten the kiss in the forest. She'd been desperate that time, thinking death was near. The lake had been completely different. Yeah, he'd blame it on the unruly lake and the enchantment that had literally glittered in the air.

Until the helicopter had swooped low and destroyed the moment.

He flung himself onto the bed, propped up two pillows behind his head and closed his eyes. Man, it felt great to get the lake smell out of his hair. And he was bone weary. Which also felt great. He wasn't one to sleep a lot, but he sensed he'd get forty winks tonight. Which was almost morning. It had been a long day.

Now they had gained one more ingredient for the witch's spell that would, he hoped, open a portal to Faery.

Did he believe after the portal was open they could simply take a jaunt through and his wings would be waiting there for the taking? Not at all. But the hope of having that entry—a place to start—was enough to keep him going. He wanted his strength and power back.

And he wanted to set foot in Faery. It was something he'd dreamed about all his life. Like any child who had ever dreamed of going to Disneyland, Kelyn had dreamed of going to his homeland. His mother had told him tales of the azure skies and many moons that could be seen at any time, day or night. How so many different species thrived, loved, fought and existed in Faery. Sprites, dragons, unicorns and so many breeds of *sidhe* they were impossible to tally.

The bathroom door opened, and Kelyn made a point

of not opening his eyes. He didn't want the tease of a wet witch in a towel to stir his desires and have him trying to hide a hard-on. If he made it through this night, he'd wake with blue balls, for sure.

"You sleeping?" Valor asked softly.

He felt the bed move when she sat on the other side.

"Almost."

"Thanks for everything, Kelyn. It's been a great trip. And while I know we both had business in mind with the lake, it was an adventure I'll never forget."

"It was awesome. I like trying new things. I've always considered myself an adventurous guy. Me, the one who's never even been Up North. But today? Rappelling down a rope from a helicopter? That rocked."

"You're telling me."

"You weren't nervous about the flight, either. That surprised me."

"Didn't have time to freak out. And I think because it was wide-open, and I wasn't stuffed into a tin can, I lost most of my fear. It was like…free-flying."

"Not even close. But I'll give you that one."

"Thanks." She lay down and he opened one eye. He could see her bare legs stretched over the folded-back coverlet. She smelled like the hotel's orange shampoo, and it made him hungry. But not for food.

She turned to her side, and he knew she faced him, so he tilted his head and met her gaze in the darkness. He could still see quite well in the dark, even without his wings.

"You know that kiss?" she asked. "Not the one at the lake but the one in the Darkwood."

"Uh…yeah?"

"In that moment, when the tree was sucking me into

the ground, I thought I was going to die. And...I haven't kissed another man since."

That had been four months ago. Really? She hadn't kissed another man? Kelyn mumbled a noise of assurance.

"I wanted you to know," she said. "I haven't felt like dating since then. I know I have no right, and I promise I'm over with the apologies, but I've sort of carried what happened as a heavy burden. But I think I'm ready to shuck it off my shoulders now."

By rights? She should have carried that burden. For a little while anyway. And that was his angry, pissed-off self thinking that. But it was a real emotion, and he owned it as it tensed his muscles and chased away any thought of touching her sweet-smelling, wet hair.

Now she rolled to her back. "I'm tired," she said. "Good night, Kelyn."

He nodded, knowing she couldn't hear that motion. He didn't know what to say or how to act around her. Because he wasn't sure what was happening between them. While he had every reason to hate the woman, every fiber of his being wanted to reach out and pull her to him and hold her close.

And while he stared at the back of her head and willed his arm to reach for her, no part of his body moved, save for his heart, sinking a little deeper into his chest.

Chapter 10

Valor woke to bright sunlight. She'd forgotten to pull the heavy curtains, and, man, did the sun look high in the sky! It must be noon. She'd slept not so long, though, because they'd gotten in early in the morning.

Wondering about room service, she pulled down the sheet to get out of bed and realized a man's arm was holding her against his body. A warm body. Rigid pectorals hugged her back. And a relaxed arm braceleted with a ring of silvery scars about his wrist hold her prisoner.

Hmm…

Attempting to move the arm would surely wake him. How had she gotten into such a position with her back against Kelyn's bare chest and him holding her as if they were lovers? His curled fingers rested below her breast on the bed, not touching her. But still…

Nice. The wish to turn back time so she could have

been awake to enjoy their closeness more thoroughly ended with a sigh. It was probably a natural movement he did in his sleep when lying next to a woman. Surely such a good-looking man as Kelyn Saint-Pierre had slept with many. She wasn't special. And they did not have an exclusive thing.

So. She'd have to do this like the proverbial Band-Aid. Rip it off and risk waking him to save her the embarrassment of simply lying there until he decided to wake up.

Not that anything could embarrass her. There was nothing wrong with snuggling with the guy. And he smelled great. The orange-shampoo scent they shared had dissipated and now all she smelled was him. The man oozed an alchemy of earth and air and something ineffable. Perhaps a masculine sort of surety. So she remained there a few minutes longer, enjoying the contact. Was it so wrong to steal the pleasure of an embrace even if the guy wasn't aware of it?

She didn't think so.

After five minutes she decided this was getting weird. Much as she enjoyed it, she also felt squicky about stealing the guy's empathy. Which was what it had felt like since they'd gotten together on this adventure. Like he was being nice to appease her. When, really, why didn't he yell at her? Accuse her? Get out the anger he had to have for what had happened?

Blowing out a decisive breath, Valor nudged carefully at Kelyn's arm and, as she did so, glided forward on the bed, which effectively lifted his arm and allowed her freedom. When his arm dropped and she sat up, he startled awake.

The guy eyeballed her, closed his eyes and smiled. "Morning."

"It is. Or maybe it's noon. Or possibly even later. Didn't mean to startle you, but we were, uh…not sure how I ended up snuggled against you like that."

"It was nice," he said. Pushing his hands back through his hair, he again opened his eyes. The bright sunshine found his violet irises and danced there. "You snuggled up to me."

"Uh, no. I don't think so. I'm sure it was you who wrapped an arm around me."

Valor slid to the edge of the bed, prepared to stand, when suddenly Kelyn grabbed her by the shoulder and pulled her down. Her head landed on the pillow, and the faery moved in for a kiss. A kiss! It was a quick one, as far as kisses being clocked went, but it was fun and landed on her lips just long enough for her to regret not snuggling with him longer.

"Okay, *I* wrapped an arm around you," he said. "The witch wins again. Now, get dressed. We need to forage for food. Then onward."

He got up and strode into the bathroom, while Valor could only lie there, touching her mouth. His kisses got better and better. Even the short and admonishing ones. And he took them whenever the moment seemed to strike him. She couldn't think of a reason to argue with such blatant thievery.

Had he actually kissed her silly?

"Yes, Marcus Welby, he did."

They managed to find another buffet restaurant, which seemed to be the witch's favorite eating style. Plate heaped with an assortment of meats, veggies, cheeses and something blue and jiggly even Kelyn couldn't identify, she was in heaven.

"I like a woman with a healthy appetite," he said while buttering the toast, preparing to smear the fried egg with the runny yoke over it. He was a vegetarian, but cheated with eggs and butter.

"I like a man who's not afraid to be weird," she said. "Eggs on toast?"

"You think this is weird?" He pointed to her blue concoction in challenging comparison.

"Hey, it's one of the food groups. Sugar. But first, veggies." She scraped up a forkload of peas and scooped it into her mouth. "Did you book a flight for us? Wales is our next destination."

"I will do that as soon as I'm done eating. Can a person fly into Wales or do we need to hit England first?"

"Not sure. Never been out of the States before, remember? And I will need to do some serious drinking before we get on another plane."

"Yes, because that worked so well for your flight here. Unless you don't mind me carrying you on as extra luggage?"

"Hey, if I could not be nervous I would. There's not a spell in my arsenal that'll chill me out, so you'll have to deal with a drunk witch."

"I have no problem with that. You're cute when you pass out and snore."

She rolled her eyes but didn't cease her eating.

"Do you think if the airplane had no sides, and all the seats were open to the elements, you'd be good? You were with the helicopter."

"I... No. We didn't go very high in the sky. Maybe it's that in the airplane you go so high and you can't see how high it is. Just...accept me as I am, okay?"

"I do. I appreciate everything you're doing for me,"

Kelyn said because he felt the need to soften that dig at her snores. "So, can you remind me of what's the next thing on the list?"

"Uh…" She sipped the black coffee then made a great show of stirring in more cream and tons of sugar and swirling it with the spoon. He couldn't quite make out what she said when she mumbled, "Mermaid's…'iss."

"A what? Something about mermaids. And I know they are not the nicest of all this realm's creatures to deal with."

"You need a mermaid's kiss," she said heatedly. "Did you hear that?"

Right. He had read that on the list. Hadn't thought much of it at the time, though. Kelyn sat back and set his fork aside, no longer hungry. From the tales his mother had told him as a kid, he knew mermaids were vicious and feral. No smart man, werewolf or even faery liked to go near them.

And then there was that other issue.

"I don't know how that's going to work," he said. "I mean, first you have to find one. Depths of the ocean? And me not being a swimmer?" He shrugged. "But even if we do manage success, how does a person store something like that?"

"Don't you worry about the storage process. All you have to do is get the kiss. I'll take care of the rest. There could be an issue with you not being a swimmer, though."

"You think?"

Lake Hillier had been shallow, at least, as far in as they'd waded. And he'd floated like a dream. But searching for a mermaid could mean greater depths, and diving, and actually knowing how to breathe underwater.

His brothers had always teased him about avoiding the waterfalls out in the back of their family land and that someday he'd surely want to know how to swim. It wasn't that water frightened him or he feared drowning. He *had* tried to swim on many occasions. But lighter-than-air bones did not make for an easy swim. He had always floated on the surface like deadwood.

No way could he manage a dive into the ocean. It would be comical, to say the least.

"We'll figure something out." She lifted a fork of the blue jiggly stuff before her. "Here's to mermaid kisses and keeping the faery all in one piece."

In one piece? Reluctant to toast to that, but ever up for a challenge, Kelyn lifted his egg-smeared toast and tapped it against Valor's fork. "And to one wily witch who intends to dangle the faery from the end of her hook."

She winked at him then, and he couldn't help laughing. The witch did have a way of sneaking in an irresistible challenge. Feminine wiles? Kind of. Sort of. Valor was a tomboy to the bone. But he had lain with his arm wrapped about her through the morning and he knew she was soft and sensual, and her hair had smelled like oranges. He wanted to touch more and more of her. And steal another kiss.

And maybe next time he wouldn't have to steal it.

It might be a good idea to up his seduction game before they got to the mermaids. Because that was one situation he wasn't sure he'd come out of alive.

Kelyn hauled the drunk witch over one shoulder and onto the plane. Once again, he'd procured first class, knowing they'd have more room and privacy for Valor to revel in her drunken nervousness. He smiled and complimented all the stewardesses as he made his way to their seats.

Depositing Valor on the seat next to the window startled her awake. She curled up her legs and tucked her hands under her chin. He settled next to her, pulling the blanket from its plastic bag and tucking it over her. "You're doing good, witch. It won't be long now."

The flight was twenty hours and included a quick layover in Cardiff, but she didn't need to know that.

"You're so good to me." Her eyes fluttered open and she smiled drunkenly. "I love you."

"I love you when you're love drunk," he stated, knowing it was the booze that had delivered such effusive adoration.

"I haven't been able to stop thinking about us, what we could have been, since the forest," she confessed.

"Me, as well." Kelyn tilted his head against hers and pulled in his long legs to allow others to get by in the narrow aisle. "I think it's time we make a go for what could have been."

Valor sighed. "If you say so."

And then she passed out.

The layover in Cardiff was more like a sprint. They had ten minutes to hop on the plane to Anglesey. Valor had made the dash on her own, but, teasing the last vestiges of intoxication for all she could manage, she had grasped for sleep again as the plane departed. With Kelyn's hand clasping hers she'd survived the flight across the ocean and Europe.

Now she thanked the stewardesses profusely as the plane landed. She'd been awake for about twenty minutes, had washed her face with a warm hand towel—man, did she love first class!—snacked on some grapes and cheese, and listened to Kelyn snore softly beside her. Bless the guy for putting up with her crazy-ass phobia.

He was too good to be true. What guy put up with stuff like that, and after having sacrificed his wings for her? She didn't deserve any of his kindness, but she wanted to earn his respect. And had he said something about them making a go for it?

A go for what? She couldn't remember what they'd been discussing when she was tilting twenty sheets to the wind upon departing the Sydney Airport. Hawkeye Pierce, that seemed like something she should have remembered.

Kelyn startled awake and looked around. The rest of first class had disembarked; the seats were littered with magazines and plastic water bottles.

"We've landed and can get off anytime," she said, "but I wanted to let you sleep. Coach is deplaning right now. How do you feel? Did you get some good rest?"

He snarled at her—actually snarled—and stood to get his bag out of the overhead compartment. "Come on," he muttered, and wandered off.

O…kay.

"Guess it's someone else's turn to be grumpy," she muttered. And instead of teasing him about it, she decided he deserved to act however he wished.

Valor followed Kelyn through the airport, loving the British accents that buzzed about her. There was something about a foreign accent that made her happy. It was so out of her usual realm. The Australian accent had pleased her, as well.

A taxi took them into town and Valor directed the

driver to a hardware store, where she intended to pick up some supplies for this leg of their adventure. She'd thought about it on the plane and had come up with as short a list as possible, yet still the essentials.

Down aisle nine, she grabbed a coiled green nylon rope and handed it back to Grumpy Kelyn. Sunglasses in place and hair tousled messily, he'd followed her into the store without a word. If he'd had a cigarette hanging out the corner of his mouth, he might have looked silver-screen cool. As it was, he was just plain annoying.

He slung the rope over a shoulder and shadowed her quietly down the aisle. The guy had a right to let loose his inner grump—why, his downright anger—toward her. It had to have happened sooner or later. So she wouldn't make a fuss and she'd try to stay out of what was surely a laser-beam glare radiating from behind those sunglasses.

Though, it took all her composure not to suggest she had a spell for his pouty face. And she did. She could whisper a man into a smile with but a few words. And that wasn't even a love spell; it was simply a cheer spell. Such a thing came in handy at the brewery when she sensed a fight was on the verge of erupting.

Down another aisle she sized up the harnesses and assorted safety gear used for climbing roofs. Holding one up before Kelyn, she checked the size, nodded and handed him the find.

They hadn't been able to carry weapons on the plane, and while she hadn't thought to look for a weapons shop along the way, she did manage to find a nifty jackknife in the hunting aisle. There were no rifles in this store, mostly traps and some camo gear. Generally she wore a thigh strap. A girl should never leave home without a blade. This folding blade was so small she could tuck it in a front pocket. It would have to suffice. When she asked Kelyn if he wanted a weapon, he merely shook his head.

So the grump continued. Fine. He'd be cursing his bad mood later if and when he needed to defend himself.

With hope, no defense would be necessary. How dangerous could a slimy chick with a tail actually be? Valor crossed her fingers and whispered a prayer to Liban, the goddess of the Irish Sea, for an easy task ahead of them.

Heading for the checkouts, she eyed Kelyn from the corner of her vision as he grabbed bags of chips and jerky from an array of brightly colored impulse items. So the guy was hungry? By the time they hit the register, he'd amassed four bags of snacks and a six-pack of bottled water.

"Good plan," she commented. "We'll need the fuel."

"Did you want something to eat?" he asked.

Valor turned her head to gape at him. "You're not going to share? What happened to you over the airspace between Australia and the UK? Dude, try a freakin' smile."

She might have actually felt his laser glare this time.

With a frustrated sigh, she handed over her credit card to the cashier, noticing Kelyn didn't offer, as she expected he might. Instead, he grabbed the stuff and headed out to the cab, leaving her to wonder if she'd done something wrong. Had she muttered something in her sleep about him?

Generally her own snoring woke her up, but she'd never been known to be a sleep talker. Hmm...she had never thought of herself as a mean or nasty drunk, either.

Must be a faery thing. Yeah, she would go with that.

* * *

Rain beat the tarmac and the sides of the hotel building as if it had a vengeance wish against the world. Kelyn paced the hotel suite, which featured two queen beds, a coffee maker and microwave and a narrow—and cracked—hot tub. He'd dropped the bag of supplies inside the doorway and was relieved when Valor said she was heading down to check out the restaurant and would bring up some food.

Thankful for a few minutes alone, he paced before the window that overlooked the weed-overgrown parking lot. This tiny town twenty miles out from the city where they'd landed reminded him of the proverbial quaint foreign village where assorted characters always got into loads of trouble with the craziest yet most down-to-earth acts. A movie set if ever he'd seen one.

Thinking about acting crazy…he'd been acting like an asshole since the plane landed. But he couldn't help it. He massaged the back of his shoulder, wincing at the pain that pulsed from where his wings had once been. Mercy, it felt like electric currents zapping in rapid beats and radiating out across his back. It had begun the moment he woke on the airplane and had not ceased since.

He spread out his arms and raised them above his head in an attempt to stretch the muscles and alleviate some of the pain. What was causing the weird phantom pain? Ah, hell. The moon must be nearing fullness. He'd been feeling this pain monthly. He'd always known his body aligned with the moon's phases. A faery thing.

The pain usually lasted a day and he then forgot about it until the next month. Pissy time for it to happen now, when he didn't mean to be so awful to Valor. She didn't deserve his anger. And he most certainly had not needed all those unhealthy bags of chips and—had he really picked up beef jerky?

A knock at the door that sounded like it came from a boot toe hurried him over to open it. Valor carried a stack of tinfoil-wrapped foods that smelled delicious.

"They offered room service," she said, walking in and handing him half the goods. "But I love sitting in a restaurant listening to others' conversations. All those cool accents! And I had a drink at the bar. And…I know you wanted some time to yourself. You feeling any better?"

"I'll be fine. Thanks for this. I'm starving." He really was in a foul mood. "Are we going to head out today?"

"It's already evening, and I'm not much for mermaid hunting in the dark. Or a monsoon. The weather report says this rain will continue through the night. There's a casino attached to the hotel. Maybe we could hang around tonight, then head out bright and early in the morning?"

"Sounds like a plan."

He set the food on the table and peeled open the foil. Savory scents wafted into the room. One of the containers held a burger dripping with cheese. He shoved that across the table. The other offered steamed veggies and white rice. It would do.

The water he'd gotten in the hardware store served them both, and, along with a couple bags of chips, they had a meal.

"You like to gamble, Kelyn?"

"Uh…" He paused with the fork to his lips. Sounded like a trick question to him.

"In the casino," she added. "I'm not much for the tables, but I do like to play the penny machines. What do they call them here in the UK?"

"Not sure. Shillings? We're both out of our element here." He winced and she saw it, so he leaned over the rice and gave it his utmost attention.

"Tell me what's up with you, Kelyn."

"Why does something have to be up?"

"Because while I don't deserve your kindness, you've been nothing but a gentleman since we set off on this adventure. So today has been a little unsettling with you playing the silent and pissed act. Did you sleep with your neck twisted on the plane or something?"

He pushed the food container away from himself and hitched a foot up on the end of the bed, tilting his head back against the chair. The position alleviated some of the pain between his shoulder blades.

"It's a faery thing," he finally said.

"Really?" Valor wiped a smear of ketchup from the corner of her mouth and guzzled down the last of a bottle of water. "Instead of spreading love, cheer and faery dust, you have a sneer and retreat day? I don't get it."

"I can feel my wings," he said heatedly. Then he cautioned himself not to release his frustrations on her and softened his tone. "It's like phantom pain. And it hits me once a month right around when the moon is full. Makes me irritable."

"Are you seriously telling me you're having a faery period?"

He glared at her.

"Sorry, couldn't resist that one. Come on," she pleaded with a growing grin. "You know that was funny."

Yeah, so she was right. But his smirk didn't quite touch mirth.

"So you're in pain. Because of your missing wings?"

"Yes. I'm sorry for being a jerk to you, but I just…"

He eased a shoulder forward, cringing at the sting. "It'll be better tomorrow. Promise."

"Kelyn, I'm so sorry. What if I give you a back rub? Do you think that would help?"

"I...don't know." He'd not thought massage could help, but he hadn't tried it before. "You don't need to."

"Let me try. Seriously. I have some healing magic in these fingers, but not a lot. I think all the working with engines and heavy-duty lifting at the brewery counters most of the vital energy I would otherwise have to heal. But I can give it a go. It'll feel like a nice warm deep-tissue massage if I work it right. Lie down on the bed. Pretty please?"

No woman had ever said *pretty please* to him before and made it so sexually inviting. She probably hadn't intended it to sound that way, but Kelyn felt her innocent suggestion all the way to his cock. And that was not so much weird as something that cautioned him.

But, really? He wanted to feel her hands on him. And who knew? Maybe a massage would bring them closer together, if not help with the pain. He wasn't averse to a little witchy healing magic.

Chapter 11

Kelyn stood and pulled off his shirt, groaning as the stretch tweaked at his back muscles.

"That bad, huh?" Valor walked around behind him and he flinched when her fingers touched his spine. "I'll be careful. Just show me where it hurts the most. Here?"

She touched gently where his wings had once sprouted from his back. When they'd been severed, nothing had remained, not even a lump. A thin scar was the only reminder he'd ever had anything back there.

He nodded. "That's the spot."

"The scars are like those at your wrists and on your chest."

"The sigils were a living, magical part of me. Sort of like stripping out my veins when I lost those. But the pain was brief and I don't feel anything on those places now." Unfortunately.

He missed having the sigils. He'd once been able to conjure air magic that might have rivaled Valor's. And the sigils had aided his navigation and enhanced his senses. Having sex with an activated sigil? Mind-blowing. Or so he'd been told. He'd never brought out his wings or exposed his activated sigils to a human woman while having sex. Just not wise.

"Lie down," Valor said. "Let me get my crystals out of my pack. I never go anywhere without them!"

He crawled onto the bed and lay stomach down. Tucking the mouse alicorn and black ring to the side, he fisted a hand under his chin and listened to her rummage through her backpack. He liked crystals and felt an affinity to selenite and tourmaline. The two were protective and cleansing stones. He wasn't sure about the circle he wore at his neck, but he thought it could be black tourmaline.

The sound of rocks clacking preceded Valor's voice. "I've got quartz, amethyst and seraphinite. Not sure how the seraphinite will react to a faery. It's a stone of the angels, you know."

"Legend tells that we faeries descended from the angels. That we were the Fallen Ones who landed on a realm other than this mortal plane, and that's how Faery was created. My mother used to tell me faery tales when I was little."

"The creation of Faery originated from angels? I like that. It's been a long time since I've seen my parents. I'm going to lay these on your back and work a little magic, and when your muscles have relaxed, I'll try a gentle massage. You good with that?"

"Work your witchy magic, witch. I'll let you know if it hurts."

"I don't hurt guys."

He laid his cheek on the bed and closed his eyes. "You just tease them, eh?"

"A chick's gotta have a little fun, right?"

He smirked. The cool touch of the crystals to his back felt great. And he knew when she laid the seraphinite on his spine between his missing wings because he immediately felt the energy in subtle vibrations that shivered across his flesh and into his muscles. It might have even permeated into his bones. He moaned with satisfied relief.

"That feels good?" she asked.

"It definitely hits the spot."

"And that's the seraphinite. Cool. Then I'll let that one sit there a bit and do its thing."

"So, your parents," he said as he felt her arrange the crystals along his spine. "You haven't seen them in a long time? Where are they?"

"Not sure. I never really knew either of them. I was raised by my great-grandma Hector in the 1940s."

"Hector?"

"Yeah, it's short for Hectorine. She is a gorgeous woman."

"Is?"

"Yes, she's still alive and intends to be so for as long as she can manage. You know we witches can achieve immortality with a spell, right?"

"I've heard that. Are you immortal?"

"I am. Or, at least, until the spell wanes. It's something we have to reactivate every hundred years."

"And how is it activated?"

She leaned over him, and the sweep of her hair shivered across his bare skin. Kelyn closed his eyes and tried not to groan at the delicious sensation, and it took a lot of effort to remain silent. "You don't really want the details, do you?"

"I do." He nudged up his shoulder blade. "Right there. Is that the quartz? It can feel it vibrate in my muscle."

Valor chanted some words in a language he didn't recognize, and as they whispered into his subconscious his muscles relaxed even more.

"Good," she said softly. "The healing energies are beginning to seep into your being. So. The immortality spell that grants a witch a century of life. Not all witches do it, just those of us who are averse to growing old and want to spend as much time as we can living, discovering and learning. It involves a vampire and his, erm…heart."

"You have to seduce a vampire?"

"Seduction can be a boon to get the vampire to comply, but no. We have to consume a live, beating vampire heart to gain immortality and stop the aging process."

Kelyn pushed himself up on the bed to glance over his shoulder at her, but she avoided his gaze.

"I know. Gross," she confirmed. "Lie down."

He did, and she replaced the quartz that had tumbled off his shoulder. Should he remind her that one of his brothers was vampire?

"We all do what we gotta do and what aligns with our morals, am I right?" Valor asked.

Like sacrificing his wings because he'd wanted to save the girl? "I guess so. No judgment. But if I ever see you eating a rare steak, I promise I will have a moment of judging you."

"Isn't that something your brother Blade would do?"

"Would you ever go after Blade for his heart?"

"Absolutely not. I sought a vicious killer when I performed the spell for myself. He had harmed so many."

"So you played judge and jury?"

"You're getting judgy now."

Kelyn laid his head down again and closed his eyes. Who was he to judge what was right and wrong?

"Let's take the crystals off and I'll massage your back…"

Setting the crystals up by the pillow, she then straddled him, sitting on his hips. Kelyn's cock responded to the intimate connection of her thighs hugging his. As long as he was lying facedown, everything would be okay. The touch of her hands on his skin felt like cool water to his aching muscles. She didn't press hard, only glided back and forth where his wings had once been and down along his spine. His core shivered and he smiled.

"You've got great lats and delts," she commented.

He chuckled softly. "You've got a soothing yet stimulating touch. You should be careful. I might respond in ways you hadn't expected."

"I think that means you're feeling better. But is the massage helping the pain a bit?"

"It is. Thank you."

Her touch grew firmer and she focused on his shoulders for a while, then slowly moved down his back. Paying attention to each vertebra, she glided her thumbs progressively downward. If he could make himself relax, he might even forget about her thighs squeezing against his hips. But his erection was not of a mind to let him off so easily. Damn.

"I have a confession to make," she said.

So did he, but he sure as hell wasn't going first with this one. "Go for it."

"Hmm…" She sighed. "Should I?"

"Yes, witch, you should."

"Okay, fine. I suggested this massage so I could touch you."

Kelyn smiled at that. Score one for the wounded faery!

"You're so strong and fierce, Kelyn. Everything about you screams controlled sensuality. Your body moves like a precision instrument. And your smiles and the looks you give me sometimes. And the way your brow furrows when you're either judging me or challenging me." She sighed. "But to see you out of sorts because you're hurting? Makes my heart hurt. And I won't go there with the *s* word. Too many *sorrys* already. But I do want to go here."

The touch of her mouth to the center of his back, below his neck, startled Kelyn for a moment. Because she lingered, her warm lips caressing his skin reverently, the tiny puffs of breath from her nose sweeping his skin. And as she leaned forward, her breasts brushed his lower back.

"You're a beautiful man, Kelyn."

Being called beautiful was weird. He wasn't. And she was being kind. The sort of kind that a person felt was necessary to make another feel good. He was lacking now. He'd never be the same man without his wings. Could he ever measure up?

The next kiss landed right where his wings should have flinched because of her touch. And he felt Valor's energy seep into him in waves of heat and violet and—hmm, a twinge of warning?

Yes, that had been a strange zap that tightened his muscles painfully. His body must remember that *she* had been the reason he no longer wore wings. *Get her off*, it seemed to say.

And yet his brain could only process the intensity of his growing desire to turn over and kiss her fully and deeply. But when he pushed himself up to begin to turn, she pressed a palm against his shoulder.

"Wait," she said. "Let me do this."

The witch's hands worked more magic than she could probably imagine. Kelyn felt her touch deeply, in his muscles and through to his bones. It wasn't uncomfortable until she skated over the places where his wings had been severed. But those glancing touches remained brief. Overall, her touch buoyed him like no pink lake could.

The urge to turn over and pull her down on top of him so she could feel all of him was strong. He wasn't crass, though. Yet her touch did not warrant patience.

"Feeling better?" she asked.

"Much." He nudged the seraphinite on the pillow and glanced aside. "It's pouring out there. We're in for the night."

"I figured that. Want to watch a cheesy movie?"

"Truth?"

"Always."

"I want to make out." He turned over beneath her and looked up into Valor's not-so-surprised grinning face. "What do you think?"

"Sounds better than a movie." She swept her fingers down his chest. She hadn't quite sat down on his hips, which was a good thing. But when her strokes lowered to above the waistline of his jeans, Kelyn hissed through a tight jaw. "My magic helped to relax you. I could feel your muscles surrendering and growing lax. But parts of you are very…"

"Tense," he said with a wink. And, grabbing her wrist to stop her from venturing lower, he pulled her down until she was nose to nose with him. He inhaled her witchy scent of sage and cheeseburger and studied her gaze. "There's only one way to ease that tension."

"Yeah, I figured. Oh, what's this?" She studied her fingers, which now glinted with his innate dust.

"You are familiar with what happens to faeries when we get aroused?"

"Right. I thought that was only when they come. Like, from orgasm."

"Close. Some of us put out dust when we're feeling… you know."

"Really? So, whenever you're turned on? Hmm…" She rubbed her fingers together, then sniffed the dust. "I could use this stuff."

"Seriously, witch? I thought we were, uh…doing something here?"

"Sorry. It's just so useful. And hard to come by."

"My dust is not included on your ingredient list."

"But you never know—"

He pushed up her shirt and tugged it off over her head, startling her to abandon her absentminded wondering. She wore no bra and her breasts were small and— the word *adorable* came to mind, but he wasn't sure she'd like that assessment. Kelyn pulled her down to lick one nipple and she quickly forgot the sparkles on her fingers. She shouldn't worry about missing out on collecting some dust for her spells. If they had sex, she'd be covered with the stuff. It made having sex with mortal women difficult to explain, so he had often tried to pick up clubbers glittered up to the nines. Come morning? Neither could determine who wore more glitter than the other.

"Oh, that's good," she said as he laved his tongue around her tight nipple. "You've definitely recovered from your grumpiness."

"That I have."

With his tongue, he teased a trail across her heated skin to her other nipple, as if indulging in a tiny treat. He was fascinated by their tightness and the barely there swells of her breasts. Every lick seemed to produce a different tone of pleasure from her. He most certainly was no longer in a bad mood, even if subtle twinges of pain had already returned to his back.

Easing his hips against hers, he reveled in the pressure against his erection. Oh, yes, if she moved her hips like that...

"Wait." She sat up, moving out from under him, and put her hands over her breasts. "This isn't the right time."

"The right—what do you mean? Aren't you into me?"

"Yes, very much so." She studied her fingers again, frowning at the dust that glittered on the tips. "But something doesn't feel right. It's like we haven't earned this."

"That's..." The strangest excuse for trying to get out of sex he had heard. Not that he'd been given excuses before, but seriously? Man, had he read this woman wrong! Kelyn blew out a frustrated breath. "I get it. You're not into faeries."

He shoved himself up and strode over to the window, pressing a palm to the rain-streaked glass. He flexed his shoulders, pressing back toward the center of his back. The ache had returned. And his cock was hard as steel, which was why he wouldn't turn to face her. Talk about leaving him high and dry.

"So, what time are we heading out tomorrow?" he asked. "Do we know where we're going?"

"Not yet. And would you chill, Kelyn? You're acting like I slapped you or something."

He turned a look over his shoulder. "Didn't you?"

"I did not!"

"Well, it felt like it. I'm getting mixed signals from you, Valor. One minute you're kissing me and touching me in all the ways that you know turn a man on. And the next?" He turned and stretched out his arms in surrender. "This."

Her eyes strayed to his obvious erection, and she inhaled deeply and let her shoulders drop. Hands still over her bare breasts, she nodded. "You're right. It is me. But it's not because I don't like you or am not interested. You're the sexiest man to walk into my life. Ever."

"Then what's wrong, witch?"

She shuddered. "You know you said *witch* like a swear word?"

"Sorry. I'm just—" he flung up his hands in defeat "—off balance right now. The moon and my phantom pain. All this travel. And I'm having trouble with this whole *us* thing."

"I get that. And they are all legitimate excuses—"

"I'm not making excuses, Valor. This is me. I expected… Hell, I read you wrong."

"You didn't. But I read you wrong. I think you're still hung up on what I did to you. How could you possibly trust me or even desire me after—"

Kelyn silenced her foolish protest with a long, hard kiss that opened her mouth and branded her with his desires. He wanted her so desperately right now. And she had lured him close enough to taste that which he wanted.

But if she didn't think the time was right, he didn't want to press. He was no man to force a woman into anything.

Reluctantly, he broke the kiss. "After?" he said to her uncertainty. "What's done is done, Valor. Move forward. I'm trying to. But it's like walking up a down escalator with you. I don't ever seem to connect."

He grabbed his shirt. Tugging it on, he strode toward the door. "I'm going down to check out the casino. While I'm there I'll give Erte a call. Good friend of mine who is an elf. He may be able to point me toward someone who knows this area and the best place to find mermaids." He paused at the door and glanced to her, still sitting there with her hands over her bare breasts. "Whatever that chip is on your shoulder about how I should feel about you? Knock it off, will you?"

And he walked out, hating that he was leaving her alone, but also knowing he hadn't the patience for her self-deprecating bullshit anymore. She needed to get over it. Or else stop trying to tease and seduce him.

The witch couldn't have it both ways.

Valor called Eryss, her best witchy friend back in the United States and also the principle owner of the Decadent Dames brewery. Eryss was in the process of opening another brewery in Santa Cruz, California, because that was where her man, Dane, lived and they'd agreed to share two places. Eryss got winter in Minnesota. And Dane was mostly okay with that. The guy was a scientist surfer dude who also worked for a secret agency dedicated to protecting paranormals from human discovery, so it was all good. Except for the part where he'd almost killed Eryss when he was carrying an enchanted witch hunter's dagger. Long story.

"Wales?" Eryss asked on a yawn. Valor hadn't done the time-change math and wasn't about to. "That sounds exotic."

"Really? The hotel we're staying in has a cheesy casino, overcooked Juicy Lucys and I don't think it ever stops raining here. But apparently it's the best place to find a mermaid."

"That it is. You have someone in the know to help you do that finding?"

"That's Kelyn's job. He might be looking into that right now. He's...not here in the room. Went down to the casino to pout."

"A pouting faery? Why? Are you two fighting?"

"Maybe. No. Yes. I don't know. Eryss, I'm such a freak." She knelt on the bed, then fell backward, head to the pillow and free arm flung out to the side. "I really like Kelyn, and I know he likes me, but...oh! Dr. Robert Chase, I feel like a sixteen-year-old angsty girl saying that."

Eryss laughed. "I don't think we women ever get over lacking confidence around men we admire. But you and Kelyn do have a history. I can understand your trouble hashing out your feelings toward him. As well, you do have the bad breakup that I know is still bugging you."

"Yeah, well, I tried to do something to alleviate that pain, but apparently it's not to be. Good ol' Valor. Just one of the guys."

"You've got to stop calling yourself one of the guys, Valor. I need to say this, and you know it's true. You push men away."

"No, I don't. I'm one of them. I'm a part of their tribe!"

"Exactly. And by infiltrating their tribe you confuse them and push them away."

Valor sighed and slapped a hand over her forehead. *Tell it like it is much?* "You know too much about me."

"What's that phrase you always say? Bros before ohs?"

So Valor preferred friendships with men. Oftentimes that meant she went without the orgasm she could have had if they'd been more than merely friends.

"You need to reverse that thinking," Eryss said.

"I'm trying to. But I'm…unlovable."

"Nonsense. I love you."

"Whoopee."

"I heard that."

"Sorry. You know I get down on myself so well."

"You do, indeed."

"It's that I think I like Kelyn. The guy fascinates me. And he's like Mr. Kind of the World. Nothing ever seems to rattle him, unless it's his faery period."

"His faery period? Do I want to know?"

"It's phantom pain he's feeling from his wings. But beyond that tiny bit of grumpiness, he's like the perfect man. And when he kisses me…"

"He's kissed you? We're talking about a new kiss, not the one in the forest when you thought you were dying?"

"Right. New kisses. As in plural. He's given me a few. And, oh, mercy, they made my toes curl."

"Then what's the problem? How does he feel about… you know, everything?"

Yeah, Eryss was too nice to just come out with

"Does he hate you for being the reason he sacrificed his wings?"

"He says he's over it and it doesn't bother him."

"Then believe him, Valor. I know how stubborn you can be about things. Will you give him a chance to be your hero?"

Now Valor scoffed. "A hero? Please, Eryss, you know I don't need a freakin' hero to ride up on his white steed and whisk me off in rescue."

"Sounds like a cool fantasy, but I agree. We women don't always need that kind of hero. Sometimes, to be a hero, a man merely needs to see us for what we really are. He needs to see our truths."

Like wanting to be accepted by a man and being really loved instead of considered just another one of the guys? Valor sighed.

"That sigh tells me you agree. But you know what? Sometimes you have to actually step forward and tell the guy what you want him to see. Believe it or not, the males of our species are not mind readers. Nor are we women. Just as I've told Dane many a time. I will never understand his always thinking I should know what he wants for breakfast. I mean, come on."

Valor chuckled. "You have found yourself an amazing man. I never would have thought you'd hook up with a science geek who also hunts witches."

"He's not a witch hunter. I thought we'd cleared that up. It was that weird enchanted dagger that was making him think he wanted to kill witches."

"Yeah, but he killed you dozens of times through your various reincarnations."

"Right? Whew! So glad that's over."

"Speaking of you and Dane, how's the little one? Kicking a lot?"

"I seriously cannot wait to get this little guy out of my stomach and into the world. I think I've got an MMA fighter in there, for all the kicking he does. And always in the middle of the night!"

"Like right now? I'm sorry I called so late. But you've cheered me up. Or, at least, you've given me things to think about."

"Relationships are hard for a reason. They're not worth having if you don't put some effort into them. But it's just the beginning for you and Kelyn. You two are on a fabulous adventure together. Enjoy it. And no matter the outcome, you need to live in the now. And speak your truths. Yes?"

"Yes! We rappelled out of a helicopter over a pink lake."

"I don't even have words for that. I can't imagine."

"It rocked. Oh, I love you, Eryss. You always make me feel better."

"Me and my snoring husband send our love. Now, go find the guy and kiss him back and tell him what you really want from him."

"I…"

"Valor," she said warningly.

"I will. I mean, when he comes back to the room, I will. I don't want to be pushy."

Eryss's heavy sigh said too much. "That means you really do like this guy. Because you generally play the aggressor in the relationship."

"Calling Dr. Bombay, anyone?"

Eryss laughed. "I love that you've finally found some-one to challenge your sense of how a relationship with a man can work. I hope he's strong enough to push back as much as you do."

"He is. Do you know he put up with drunk preflight me? Twice."

"Give that guy a medal. Okay, take it slow but steady. And let him kiss that mermaid."

"I will. Talk later, Eryss. Night."

"It's three in the morning, sweetie. I owe you one for this wake-up call. You'll be hauling grains for weeks when you get back to town."

"Who is doing it now?"

"Mireio talked Dane into helping her. I think she batted her lashes at him. She's a kook. But you know we could never convince Geneva to lift a forty-pound bag of barley. She might chip her nail polish."

Valor laughed. "Well, then, she could get one of her billionaires to buy her a new manicure."

"She's off the billionaires, didn't you know?"

"I didn't. That's... Really? That chick never dates any man whose worth is less than ten figures. What's up with that?"

"She wants to see what it's like to date rustic. Those were her exact words."

"Oh, that is so Geneva. I can't wait to get back to town and hug all you girls. Give everyone a hug and kiss for me. Good night!"

Valor hung up and pressed the phone against her lips. She'd needed that conversation. And the encouragement. Maybe she did need to view this adventure with new eyes. Live in the now and not worry about what could never happen.

But as for telling Kelyn that she needed him to see

her? That felt difficult. Like exposing herself to a crew of hungry hyenas. No, she couldn't go that far.

"Slow," she muttered. "That's how we're going to do this."

Chapter 12

Valor woke to find that Kelyn had not returned to the room. She glanced out the window. The sun shone and the parking lot was drying up after yesterday's rain. Could they get lucky enough to have sun for their mermaid hunt?

She couldn't find hope without knowing if Kelyn had returned last night while she was sleeping, or maybe he'd not come back at all. Had he been that angry with her? Maybe Eryss was right. She needed to talk to him straight out.

Or not.

"You gotta stop being a flake," she muttered as she wandered into the bathroom. "Be you. The tough chick who takes what she wants and gives as good as she gets. Yeah," she said to her reflection.

She'd put the whole guilt thing aside and give Kelyn

the respect he deserved. And maybe she could loosen up the tough act. Just a bit. Let the guy in? She didn't always have to be one of the guys.

"Maybe," she said on a whisper that ended in a wink at her reflection. She patted down a tangle of hair above her ear, then decided the gray T-shirt she'd slept in and the skinny black jeans were good to go.

Ten minutes later, she wandered through the casino, cautioning herself not to look down at the crazy carpeting that resembled Scottish tartan on crack. The pattern alone could mesmerize a person and set her off course to crash into a nearby slot machine.

Not many people were in the casino. In fact, she saw fewer than half a dozen sitting before the slots. It was early. Probably most were in the restaurant eating or enjoying their vacations by lingering in bed. She didn't have to go far to spy the blond faery slumped in a chair before an electronic slot machine that flashed neon-haired women with purple kitty ears and tails. His feet were propped up on another machine, and one arm hung down the side of the chair, his knuckles brushing the floor.

That man was going to have one hell of a neck ache when he woke. Of course, if it gave her a chance to exercise her massage skills again, this time she would not balk when he tried to take it further with kisses and bare skin. Because she wanted to put her hands on him again. His muscles were so hard, and it wasn't often she got to practice her healing magic, either.

Valor glanced to a passing attendant who was polishing the chrome-edged slot machines with a cloth and spray. The elderly woman wearing a pink apron and bright white high-tops offered her nod to Kelyn and a shrug. "Didn't want to wake him," she said quietly. "He yours?"

Valor shrugged. "I guess so."

If only!

Then again, there was a lot she didn't know about this man, and the fact that he'd rather spend the night camped out in a cheesy casino than up in a comfy bed beside her said so much. Had she hurt him that much with her flaky refusal to push the make-out session to the next level? Or was he one of those sensitive types whom a woman could never please no matter what she did?

Goddess, but she'd had enough of that type of man. Yet tops on her list of not-wants was the man who could never see beyond her as just another one of the guys. How to change that impression? She couldn't do frills and makeup. That was so out of her realm of talents.

Valor slid onto the vinyl seat next to Kelyn and clasped her fingers about his wrist. The silver scars where his sigils had once been were not raised, but she sensed some minute power within. It seemed to poke at her own magic as if trying to shrug her off. Interesting. Could he have a bit of magic left within that he wasn't able to consciously access?

Kelyn startled and then groaned. His body eased into a stretch, his long legs bending and his feet slipping off the slot machine with an ungraceful thud. That prompted another groan from him.

When he finally popped open one eye, he managed a smirk. "Morning."

"That it is. I'll reserve the *good*, though, until I can assess whether or not you're going to have a screaming neck ache."

"Sorry," he mumbled. He cracked his neck one way,

then the other. His wince told her he wasn't pain free. "Should have returned to the room. I thought I was going to close my eyes for a few minutes. Guess all this traveling has worn me out. What's up for today? You ready to go?"

"Uh, sure. But it's early. We've time to catch some breakfast. You know how I do love a buffet."

"That I do."

"Unless you want to hang in the casino a little longer. I didn't think you were the gambling type."

"I'm not. But a few plays were necessary. Just to see if I could get all the purple kitties." He smiled a ridiculously charming yet tired grin.

"Did you find someone who can take us to mermaids?" Valor asked.

"Never."

"Oh. Uh, do you want me to give it a try?"

"Guy's name is Never." Kelyn sat up, wincing, and stretched his arms above his head, which tugged the shirt across his hard pecs right at about Valor's eye level. The ridges of his abdomen pressed against the shirt, as well.

Yeah, she was over the guilt and the weird need to push the man away. She wanted this guy. To touch and kiss and…whatever came next. No strings or expectations attached. *If* he would give her another chance.

"Never is an Unseelie who left Faery years ago," Kelyn said. He stretched back an arm, then swung it forward, working at the tightness. And then he leaned in close to her. "Erte told me about him."

"I've heard that name before."

"He's my best friend. Elves in the mortal realm are rare. He lived in Faery ages ago, but he prefers our realm. Go figure."

"And by ages, do you mean centuries?"

"I do. But the guy didn't have to consume a vampire's heart to live as long as he has. Long life is natural for elves. I trust him, but he said we should not trust Never."

"Great. Untrustworthy faeries. And vicious mermaids. Just what we need to make this adventure unforgettable. You hungry?"

"Always. Should we head to the buffet?"

"Sure, but first…" She wrapped her fingers about his wrist again and paused to summon her courage. Eryss's words resounded, yet she wasn't quite ready to go all in. "This is the last time I'm going to say sorry to you, but you do deserve this one. I've been kind of flaky around you and it's going to stop."

"Valor, I understand—"

"You might think you do, but that doesn't mean I can't aspire to a different tactic and try to be…" A real girl. Someone with whom a man could see relationship potential. "I want us to be good."

"We are good."

"All righty. But maybe I want us to be better than good. Like, you know, good is for friends. Something a little beyond that kind of good?"

"Such aspirations are a fine thing to have," he said, standing. "Beyond good it is." He offered her his arm and Valor stood and hooked hers in his, pleased he'd agreed so easily to her not-so-definitive suggestion about their relationship. "Can I take you out on a breakfast date?"

"I'd like that. Oh, hey, look." Valor ripped the paper tag from the slot machine. "You won twenty pounds from the purple kitty chicks."

"Nice. We are definitely getting the plate-size upgrade."

"Whoo!"

"What's a thin place?" Valor asked Kelyn as, two hours later, he navigated to the village for which the faery Never had given him GPS coordinates. "I've heard it mentioned and suspect it's to do with Faery."

Kelyn possessed an ease driving the car, one wrist propped on the steering wheel and his eyes taking in the periphery, as if he were adventuring and searching for great sites. She found it sexy, so casual and sure of himself.

"You know Faery is everywhere?" he asked. "Though it's not as close in the more populated places, like big cities."

"It's another dimension, of sorts, that overlies or underlies the mortal realm."

"Right. But you can only get there through a portal and you must be *sidhe* or have another means, such as a spell." He winked at her.

Valor caught that wink as if he'd given her a hug. She smiled to herself and felt that, whatever happened between the two of them, it was going to work. It had to.

"A thin place is where Faery bleeds into the mortal realm. It's not Faery. It's not the mortal realm. It's sort of both."

"Can you get into Faery through a thin place?"

"Maybe. It's not a portal. It's a place where the *sidhe* exist without being seen by human eyes. Sort of like FaeryTown in Paris. And like the Darkwood. That's a thin place. You did know that about the forest before you went there, right?"

Now he didn't offer a wink but instead a sideways glance.

"Maybe? First time I've heard the definition for thin place was today. But I get it now. Faery exists on top of the mortal realm. And woe to those who try to exert their power there. Or borrow a few mushrooms."

"Borrow? What about invoking a dangerous spell?"

"Dangerous?" Arguing would open a can of worms she wasn't willing to shake. Valor could but offer a guilty shrug.

"I understand pretty much the entire shoreline of Wales is a thin place," Kelyn said, "though not the major ports. That must be the village ahead where those thin puffs of dark smoke are curling out of chimneys. Quaint. And *that* is what we are looking for."

Valor looked in the direction Kelyn pointed. A long, winding fieldstone fence hugged the road, looking ever so Old World. And atop it crouched a man with dark hair and wings.

"Seriously? He sits out in the open with his wings revealed?" Valor wondered.

"I suspect he's wearing a glamour against human eyes." Kelyn pulled the rental car over to the side of the road thirty feet away from the faery, who hadn't moved from his perch. "You ready for this?"

Valor shrugged. "Are you?"

"I am. And so you know, he requires payment for this venture. Which I'm perfectly willing to pay."

Kelyn got out and strode ahead. While Valor, gripping the door handle, wondered exactly what sort of payment a faery would ask of another for the map to a thin place.

Chapter 13

As they approached the faery crouched on the stone fence, Valor invoked a white light of protection over herself by grasping the moonstone amulet and drawing her other hand from her crown and gesturing downward to the ground until she felt the energy clasp about the bottoms of her boots.

The air was heavy with a promise of rain. The gray sky flashed with intermittent peeks of sunlight through clouds. Valor noticed the black markings on the faery's neck and the backs of his hands. Delicate tracings that resembled some kind of *mehndi* creation, but she knew they were sigils. Most faeries wore them and used them to conjure their own kind of magic.

Kelyn's sigils were gone. No amount of massage or restitution could erase her guilt over that. She'd only once seen him in all his wondrous faery magnificence, that night when he unfurled his wings and went after the troll in the Darkwood. Magnificent.

Damn, she hated herself sometimes.

"Never," Kelyn said as he arrived before the faery, who jumped down to clasp hands in greeting. "Erte sends his respects."

"I return them," Never said. Dressed in tight black leggings with tears in the knees and a ripped black T-shirt, he looked like a punk rocker abandoned by his crew after a night lost in the wild. The dark faery's violet gaze, outlined in thick kohl, moved to Valor. A breeze tickled through his spiky black hair. A smirk of challenge lifted the corner of his mouth. "And this is the witch?"

"Valor Hearst," Kelyn introduced her.

Never stepped forward with a limber bounce that was almost imperceptible and yet Valor thought perhaps his jerked moves indicated a few cels from the film strip had been removed. It was a faery thing, that rapid movement that seemed to jerk and alter space and time. Though she hadn't seen Kelyn move so quickly.

She offered her hand to shake, and Never bowed and kissed the back of it. His dark menace whispered over her skin like gray soot.

The faery released her hand quickly, stepping back. He winced. "You needn't ward against me, witch."

"Probably not," she offered. "But all the same, I'm more comfortable wearing one in new places."

"Of course." He acquiesced with a tight smirk. "So, mermaids." He turned to Kelyn. "It's not often I hear of a fellow *sidhe* with a hunger to make out with one of those scaly bitches."

"It's for a spell," Kelyn said. "My wings were... I gave

them freely to another and now I want to get them back. The mermaid's kiss is an ingredient in a spell that'll open a portal to Faery."

"I see." Never walked around Kelyn, his dark clothing and hair making him look like a gothic punk rocker plopped into the setting of old-world charm, green fields and even a few white sheep grazing in the distance. "Why would you give a part of you away so freely?"

"It's not your concern."

"Probably not. But that cipher you wear at your neck could be my concern. Why have you a cipher that only the Wicked can use?"

Kelyn touched the leather cords about his neck, his fingers glancing over the mouse alicorn before he pressed the black circle between his fingers. "This? I don't know what it is, actually. A friend gave it to me."

"A friend? One of the Wicked? Though why one of those terrible things would give up such a thing surprises me. You don't know what you have? That—" Never pointed to the tourmaline circle Kelyn still held "—is a cipher that can be activated by the Wicked. It's a navigational device used in Faery. It leads to dark and dangerous things, my friend. One such as you has no power to use it. Though—" Never tapped his jaw in thought "—it does connect you to something. I'm not sure what, exactly."

"A cipher." Kelyn shrugged. "Then I'll be sure not to hand it over to a Wicked One. If it has no power in this realm, it's but a trinket, isn't it?"

"I suppose so."

Kelyn stepped before the faery to stop his circling pace. "Are we going to do this or not?"

"Of course. The thin place is close," Never said. The

faery's eyes scanned the steel-and-rose horizon. The sun was falling in the sky, despite their early start. "But first I'll ask my payment, as you've promised."

"If this is going to cost a lot…" Valor started, but Kelyn's sudden chiding glance stopped her cold. *Step back, witch*, was the feeling she got from him. Let him handle this.

All righty, then. She put up placating hands and took an exaggerated step back. She'd leave the faery business to the experts. It was all a part of the new and untested not-so-aggressive Valor. A girl the guys could see as more than one of their tribe.

Whatever.

"It'll cost no more than a swoon and a smile," the faery Never said as he walked around behind Kelyn and toyed with the man's blond hair. He eyed Valor from over Kelyn's shoulder. "All I ask is ichor."

"Ichor?"

"This is not a problem," Kelyn said to Valor with that same chiding tone touching his voice. "He's half-vampire."

The faery winked, and now Valor noticed that within his violet pupils were red stars. So, a half-breed Unseelie escapee was going to help them find mermaids? For ichor? She didn't get it. And generally she was pretty quick on the uptake.

And then she did get it, when the faery opened his mouth to reveal fangs.

"Make it quick," Kelyn said to the faery hugging him from behind, but he maintained eye contact with Valor. "We haven't got all day."

Crossing her arms, Valor stepped back. She didn't want to watch this. But when the faery lunged toward

Kelyn's neck, she could suddenly imagine nothing more than watching. Pearly sharp fangs sank into flesh, and Kelyn winced at the intrusion. The faery gripped him up under the chin while he fed from his vein. Faery blood wasn't red, nor was it even blood, but instead, ichor. A clear substance that sparkled with the faery dust that coursed through their systems. Ichor could be extremely addictive to vamps. But to a half faery, half vamp? Valor couldn't fathom what Never got out of such a drink.

And then she could, as the faery moaned a long and sexually pleased tone. The hand that grasped Kelyn's chin seemed to stroke lovingly. Even Kelyn hummed out a satisfied sound, mined deep from his chest. It was as if Valor were watching something illicit.

And she could not look away.

When she placed a hand over her heart, the thuds startled her. And she realized her skin had warmed even though the breeze was cool. Was she...turned on by watching such a thing? No. That wasn't her style. Maybe?

Kelyn stepped backward, as if losing his balance. Never gripped him surely and licked at his vein. The red-eyed faery caught Valor's interest and smirked against Kelyn's neck. He enjoyed that she was watching.

When, finally, Never released his ichor donor, Kelyn stumbled and put out his arms to right himself. He tossed Valor a loopy grin and she knew he was in a swoon from the powerful bite. As was Never. The dark faery reeled around and caught his hands on the stone fence, laughing and then falling to his knees in a wicked spin of orgasm.

"Well." Valor stretched and twisted her neck uncomfortably. She announced, "That was inappropriate."

Both faeries chuckled as she strode back to the vehicle.

* * *

From the back seat of the Jeep, Never directed the two of them to a sparsely wooded area that fronted the Irish Sea. Sure the rains would begin soon, Valor hoped they could get this done before that happened.

Kelyn found a clearing of jagged rock scattered with boulders—one the size of a VW—and parked the vehicle.

Tall grasses hugging the olive trees dashed in painted streaks greener than emeralds. Skylarks soared overhead. And the air seemed kissed with a fragrance Valor could only call life and breath and vitality. Her hair blew in unnatural flutters about her as she stepped out to look around. Her air magic sensed the intensity of the vita about her and responded like an electric force.

"That's interesting," Never commented on her hair. "Air witch?"

She nodded. "So tell me this. Why ichor? If you're half-vamp."

"Human blood makes me sick," he offered. "Iron and all."

"Ah." Faeries and iron did not mix. "Got it. So, are you going to stick around for the fun?" She opened the back of the Jeep, where they'd stowed the rope and harness.

"Wouldn't think of it. Even if I did have access to Faery—which I do not—the last thing I want to do is return to Faery. Don't want to end up working for dear old Daddykins. But you…" Never walked up to Kelyn and stood so close Valor wondered if he might kiss him. The two had bonded in some weird way with that bite, but she didn't want to question it too much. Never placed his palm over Kelyn's heart. "You do know what will happen if you manage to retrieve your wings from Faery?"

Kelyn set back his shoulders proudly. "I'll be whole again."

"Not necessarily. If someone else is wearing them, those wings will be tainted by that creature's essence, be it good, evil or merely malicious."

"Merely?" Valor prompted.

The faery smirked. Of course, faeries were big on malice and menace. And, apparently, black eyeliner.

"Be wary," Never said, and stepped away from the two of them. "If you're ever eager to donate to the cause again…" He winked at Kelyn.

Spreading out his arms dramatically, Never then released his wings in a whoosh of gray, black and red. With but a jump backward, the faery took to air, transforming to small size within a blink and zipping off across the lush emerald countryside. He looked like a dragonfly darting off to Wonderland.

"Cool," Valor commented. "I guess he wasn't so bad."

"If you say so." Kelyn grabbed the rope from her and wandered toward the trees.

She probably shouldn't press regarding the bite, but…

"Wait up!" She grabbed the harness from the back of the Jeep, checked that the jackknife was tucked in her back pocket, then ran after Kelyn. "So, are you going to tell me about the bite?"

"What's there to tell? You saw the whole thing."

"I did, and it was…"

"Inappropriate?" He chuckled and winked at her. "You know what it's like when someone is bitten by a vampire."

"I do. Not from personal experience but from hearsay." It was supposed to be orgasmic for the vampire, and the victim was generally left in a swoon, as she'd witnessed with Kelyn. "It's got to be a bummer for a faery who needs to drink blood but can't. That's just weird."

"I'm not going to question too much. It was what he required for payment. It was something I was willing to offer."

"So, did you, you know…?"

He hefted the coiled rope over a shoulder. A waggle of his brow teased at her. "You know?"

"You're going to make me ask it?"

"I am."

"Fine! Did you get off?"

"I did." And with that he wandered ahead of her toward the granite cliff.

Valor followed with a muttered, "Exceedingly inappropriate."

Chapter 14

The inky green sea swirled before Kelyn as he stood at the edge of a granite ledge that hung over the water. The drop to the water's surface was two feet from the stone. Never had referred to finding the *tongue* of stone that licked over the waters as an excellent vantage point from which to locate mermaids.

The air was heavy with moisture and brewed the salty ocean scents to a heady elixir that even he, with his muted senses, smelled all over, as if his skin were the nose. The sun had disappeared behind clouds, though a weak half circle of muted gold glimpsed out once in a while. It would rain soon, so he hoped to get this done before the deluge.

He checked the blue nylon harness he wore, which strapped about him like a vest. Attached to it were a couple D-rings, through which he'd threaded the length of rope.

Turning, he followed the rope along the granite surface about thirty feet to where the two of them had wrapped the other end of the rope around a massive boulder that had only budged a little when Kelyn testingly shoved against it. Valor had knotted the rope expertly, commenting she'd learned sailor's knots when she dated a seaman in the middle of the last century. It should provide a good hold.

And beside the six-foot-high boulder stood Valor. When his gaze met hers she shrugged, and with a wave, she called to him, "What could possibly go wrong?"

The chick was damn cute when she was working the false hope.

Turning back to the sea, Kelyn sighed heavily and took stock of this crazy venture he was about to literally dive into. He could not swim. His light bones made a free dive difficult, if not impossible. He wasn't even sure how long he could hold his breath underwater. And he was now only as strong as a human man.

Another glance over his shoulder to wink at Valor felt necessary. The witch had a way of challenging him. And he loved it. But was it worth the risk to get back wings that could be tainted by an unknown evil, as Never had suggested?

"Yes," he murmured. "I want to be whole again."

"I want that for you, too."

Kelyn startled at Valor's voice beside him. He hadn't heard her approach, which proved he was out of sorts and not on his game. He'd better check that if he wanted to survive this next challenge.

"This will work," she said.

Standing up on her tiptoes, she kissed him. It was a long, lingering kiss that said so many things he wanted to hear but dared not put into thought. Hope and want and desire. Better to feel it than have it spoken. Yes?

Could he allow himself to want the girl? He'd stayed in the casino last night because he'd been miffed at her rejection, but he'd also felt he was pushing her too quickly into something she didn't want. He was supposed to protect the woman. But he knew she didn't need protection.

Part of him wished she could need him a little bit. How to win over a woman who was her own hero?

Ending the kiss, she asked, "You good?"

"Yes, of course. But, uh…" He swiped the back of his hand over his mouth. "Better wipe that one off so the mermaid kiss will stick. A shame, though. Your kisses are something a guy wants to keep for much longer."

"I promise you another one after you've secured the prize." A gentle punch to his shoulder sealed her word. With a wink, she tugged at the rope, making a show of checking the secure knots. She patted her gray-and-black-camo coat pocket. "Got the vial and sticking paper right here. Soon as you've been deflowered, I'm moving in. I think I should put a protection spell on you."

"Not a good idea. I want the mermaid to kiss me, not be repelled."

"Right. As soon as you get that kiss…"

"I'm getting another one from you." He winked at her and she almost punched him again, but withdrew and instead bowed her head, smiling.

Yeah, she liked him.

"You might want to stand by to tug me up in case the mermaid's kiss disorients me," he suggested. "Never been kissed by a mermaid before, but I suspect it's not as delicious as yours."

"There you go being a sweetie again. It's gotta taste like fish, right?"

"I hate fish."

"We'll dine on veggies and cake later to celebrate."

"Sounds like a plan." He clapped his hands together and nodded with decisiveness. No more stalling. Time to either sink or swim. "Let's do this!"

Kelyn knelt at the edge of the stone tongue and gave a look to Valor so she stepped back about ten feet, giving him space. Good call. Should the mermaid see her, the creature might be frightened away.

He lay on his stomach and reached down, but his fingers barely touched the surface so he shoved himself forward until he could cup the cool water in his palms. The granite he lay on smelled like old civilizations. The sea smelled rich and steeped with ages of secrets only dead sailors could tell. He wasn't sure how to call up a mermaid, and Valor had no clue, either. Probably something they should have researched before coming out here.

He'd wing it. Wingless as he was.

Searching the metallic green surface, Kelyn could not see far into the depths. Murky waters. That did not seem to bode well. What had Valor cracked about him getting this kiss? Deflowered? Yikes, this would be the first time he'd ever kissed a fish.

But he was approaching this the wrong way. He needed to remain positive. The kiss was another ingredient to check off the list. And then he'd be that much closer to getting back his wings.

Stirring his fingers in the waters, he closed his eyes

and focused on aligning himself with the sea and the creatures within. As faery he had an intimate connection to nature and all her inhabitants. He could tap into a hummingbird's heartbeat and direct it to the best source for food. He could race an elk through the forest and oftentimes win. He could count a bird's chirps and determine whether it was a warning or a greeting.

And he could call a mermaid to kiss him if he desired.

That was the key. He had to want it and believe it was possible.

Feeling the ancient memories of the waters bestill him and calm his heartbeat, Kelyn hummed from the base of his throat, tapping into the Celtic rhythms he had never known, but that had been imprinted on his soul through the ages as a collective message from the universe. He did believe in mermaids. He believed in every myth about which the humans liked to tell stories. They were all real.

He wasn't sure how long he lay there, humming, stirring the waters with his fingertips, but he forgot the witch standing nearby and didn't notice the sun glimmer on the horizon with a wink before a fine mist began to wet his hair and back.

A bubble rose and broke the water's surface. And then another, and another.

He stretched his fingers through the water, and when the cool, wet hand clasped his, Kelyn cursed quietly. In for the ride, he reminded himself. No matter the slimy scales that abraded his skin. He leaned forward more until his entire chest hung over the waters. He could feel the rope tug against the rock and felt secure, so he inched forward a bit more.

The mermaid's head rose, pale green hair spreading

across the surface and forming liquid arabesques about her. Within the seaweed-like hair, bubbles formed, and Kelyn saw a tiny fish bob up briefly within the strands. She emerged to her nose, which was flat and gilled on both sides instead of sporting human-like nostrils. At her cheeks gills also flapped. Otherwise, she looked quite human, save for the green hair.

"Hello, pretty," he offered as charmingly as possible.

Her head rose a little more and her mouth curled into a smile. It was a soft mouth, shaded green as her olive skin but with a tint of rose to it. She tilted her head, brushing it against his open palm like a cat seeking a nuzzle. Kelyn slipped a heavy ribbon of her hair over... well, she didn't have an ear that he could see, so he dropped the hair and offered her a smile.

He wasn't sure if she could speak his language, so he didn't think conversation would be important. Instead he softened his gaze on her and winked.

The mermaid chirred out a giggly sound and behind her, her caudal tail fin slapped the water in a bejeweled display of opalescent scales. Water splattered Kelyn's face, but he laughed as a means to calm his nervous jitters.

"Your tail is beautiful," he said. "As are you."

And then he leaned forward even more, daring to close his eyes and hope upon hope she would understand he wanted a kiss. For ages, mermaids had been known to seduce sailors into kissing them, and then they'd drag them to their deaths at the bottom of the sea.

He'd have to be cautious he didn't become another statistic to fortify the legend.

When a wetness touched his forehead, Kelyn realized she'd touched her forehead to his. Her flesh was soft and slimy, exactly like a fish. And then it happened. Her mouth landed on his in a cold, yet sweetly exotic touch that shivered through his system like nothing he'd felt before. It wasn't as intimately surprising as the faery vampire's bite had been, but it did sharpen his senses to the salty taste on her mouth. She slid her webbed hands over his shoulders, pulling him closer to her until his face was in the water, lips still kissing hers, and then...

He didn't so much drop into the water as get tugged from the granite ledge like a sack of valuable pearls the greedy bitch wanted for herself.

The harness squeezed his chest as the rope resisted. Kelyn felt the mermaid wrap her arms tightly about his shoulders as the murky water engulfed him. His feet kicked at something slippery. Her tail felt as though it had wrapped about his shins. And then the rope gave a little more.

And a little more.

And soon it was as if the rope might have snapped or come untied, for the mermaid swam swiftly downward, taking him along. The kiss broken, he struggled to shuck off her hold about his shoulders. A shout released his air. Water bubbled about him, and her tail lashed roughly at his legs, beating at them wickedly.

Suddenly he was jerked out of her grasp. Snapped upward by a force about his chest, he realized the rope was still secure. Kelyn stretched his arms, aiming for the fading glimmer of the surface. His fey weight buoyed him swiftly upward.

As he ascended, the mermaid circled him, swishing her tail at his face. The scaled fins cut his skin and he struggled to push away the menacing weapon. It was as if a jellyfish were stinging him. He cried out, releasing his last gasp of breath as he surfaced. Thank goodness for his lightweight faery bones!

Yet, from below, the mermaid pushed up on the soles of his boots, rocketing him out of the water to land on the rocky outcrop right beside the boulder that had apparently rolled to the edge.

Kelyn landed on his stomach, grunting at the incredible pain of his body colliding with the solid surface. He rolled to his back and splayed out his arms, gasping for redeeming air and sputtering up the foul water.

"Wait! Don't spit." Valor's voice sounded above him. "Remember the plan. Let me take care of this."

The plan. She'd devised a simple way to retrieve the kiss. Using a piece of rice paper that she now pressed to his mouth, she carefully peeled it away and held it up to study. Scales glinted on the transparent paper. "Got it!" She curled the paper and stuffed it in a glass vial, then stood. "I'm going to put this in the car so I don't lose hold of it. Be right back!"

"Sure." Kelyn sputtered more water. Man, the sea did *not* taste good. "You do that. Leave the half-drowned faery here to die!"

Then he laughed a wet and weary laugh. He'd survived that challenge. He wasn't going to die and end up buried in some rotting shell of a ship filled with hundreds of other unlucky souls. Davy Jones had lost this one. How's that for a guy who had never taken a swimming lesson?

Pushing the hair from his eyes, he winced as his fingers traced the cuts marking his forehead and cheeks. He would heal, but not as quickly as usual.

The crunching of stone and the sudden wobble of the boulder beside him alerted Kelyn. Accompanied by a rush of sudden wind and rains from above, the boulder wobbled…

Tilted forward…

And dropped into the water, breaking off the granite ledge as it did so.

The rock fell away from under Kelyn's legs. Frantically, he shuffled backward. Then he slapped a hand to the harness and the rope knotted so expertly by Valor.

"Shit."

Chapter 15

Pulled with great force into the depths by the heavy boulder, Kelyn focused his intent on the rope in hopes of severing it with sheer strength. Ah! He had no sigils to access his former strength. Water rushed into his mouth, nose and ears. The only way out of this was to swim to the boulder and shimmy the rope from around it.

And that would prove much harder than expected as the flap of a mermaid's tail brushed his cheek and his ichor spilled out into the water.

Valor ran from the Jeep toward the ledge. She'd heard the crushing sound of rock breaking. And the abruptly muffled yelp of one very soaked and defeated faery. She stopped where the granite had broken and crumbled into the sea, stepping back to avoid the loose shards. She should have untied Kelyn immediately. *Fool!*

Kneeling at the rough stone edge, she studied the green water. The surface was remarkably smooth and calm. He must be quite far down already. She wasn't sure if faeries could breathe underwater as vampires could. Would he be able to release himself from the harness? She slapped a hand to her pocket and palmed the blade. It would serve no good in her hand.

What could she do to help? She was no swimmer. And she did not practice water magic. Her expertise was air magic.

"Maybe…" Air *could* be used as a tool.

Standing, she planted her feet squarely and bowed her head to focus her energies. Spreading out her fingers, she slowly raised her arms as she chanted a powerful spell to summon the wind from within the nearby forest. And to harvest the misting rain with that wind. Focusing her vita out through her fingers, she channeled the air elements. Lifting her arms high, she dashed her hands in a swirl that plucked out a tail from the air, collected the rain and swirled it into a tornadic spin of energized magic.

The tornado spun above the water, faster and faster, until the force of it began to open up the waters as if drilling down into rock. And when a column of open water had formed within the sea, Valor sent the tornado down, spinning, spiraling, mining deep, until she felt it connect with the boulder. Like a suctioned tentacle, the end of the tornado grasped the boulder and she commanded it to rise.

Water splashed up over her body as the wind tunnel carried the rock high into the air. And in the next moment, Kelyn stepped onto the broken granite ledge beside her, dropping the frayed rope that tailed behind the boulder.

With a sweep of her hand, she sent the boulder off into the sea and dismissed the tornado. A heavy fall of water that had been corralled into her weapon now released and beat upon their heads. Kelyn's knees buckled. He collapsed and splayed onto the stone.

And then all grew calm. Even the sky seemed to suddenly brighten, thanks to a thread of lingering sunlight. Valor looked over Kelyn's body; ichor covered his face and had started to puddle below his head.

"Dr. Bombay, this is not good!"

She dropped to her knees beside him and pressed an ear to his chest. She didn't feel his chest rise. That couldn't be right. He'd stood next to her, had even smiled. He couldn't be dead. Closer inspection saw the cuts on his face, from which all his ichor flowed. Had he lost too much? The man must have battled with the mermaid within the depths.

Talk about a fickle kisser.

Frantic, Valor clutched her hands before her as she scanned Kelyn's inanimate body. The charms at his neck were still there, the mouse alicorn and the—whatever the thing was that only the Wicked could use. Did it connect him to something? She reached to touch the black circle, but then did not. Now was no time to get curious.

But how to help him? Her healing magic wasn't able to bring back life, not even lure life to remain in a dying body. She could fix boo-boos and even mend the occasional broken bone. But how to give a man back his breath?

"CPR," she muttered. "Yes, how did that go?"

Years ago Mireio had convinced Valor to attend a

CPR course with her. Said it would be a good skill to learn if it was ever needed at the brewery for a customer. Because they certainly couldn't whip out the healing magic with a crowd of humans observing.

Pressing her palms over Kelyn's chest, she pumped once. Then again. Then a few times more rapidly. Bowing over his head, she tilted it back and, clamping her fingers over his nose, breathed into his mouth. Once, twice. Listened for breath. She repeated the sequence over and over, crying out to all the television doctors she had a habit of invoking when life pissed her off or challenged her.

"By all the TV doctors and Dr. Bombay, I will save him. I can't lose him. Not this guy. He's the nicest man I know."

He was the only man who'd ever given her a chance when she least deserved one.

Placing a palm over her other hand, she compressed his chest a few pulses. And this time, when she breathed into his mouth, she invoked all her powers of air magic and infused his system with her vita, her life. Conjuring a violet essence of vitality, she breathed that into him, blessed air that had originated from the universe, representing centuries and millennia of existence. Everyone breathed and walked in the life-giving elixir.

Gasping, Valor pressed her hands to Kelyn's chest again. This time when she pumped, her wrists weakened and her palms slipped from his wet chest. She was growing weak. Had expended too much magic. And...

"No, gotta keep going." Another breath escaped from her exhausted lungs. Valor lingered at Kelyn's mouth, her lips brushing his. "Please..."

A seabird soared overhead, cawing out a mournful

cry. Rain spattered his eyelids, and Valor thought maybe she saw one of them wriggle…

Kelyn choked up water. His body jerked and pulsed upon the wet stone. He groaned and with a choking contortion, rolled and spat out more water to the side. "Oh… scales."

"Oh, yes, thank you!" Pulling him to lie on his back, Valor hugged him across the chest. His fingers grasped at her wet hair, but he didn't move much more than that. "You're alive. I'm so happy. I thought… No, I knew you'd survive. Blessed be!"

"Valor," he said as if in a prayer. "I'm not dead."

"No, you're not. You're lucky I remembered CPR. That came in handy more than I ever expected it would."

"You gave me your…breath."

She shrugged. "It was the least I could do. But know this. That is the last time I let you kiss a mermaid, buddy."

His chest bucked as he laughed and then the faery wrapped his arms across her back and hugged her tightly to him. "No more mermaids. Promise."

Eyes closed, Kelyn lay on the wet, cold stone for a long time. The misty rain continued, and he didn't care. He'd gone beyond soaked. So long as he was not strapped to a big rock and tossed in the ocean again? He was good.

Valor's heat snugged his side. She hadn't said a thing after he closed his eyes. She understood he needed to restore, get back his meager strength and process what had occurred. He'd been dragged to the depths—so close to death—yet he knew Valor's air magic was what had brought him to the surface.

As well, the air from her lungs had ensured he did not die. She had literally given him a kiss of life.

He also sensed that such rescue had fatigued her. Magic extracted a price each time it was used.

But they'd done it. And now elation surged through him as if it were an electric current. He clasped Valor's hand and kissed it.

"You're amazing," she said. They both lay on the granite outcrop, looking up at the gray sky streaked with silver clouds and stitched with the flight of a dark bird soaring beneath the clouds. The moon held reign above the tree line somewhere behind them. "You feeling any better?"

"I am." He rolled onto his stomach and peered into Valor's eyes. Her hair was wet and looked like violet silk. He felt like a soggy piece of seaweed, but that didn't lessen his attraction to the witch's soft, parted lips. "I feel revitalized, actually."

She nodded. "The whole elation-following-death thing?"

"That's a thing?"

"Apparently. Guy gets close enough to kiss death. He survives. He embraces life with gusto."

"If by embracing life you mean this…" He stroked his fingers down her neck to her breast above where the soaked fabric highlighted her tight nipple. "Then I'm in."

She tilted her head to eye him. Moonlight glinted in her big beautiful browns. "You think so?"

He leaned over to kiss the hollow curving at the base of her throat. She swallowed against his lips. Tasting of the sea and air, she felt warmer than fire. The need to devour her so that he could feed the energy that had been taken from him was strong.

"I want you," he said softly, and tugged at her shirt with his teeth.

"Yes. I want you, too. Right now. Here, at the edge of the world." The witch pulled him down for a kiss.

Kisses salted with their fear and a new dose of accomplishment, they greedily took from each other. Kelyn peeled off her wet T-shirt and unbuttoned his jeans. The denim was soaked, but he managed to shove them over his hips. Valor pushed his chest and he rolled to his back. She straddled him and bent to kiss his chest, nipping at his skin and nipples as she did so. The erotic sensation and the sudden rush to grasp pleasure rocketed all feeling to his cock. He sat up, and she slid her legs about his hips. His hands clutched at her hips, then at her breasts and then her hair as he frantically sought to touch all of her, know every part of her.

Then he decided now was not the time for a thorough and detailed exploration of her body. Right now he simply wanted.

"I want to be inside you," he said. "Can we do that?"

"Yes." She shuffled off her boots and pants, then knelt before him, naked. A wet witch had never looked more appealing. "Let's take life and crush it between us."

"Now, that sounds worth the dive."

So he dived for her, gently laying her down on the granite. His heavy erection landed in the soft nest of her curls and he groaned at the sweet, tickling sensation. She wrapped her thighs about his hips and ground her mons against him. He wasn't going to take his time. Already his body trembled in anticipation of release.

"Come inside me," she whispered urgently, reaching for his cock.

Ah, that firm grasp was what he needed right now.

Bowing his head to her breast, Kelyn licked at the tiny swell as, with her guidance, he glided between her legs and inside her tight, squeezing heat. She might have whispered a doctor's name; it might have been some other name entirely. Didn't matter. He felt much the same. This was bliss.

She wrapped about him, embraced him, consumed him. And he didn't ever want to rise from such a place. Pumping slowly within her, he drowned a second time, only this time he enjoyed every gasping breath of it.

Her fingernails dug into his back. The pain sweetened everything and he thrust faster, seeking oblivion.

"Yes," she gasped. "Do it. Fly us both into the stratosphere. Oh, I'm so close, Kelyn. Faster!"

Being told what to do by a woman had never felt more right. Kelyn crushed himself into her, against her, about her. They crushed life together. Let the mermaids wail in jealousy, he'd chosen the woman he desired. And with a few more thrusts, they came together on the granite ledge overlooking a dangerous sea that he had taken on and defeated.

The rain picked up, forcing them to seek a different, less exposed, place for their sexual antics. The granite ledge was fine, but it was growing slick and cold. Welsh summers were never tropical.

Tugging up his jeans so he could walk, Kelyn hoisted Valor over his shoulder and bent as she gathered their remaining soaked clothing into her hands. He raced back to the Jeep, confident they had this little cove by the sea to themselves, but not caring right now if anyone had spied their naked gyrations.

The Jeep was open, though it did have a roof. Still, the

rain had blown diagonally for a while and much of the vehicle was wet inside. He set her down and Valor began to sort through their clothes. Kelyn dipped his head to kiss her on the neck. She giggled, and that giggle ended in a snort.

"I love that laugh!" He picked her up and she wrapped her legs about his hips. Leaning her against the side of the vehicle, he bowed to lick her rain-slick ichor-bedazzled skin. "I also love the taste of a wet witch."

"Oh, yeah? I can take that so many ways."

"This is the way I meant it."

Opening the back door, he laid her inside on the seat, but kept hold of her legs to pull her to the edge of the seat before she could sit up. He stretched out a leg and didn't quite kneel on the ground to get a good position. Valor hiked up one foot onto the open door top, the other she put on his shoulder. Dashing his tongue along the inside of her thigh, he licked away the rain and ventured higher, seeking the treat he desired to taste.

She squirmed but didn't push him away. Instead she scrunched her fingers through his wet hair. Everything was wet. The car, the dirt squishing between his fingers, her skin and, mmm…right there.

"Oh, Kelyn, yes. Just a little lower. And to the left."

He smiled against her thigh and kissed her there quickly. He appreciated a woman who knew exactly what she wanted and wasn't afraid to tell him how to get her there. And since his navigation skills had been lacking of late…

He suckled her swollen nub, tasting it, luxuriating in the moans and rocking hips that resulted from his intense ministrations. And that was the thing that sent the witch reeling. Now, with both feet hooked at his shoulders, she used the leverage to tilt up her hips. He followed her demanding movements, tending that sensitive spot with as much focus as she deserved.

She muttered another doctor's name. Should he be jealous? No. The crazy witch.

And when she cried out a triumphant "Yes!" that was followed by a quick, gasping "Inside me now, faery!" he popped up his head and flashed her a wink.

As the witch wished.

Kelyn stood and shoved down his wet jeans. His hard-on stood at full mast, ready to please. Grabbing one of her legs to pull her closer, he guided himself inside the hot, groaning witch. The wicked tightness of her, and her heat—she was molten—lured him to the edge, where he met her in an orgasm that surely the mermaids would be jealous of for their shouts of ecstasy.

Chapter 16

The bed was blessedly dry. Well, mostly dry. And it...
sparkled. As did Valor. She rubbed a palm over her glinting forearm. When Kelyn came he literally spumed dust
from his pores. Way to score with the faery. This trip
was turning out much better than she had expected.

She'd expected a tense relationship between the two
of them, if any at all. But what had developed proved
more than magical. It was actually kind of enchanting.

"What?"

Valor realized she'd been staring at the side view
of Kelyn, who sat naked in a chair before the window,
watching the rain pummel the tarmac outside. He had
an erection, and his fingers rested about the base of it.
He'd occasionally stroke it, but not with any determination, sort of a reassuring move.

It was ridiculously sexy to know that he'd forgotten

himself while she was in the room, and had kicked back, lost in his own thoughts. Or maybe he hadn't.

He turned a look over his shoulder at her and, with a flick of his wrist, waggled his cock. They'd had sex again after returning to the hotel room and showering. But they hadn't used towels to dry off. In fact, she was still moist. Everywhere. The bedsheets were wet, too, but she didn't care.

"You're sexy." She pushed herself up to sit against a pillow. Bowing forward, she wrapped her arms about her bent legs and rested her cheek on a knee.

"And you have purple hair." His brow furrowed, but with more of a seductive concern than consternation. It was the sexiest move she'd ever watched a man make.

"That I do."

"Is it natural?"

"No. It's a spell. I can streak it any color I like for months at a time. This color is my favorite. It reminds me of a '64 Chevy Impala that I owned a long time ago."

"If it was a '64, then it has been a long time. Did we ever establish your age?"

"We did not. And I don't think it's important, is it?"

He shrugged. "Nope." Another gentle stroke of his erection. It wasn't quite full staff. Relaxed, his body was a study in curved muscle and hard, angular bone structure. "You like cars and motorcycles and all things greasy, including fries and steaks."

"That I do."

"Want to know what I like?"

"Besides running races with deer in the forest and being a super nice guy to everyone you meet? Yes. What is it that Kelyn Saint-Pierre really, deeply, honestly likes?"

"I like a certain witch." He shot a wink over his shoulder. "With purple hair."

The urge to rush over and wrap her arms around him was strong. But Valor decided to simply sit there and take it in. How many times previously had a man complimented her so sweetly? It was a nice moment. One to cherish.

They had spent the early evening risking their lives—okay, so Kelyn had—and by facing death they'd fallen into incredible sex. That whole passionate *la petite mort* thing. So the man was probably on some kind of high right now.

As was she.

They'd lie around a bit longer and come down from the sex endorphins. And then they'd head back to business. Just friends.

Maybe?

"Come here," he said lazily. "Come sit on this."

"You think so?"

"We're not going anywhere until the rains stops. Well, we can, but I like sitting here watching it streak the window. The thunder is relaxing, too."

Valor wandered over to settle onto his lap, back to his chest, directing his now-hard-again erection between her legs to squeeze it tightly with her thighs. That eased up a deep-throated moan from him. She leaned her head against his shoulder and he cupped one of her breasts with his wide, powerful hand.

"Did you think you were going to die?" she asked quietly while tracing the silver remnants of his missing sigil. Outside, lightning streaked the sky in brilliant gold.

"Yes. No." He exhaled against her cheek, and that

ended with a chuffing laugh. "Yes. I regret never taking swimming lessons when I was a kid."

"Adults can take them."

"They can? I suppose. I'm thinking maybe avoiding mermaids is probably the thing to do from now on. And always wear a life jacket."

"Good call. I thought you had died, too. For a few minutes there…"

He pulled strands of half-dried hair away from her face and pressed his lips against her cheek. "I didn't die. And you didn't die when you were pinned in the Darkwood. We're both alive. The universe is not done with us yet."

"Do you believe the universe has a plan for everyone?"

"Yes," he said. "Or rather, that we made the plan before we ever came into our bodies. Our souls wanted to find each other."

"I believe that, too. But we didn't have a very auspicious beginning. And you never know, the ending could be pretty crazy, too."

"Then we'd better enjoy what we have while we can. Yes?"

She reached down to grip his penis. The man beneath her groaned and rocked his hips. Time to drive.

Valor packed her things and took inventory of the magic ingredients they'd collected so far. The mermaid's kiss was tightly capped and secure. The pink water…

"Trapper John! See? What did I tell you?" She waggled a broken vial at Kelyn as he picked up the room.

"Can't you bespell the glass not to break?"

"I could—well, uh…" Why hadn't she thought of

that? Valor bristled at his knowing chuckle. "Cocky faery."

With a few Latin words, Valor spelled the remaining three glass vials not to break. It was a *duh* moment that made her chuckle, as well.

And Kelyn's head rose from packing his things to home his bemused gaze on her like an arrow to the target.

"You really like the way I laugh?" she asked.

"It makes me horny."

"What?" That information made her laugh even more robustly.

And Kelyn dived for her on the bed, pinning her wrists down and kissing her hard against her neck. He licked under her jaw and gave her a gentle nip, which spurred on her laugh even more.

"Let's see if you're ticklish, eh?"

"Oh, no!" She was. And he learned that quickly.

The faery went at her relentlessly, finding all her sensitive spots—goddess, behind her knee!—until she was gasping and pleading for mercy.

"Very well," he said, and his tickles softened to kisses.

A soft touch landing on her breast made her sigh and clutch his hair. "That's so weird that laughter makes you horny."

"Not any laughter. Only your silly, snorting chuckles." He kissed her forehead. "They're amazing."

"No one has ever told me something like that before."

"What? That you're amazing? I can't believe that."

She shrugged. "Maybe it's the company I keep."

"Just one of the boys, eh?"

"Bros before ohs."

"What?"

"Eh, it's something I say. I like my guy friends, and I like that they accept me into their confidence as just another guy. Not a frilly girl that might threaten their man cave."

Except...when she wanted more and the man couldn't understand that.

"What's wrong with being frilly?" he asked. "I like a little frill once in a while."

She shrugged. "Too much work. Seriously, Kelyn, if frills are what you need—"

He kissed her deeply, dancing his tongue with hers. Stealing away her protest. And Valor took that as a hint to shut up and let the man like her.

She could do that.

Another flight was met with but one dirty martini and a firm clasp of Kelyn's hand through most of the quick jaunt across the English Channel to France.

He kissed her as they landed at Charles de Gaulle. "You're getting braver." Then he shook out his hand, the one she'd had a vise hold on through the flight. "And I may not have feeling in my fingers for a few hours."

A snorting laugh from Valor was rewarded with a kiss. It felt wrong that such an awful sound should be answered with a hot, lush kiss, but she'd get used to it. Hell, she already was. And she intended to laugh at every opportunity.

"The ingredients in this spell are so specific. Occipital dust from a skull?" Kelyn asked as, an hour after landing, the taxi navigated central Paris toward the Île Saint-Louis, as he'd directed.

"Better specific than vague. We want this to work, right?"

"Yes." He clasped her hand and kissed the back of it. "You smell great."

Valor smirked. "I smell clean, not like mermaid slime or a pink lake. Is that what you're getting at?"

"Probably." He tilted his head onto her shoulder and nuzzled his nose against her neck, which felt so deliciously exciting Valor had to keep from turning to kiss him. She was not one for PDAs. "You know people are attracted to one another by scent? We select our mates that way."

"Hmm… But how do you know you've the right-smelling person?"

"It's instinctual. We know when we know."

"I see. And what do you know right now?"

"I know that you smell gorgeous." He kissed her neck and licked her skin. A shiver traced her body and coalesced in her nipples, tightening them. He noticed and tweaked one with his fingers.

"Kelyn," she admonished, and gestured toward the front seat.

"He can't see."

"But he *knows*."

"How do *you* know he knows?"

"I just do."

"Fine. Hands off. But this is the hard part."

"Yeah? I thought *that* was the hard part," she said with a glance to his crotch.

"Do you purposely do that?"

She nodded, knowing he was now horny with no means to alleviate that condition. Because of her. "Probably."

"Did I mention we're heading to my aunt's place?"

"Uh, no. I thought we'd grab another hotel room."

"Nope. Kambriel is my dad's twin sister. She and her husband, Johnny Santiago, live on the island. They own a huge place. I'm sure they won't mind putting us up for a day or two."

"They don't know we're coming? Great."

"They're cool. They're both vamps, so you know. They both sing in a goth band and travel the world a lot."

"I like vamps. I look forward to meeting them. Your family is such an interesting mix. Your dad is a werewolf and your mom a faery. Yet your dad's sister is vampire?"

"Grandma and Grandpa are werewolf and vampire."

"Right, Blu and Creed Saint-Pierre. I've met Blu once or twice. She's awesome."

"Grandma rocks. And she won't let Grandpa forget that. As for the rest of our eclectic mix, I used to be the only faery in the family until Daisy Blu chose faery over being a werewolf. She was once full werewolf with only traces of faery in her. She was forced to choose between the two. It goes back to the Denton Marx thing."

"The time-traveling wolf hunter. Wow. I guess I wouldn't be able to pick if I had more than two breeds running through my veins. We witches are pretty solid. So you're full-blood faery? Not a bit of wolf from your dad?"

"I've never exhibited any werewolf-like behaviors, but Dad always says I've the wolf in my soul because I'm the strongest of all the Saint-Pierre boys. But don't tell Trouble that. He likes to think he's the toughest."

"The way I understand it from Trouble, he's fully aware of your strength and respects that."

Kelyn shrugged. "The faery is always the last one invited to the fight because my punches tend to knock a guy out cold. At least, they used to."

Valor kissed his forehead. "You'll get your strength back. Soon. I'll do everything in my power to make it happen."

"You've already done so much. Thank you, Valor."

The look he gave her went all melty and worshippy, and Valor, for not the first time, had to catch herself from laughing in disbelief. He was so different from all the other men she'd ever dated or chummed around with. How had she gotten so lucky? Oh, right. He'd committed a brave and noble act to save her life, and now she was trying to catch up with him and make it all right according to her logic.

She was almost there. Almost.

The cab pulled over and, after paying and locating the right building, Kelyn knocked on the door to his aunt's home. The vampire who opened the door was dressed in skintight black latex and a silver hip chain dotted with rubies. Long black hair coiled on her head in pseudo demon horns, and her black lipstick looked as seamless and smooth as the latex. She squealed at the sight of Kelyn and lunged to kiss his cheek.

"Sweetie! Come in, come in! I can't believe you're in Paris."

"Hey, Aunt Kam." Kelyn smeared the back of his hand over the black lip print on his jaw, but was successful in only removing half. "Sorry to surprise you like this, but Valor and I are in town for a day or two and I was hoping we could crash here?"

"Of course! And Valor, eh?" The gorgeous vampire with pin-sharp black fingernails eyed her from head to toe. And for once Valor felt her lack of glamour as a bone-deep affliction. "Sweet," the vampiress commented, lacking enthusiasm. "Oh, but Kelyn, you'll have the place all to yourself. Johnny and I were heading out the door to Brazil for another honeymoon."

"Another?"

"We celebrate one every year. Honey!"

A long, lanky man with coal-black hair shaved along the sides and above his ears, and wearing black leather pants low at his hips, swung around the corner. On his shoulders glided a green snake half the size of a healthy boa constrictor.

"Kelyn!"

"Uncle Johnny." Kelyn clasped Valor's hand. "Is that your dad's snake?"

"Yeah, Green Snake the Third. I borrowed him for a show we did last night. So, who is this?" Johnny smiled expectantly at Valor.

"This is my, er, friend, Valor. She's a witch."

Valor offered a little wave over Kelyn's shoulder. She wasn't too sure about getting close to that snake. With its pink forked tongue flicking in and out, it looked suspiciously dangerous.

"Kam said it would be okay for us to crash here, but I'm bummed you two are leaving."

"The cab will be here in half an hour," Johnny said. "And we need to stop by Dad's house and drop off Green Snake along the way."

"Ah! I need to do my lashes," Kambriel said. With another quick kiss to Kelyn's other cheek, she skittered off, down the marble hallway on six-inch heels. "Love you, sweetie! Next time call ahead and we'll plan to be here."

"Sweetie?" Kelyn looked to Johnny, who, surprisingly, blushed.

"She's been calling everyone sweetie and honey since she found out," Johnny said. "I think it's hormones."

"Found out?" Kelyn asked.

Valor offered, "She's pregnant. She absolutely glows."

"She is," Johnny said proudly. "We're going to have a tiny bloodsucker. And I will call him Stoker." He winked at them. "Just kidding. So, what are you in town for? Vacation? Love tryst?" he asked, pronouncing the word *love* with a roll of his tongue.

"We're hunting for spell ingredients," Kelyn offered. "We've determined what we need is in the Council Archives, which brought us to Paris. You have any contacts there?"

"Uh, yes?"

Valor and Kelyn exchanged glances at that unconvincing reply.

"You can try Certainly Jones, who is lord and master over the Archives," Johnny offered as he stroked the snake easing along his shoulder. "He won't be an easy one to convince to let you dabble with the cool old crap collected within the Archives. Which, I'm guessing, you'll want to do. Dabble and/or remove something?"

"Just borrow a little portion of something," Valor explained with a close pinch of her fingers.

"Right. Certainly is not going to approve that. So then I'd go with Tamatha Bellerose, who works with CJ. She does most of the filing and labeling of the items they receive for storage. I'll give you her number and—hell, I wish we had more time, Kelyn. You look great, man. But I heard about your, uh, situation."

Leave it to his mom, Rissa, who spent a lot of time on the phone with her sister-in-law Kambriel, to spill the beans all the way across the ocean. "That's what we're trying to rectify."

"Yeah? I heard it was a nasty witch who caused you to lose your wings."

Valor offered her hand to shake, and as Johnny took it, she said, "Nasty witch, right here."

He retreated from the shake with a wipe of his palm along his thigh. "I see." The vampire eyed her with a discerning quirk of eyebrow, then flashed a glance to Kelyn.

"We're good." Kelyn put an arm around Valor's shoulders. "Get me that number and then you two should head out. Promise we won't trash the place."

"The guest bedroom is down the hallway. It's the gray room," Johnny noted. "Stay out of our bedroom. Unless you want to see things you'd rather not see. You're my nephew, so, yeah, I'd say stay out of that room." He winked again, but Valor did catch his concerned look at her.

"How much time do I have?" Kam called out from down the hallway.

"Ten minutes, lover!" Johnny blushed again. "Oh, there's no food in the house. Vamps." He thumbed his chest. "So you two are on your own for that."

"Not a problem. Thanks, Johnny."

"I gotta go grab our bags. Hold Green Snake, will you?"

Kelyn allowed the snake to slither over his arm and across his shoulders. Johnny sprinted down the hallway and out of view.

When her lover turned to her with a big grin on his face and a snake tongue flickering not far from that grin, Valor stepped back until her shoulders hit the wall.

"Really?" Kelyn said with surprise. "Grease Girl is afraid of a little snake?"

She couldn't even find words because the snake kept flicking out its tongue and eyeballing her with those big gold eyes. Very suspicious.

"Wow. I guess I found your weakness. Don't worry. Green Snake is harmless. I think." He winked.

And Valor walked a wide curve around the guy and his snake, and headed toward the gray room.

Chapter 17

Valor spoke to Tamatha Bellerose on the phone as she and Kelyn walked down the tree-shaded Rue Henri to the eleventh arrondissement where the Council's headquarters was located. A division of the Council, the Archives was a collection of articles, spells, grimoires, objects of a magical nature, creatures of mysterious origins, and other nefarious and possibly deadly items an organization such as the Council should keep in hand and under lock and spellbound key. Some things had been collected by Retrievers, other stuff was donated.

The Council was an overseeing body that didn't so much govern the paranormal nations as watch and keep tabs.

Valor had heard the Archives had rooms designated for objects and history related to each species, and that the witches room was filled with every spell, grimoire and alchemical instrument a witch could ever dream to know. She was excited to look it over, but Tamatha had warned her she and Kelyn didn't have clearance to simply browse about and take what they wished. Tamatha would have to obtain the skull dust—and she would, because she was behind helping Kelyn after Valor had explained the situation about his wings. And any family member of Johnny Santiago was a friend to her.

The only problem? Certainly Jones headed the Archives and he kept a tight hand on the contents. Visitors simply weren't allowed access.

The good part of that problem? He wasn't due in until later in the evening. He'd pulled babysitting duty for his twins this afternoon while his wife was out on a cleanup job. So Tamatha had suggested Valor and Kelyn hurry over. *An infinitesimal amount of bone dust scraped from a skull? No one should miss that.*

The headquarters was located in an unassuming four-story building that they only found because Kelyn suddenly paused and put out his hands as if to stop the ground from rising up.

"What is it?" Valor asked.

"I can feel it."

"Feel what?"

"Everything." He met her gaze with a wondrous little-boy grin. "It's amazing."

"Cool. You getting some of your navigation skills back?"

"Maybe. Paris does have a lot of ley lines running through it. The earth's energies feel…welcoming."

"That's awesome. So…down that alley, you think?"

"Yes." He took the lead, angling down a dark alley-way paved with uneven cobblestones. "You know, since we're in Paris," he called back, "maybe we should check out FaeryTown? I didn't get a chance when I was here years ago for Johnny and Kam's wedding."

"Is that the place where Faery overlies the mortal realm? It's a thin place, right? Maybe you can get to Faery through FaeryTown?"

"Not sure. I don't think there are portals there. And if there are, you need to be in the know. You know?"

"Right, got it. This chick is so not in the know."

"FaeryTown is just a sad, sorry place where faeries exist in mortal space." Kelyn's long strides moved him so swiftly Valor had to double-time to keep up. "The inhabitants either left Faery or were born here. Lots of dust addicts there, too, or so I've heard. You know Johnny's dad, Vaillant, used to be addicted to ichor?"

"Yeah, vamps and faery dust. Not cool." Valor joined him at a metal door set into the brick wall, but neither of them knocked, as Tamatha had requested. "So, are you going to take me to an ichor den later and show me a good time?"

"How about we climb the Eiffel Tower and kiss at the top of the world?"

"I like that idea. How'd you get to be such a romantic?"

"It's easy around you, Valor." Leaning up against her, he blocked her in against the wall. His violet gaze enchanted her. "You challenge me, and yet you always accept, as well. Even when I'm doing the grumpy faery thing. Do you know how rare that is for a guy who's always had trouble dating?"

"Why the trouble?"

He swiped a trace of faery dust from her neck and showed her. "I'm so over dating club girls with glitter makeup in order to hide my dust."

"That must be difficult."

"Exactly."

"I'm not much for dating, myself," she lied. "Too complicated. So many expectations."

"Right?"

"I mean, who wants to fall in love and have to commit to the one person?" She did! She so wanted that.

"Commitment." Kelyn shook his head with disdain. "So, uh, we're not dating, right?"

She hadn't expected that one, but Valor shrugged and forced a nod. "'Course not."

"But we're lovers." He tucked a kiss at the base of her earlobe.

"So you're thinking more like friends with benefits?" *Please say no*, she thought.

"Honestly? I'm not cool with that."

His kiss melted her tensions and Valor relaxed against his hardness. She shouldn't have lied to him, but she didn't know how to put that intimate desire out there. To be mocked and disregarded.

"I want you as more than a friend," he said.

"I want the same thing."

She was ready to show him exactly how much she wanted him by sliding her hand down his jeans when the door creaked open and out popped a silver-haired witch. The twosome straightened and tugged at their clothing as if they'd been caught making out behind the pews by the Sunday school teacher.

Tamatha Bellerose resembled a retro rocker with her green wiggle skirt and white-and-black polka-dot blouse that revealed tattoos on her arms, fingers and neck. She wore her silver hair in victory rolls and had a lovely rose blush to her cheeks that drew attention to her bright green eyes.

"Valor Hearst?"

Valor shook her hand. "Indeed. Wow. You've got some power in that hand. More than air magic?"

Tamatha pointed out the sigil for the elements on each finger as she said, "Earth, air, water and, on occasion, fire. I can feel your vita, too. You've walked this soil almost as long as I have. Nice to meet you. And this is?" She turned an admiring gaze up to Kelyn, who thrust back his shoulders at the feminine attention.

"Kelyn Saint-Pierre." He shook her hand and she held it.

"Of the infamous Saint-Pierres? Wow. You all get around this planet, don't you? But you're not wolf. You're faery. Nice." She rubbed his hand with her palm. "I can feel what's missing from you. Oh, darling, you need to get back your wings before it's too late."

"Too late?" Valor hadn't thought there was a deadline. "What do you mean?" Kelyn asked the witch.

Tamatha took his other hand and closed her eyes. Valor guessed she was reading his vita. Something she'd not thought to do. She could do that, but she wasn't expert at delving into past lives or anything beyond current events.

"You've been weak and unable to shift since it happened," Tamatha said, but the statement ended as a question.

Kelyn nodded.

"A faery's wings are his life. As strong as you are, you will only grow weaker. I'm sorry." She dropped his hands. "Sometimes I get feelings about people, and they're always accurate. Anyway..." She tugged a blue glass vial out from the waistband of her skirt and handed it to Valor. "The Skull of Sidon was discovered a few years ago by archaeologist Annja Creed."

"Why does that name sound familiar?" Kelyn asked.

"She used to have a TV show about history and archaeological stuff."

"Oh, right. *Chasing History's Monsters*," he said. "I loved that show. Used to watch it all the time when I was a kid."

"I watched a few reruns after we obtained the skull, for curiosity's sake," Tamatha said. "That woman can kick butt and she's smart. Anyway, the skull was rumored to have been destroyed after Creed found it, but of course, we stepped in and made sure that didn't happen. Gotta keep tabs on all the supernatural stuff floating about in this realm, ya know?" She tapped the vial. "I scraped that from inside the left occipital hollow. No one is ever going to know it's missing."

"Unless of course…"

All three turned at the deep male voice that echoed from down the alleyway.

Certainly Jones's tall, lithe figure flashed out of shadow as he straightened his shoulders. "That *no one* is me."

Chapter 18

Kelyn heard Tamatha swear under her breath. Turning, he lifted his chest defiantly, yet he knew they were the ones in the wrong. Still, he wouldn't allow Tamatha to take the blame.

"I recognize you," Certainly Jones said as he approached. The man was dark, as were his hair, his clothing and the tattoos that covered virtually every portion of exposed skin, save his face. Kelyn could feel the magic waver off from the man, and it wasn't a pleasant feeling. "Weren't you in town a few years back for..."

"A wedding." Kelyn offered his hand, and the witch shook it. Strong grip, yet Kelyn could feel the malice in his magic vibrating in the touch. "I'm Kelyn Saint-Pierre. Kambriel Saint-Pierre is my aunt. She married Johnny Santiago. I think we may have met at the wedding. Uh, my friend and I—this is Valor Hearst—we meant no harm, Monsieur Jones. You shouldn't blame Mademoiselle Bellerose for this."

Certainly tilted his head, eyeing all three of them in slow but judging perusal. "Did I hear correctly that what is in that vial was taken from the Skull of Sidon that is under protection by the Archives? Who's working a spell?"

"I am." Valor shook hands with Certainly, but Kelyn noticed she didn't offer to hand over the vial. Good girl. "It's a spell to open a portal to Faery. Kelyn needs to get his wings back. We have to go to Faery to find them."

Certainly again looked Kelyn over. He'd never felt a gaze so deeply. It was as if the witch could read things about him even he didn't know. "What happened to your wings?"

"It's a long story. Suffice it to say, we've been gathering ingredients for the spell. We should have asked you for the skull dust. I know that's wrong. But I'm also not willing to give it back. And I will stand strong if you insist."

Certainly smirked. "I could take it back with a flick of one finger." He waggled a tattooed finger before them. "A portal spell? What are the other ingredients?" he asked Valor.

"Uh, well, a werewolf claw. We got that. Mermaid's kiss. Just barely got that. Water from Lake Hillier, it's pink. Pretty cool—"

Certainly hissed. "What in all of Beneath kind of spell requires such water? Don't you know that stuff is volatile when mixed with the light sort of witchcraft?"

Valor exchanged gazes with Kelyn. He sensed her sudden anxiety. And also that she hadn't a clue what

Certainly was talking about. "Why would the spell require such an ingredient if it doesn't work?" he asked.

"Oh, it'll work. But in the hands of a light witch, it could produce a catastrophic effect, as well." Certainly opened the door and turned to them. "Let's check this out. I've the *Book of All Spells* inside. If you're going to steal from me, I want to make sure you don't end up blowing away half the population in the process of invoking the spell."

The storage room dedicated to witches was three stories beneath the surface of Paris, and it was a marvel. Valor followed Certainly into the room, and when he said she could look but not touch, she took that to heart and started down the first aisle, forgetting that she'd left Kelyn at the door. The air was dark and heavy with dust, and there were shelves upon shelves of books and compendiums and grimoires. It reminded her of some kind of fantasy library, in which anything on the shelves might get up and dance as soon as she turned out the lights and closed the door. Of course the lights were oil lamps. CJ had explained electric lighting was iffy with this much magic in storage.

"Don't go that far!" CJ called as Valor neared the dark end of the first aisle.

Ahead of her, the walls appeared black, and yet when Valor squinted she saw into the depths. The book spines were black and…*things* seemed to be moving. Vines? Or were those tentacles? Did she smell sulfur?

Compelled to take a step forward, she startled when someone gently grabbed her arm. Kelyn leaned in and said at her ear, "You should listen to the dark witch who can take us out with a flick of his tattooed fingers, yes?"

"Yeah, but look." She gestured toward what might have been pinpoint red eyes peeping out from between two books.

"This way." Kelyn tugged her back the way she'd come. "There's a wall of herbs and other nasty things like bones and rat skulls I'm sure you'll be interested in."

"Really?" She turned and passed him, veering toward a dully lit corner where the ceiling grew thick with ancient herbs, some hung and dried, others growing in *kokedama* Japanese moss balls or delicate hydroponic glass balls. Her witchy senses were drawn toward the scent of dragon's blood and she touched the long, narrow vial that glittered with violet substance.

"I said don't touch!"

She waggled her head at CJ's admonishment as Tamatha joined her side. The witch was glamorous, yet seemed more down-to-earth than even Valor's best friend Eryss, and Eryss was an earth witch.

"It's like being a kid in a candy store, isn't it?" Tamatha whispered.

"Oh, yeah. What's that?" Valor almost touched a vial in which something phosphorescent blue wiggled inside red liquid.

"Dragon parasite. Excellent for stanching fire spells. And did you see the gargoyle's eyes?"

Valor studied a jar of stone eyeballs that pulsed with red veins. "Nice."

"Oh, this is not good."

At Certainly's dire utterance, both women lifted their heads. Tamatha gestured for them to join the dark witch, and they walked over to stand beside him and Kelyn. The group perused the massive *Book of All Spells*, which was, when spread open, about six feet wide and four feet tall, and stuffed with tissue-thin pages. Yet the page it was open to seemed alive as the illustrations danced, and Valor even picked up cinnamon and some darker earthy scents from its content.

"Water from Lake Hillier reacts to light magic unless it is blessed by a dark witch," CJ recited as he read the page. "And you've got all five ingredients? The claw, water, kiss, skull dust and tear?"

"Heading home tomorrow to check on the tear," Valor confirmed. "I'm sure I have it in stock. But if the water merely needs to be blessed by a dark witch…?" She gave him a hopeful grin and exchanged nods with Kelyn, who stood at one corner of the book with his arms crossed.

"Where do you intend to perform this spell?" Certainly asked.

Valor shrugged. "Probably at home in my spell room. Why?"

"That's not what is required." He tapped the page. "Didn't you read it all the way through?"

Valor leaned over the book and scanned through the ingredient list and the basic incantation, both of which she was familiar with. And yet it went on to describe summoning location and conditions. And there was even a warning about the lake water that was new to her.

"That information wasn't in my grimoire," she said.

"You must have an abridged edition."

"No. It was once my great-grandmother Hector's grimoire. She passed it down to me. It's original. Sometimes I can even smell her perfume in the pages. Everything was handwritten."

"Not according to this." CJ tapped the page. "This book is the master book of all spells ever created. The moment a new spell is written, spoken and/or chanted, it is recorded here. Your great-grandmother must have removed some pages from her grimoire. It's the only explanation for your missing information."

"Now that you mention it, there are a few places where I've wondered if a page was torn out. Well, can I get a copy of the spell from this book?" Valor asked.

CJ stood straight and eyed her with the darkest jade eyes she had ever seen. No compassion in them, and yet she could feel a certain softness emanate from him, as if he wanted to be kind, to assist her. Surely if she told him about Kelyn's desire to get his wings back, the witch would sympathize.

"Please," Kelyn said. "We wouldn't ask unless it meant more than life itself."

And all in the room felt Kelyn's heartfelt desire to be whole once again. He didn't even have to explain.

"Of course," CJ said. "You've already stolen the skull dust." He shot a condemning look at Tamatha. "Not like we can actually put that back, is it? I'll have a copy of this spell made. Tamatha, can you get the handheld scanner?"

"You mean you can't magic a copy into her hand?" Kelyn asked.

"I am not a Xerox machine," Certainly commented, and followed with a heavy sigh. "As for performing the spell at your home, Valor, it'll never work. It has to be at the place in which you wish the portal to open. In a thin place."

"Like the Darkwood," Kelyn offered hopefully.

"Exactly," CJ agreed.

And Valor cringed to imagine returning to the forest where it had all begun. Was she even allowed back in?

Would the wicked trees pin her once again? It was too risky. And it would dredge up so many awful memories of her dreadful beginning with Kelyn. They'd only just engaged in something wonderful. Why ruin that with something bad?

She met her lover's gaze across the massive book. His violet eyes twinkled, yet he didn't quite smile. He was trying to read her and had probably seen her reluctance, so she pulled on a smile.

"Sure," she said. "The Darkwood it is."

"Great," CJ said. "You have the lake water that requires blessing on you?"

"It's at Kambriel's apartment on the island."

"Bring it to me and I will bless it. I was on my way home, actually, when I had a feeling there was a reason I needed to return to work." Again, he cast a condemning gaze at all three of them with the ease of dealing out cards.

"Tamatha said you were watching the kids?" Valor said.

"Vika got home from work early. Now, I'll give you my address, and you'll come to me if you want this done."

"Of course." She tugged out her cell phone, scrolled to Contacts and handed CJ the phone to enter his info.

Tamatha returned with a scanning wand, and in but a minute the spell had been scanned and digitally sent to Valor's phone. She verified she'd received the complete file, then shook CJ's hand. "I owe you for this."

"Of course you do. We'll meet again someday. And when you do get back your wings?" He turned to Kelyn. "Be cautious. If someone else has been wearing them, they will be tainted."

"So I've been told. I will be careful. Thank you, Monsieur Jones. We both appreciate everything you've done for us, and I am at your beckon, as well. Whenever you need it, let me know."

"I consider myself richer for the friendships I've gained today. Now, out with you." CJ gestured for them to leave and bent over the massive spell book. "I'll be home in a few hours."

Once outside and in the cobblestone alleyway, Kelyn pulled Valor into an embrace and kissed her there against the brick wall in the darkening midafternoon shadows. Their kisses had become so easy, yet never simple. Each time his mouth fit against hers, Valor felt it in a different place. This one seemed to focus on her nipples, teasing them hard, so she rubbed them against his chest. His moans always spoke so much more than words. The man could kiss her anywhere he wanted. She might even let him kiss her in the back of a cab next time.

"You sure about having the fifth ingredient at home?"

Valor nodded. "Ninety-five percent sure. Should we go grab the water and head over to the dark witch's home?"

"I'm curious to see a dark witch's place. Let's do it!"

The dark witch blew a haze of whiskey-tainted smoke over the opened vial of the Lake Hillier water. The vial briefly glowed pink before he capped it and handed it back to Valor.

"It's done. Blessed," Certainly said. "It shouldn't prove an issue to work with it now. Unless the dark blessing is warded between now and when you perform the spell. If you've wards up on your home you should remove them before entering. And most certainly do not enter the thin place warded. Got it?"

"Thanks, CJ." Valor handed Kelyn the vial, who tucked it in the backpack in which all their valuable finds were stored. "So, before we go, can I ask about the chandeliers?"

The dark witch sat back on the velvet sofa, stretching his arms over the back and tilting his head to take in the constellation of glass chandeliers that hung in the two-story open-space loft he and his lover, Vika, and their twin one-year-old sons, had commandeered in the seventh arrondissement of Paris. *There must be hundreds*, Valor thought. A few were actually lit, providing more than enough lighting.

"It's a long story," Certainly said. "But I once required prismatic light to keep away the demons that had infested my soul after a rather unwise venture into Daemonia. There are always consequences to using dark magic. But Vika still loves me."

Vika was Viktorie Saint-Charles, a light witch who lived with CJ and who operated a cleaner operation with her sister, Libertie. Cleaners were available to do just that—clean up dead paranormal bodies best not left lying out for the public to stumble over.

"It's beautiful," Kelyn commented, hooking an arm over Valor's shoulder and leaning in to nuzzle his nose at her hair.

The door opened and in breezed a red-haired witch wearing a long black Morticia gown and a bag of groceries.

"Vika, Queen of My Heart." CJ rose to kiss his lover. "We've friends for a little whiskey and magic." He glanced to Valor and Kelyn. "You two up for that?"

Kelyn exchanged looks with Valor, and his smile grew quickly. A challenge, if either of them had heard correctly.

"Oh, yeah," they said together.

Chapter 19

"Will your boyfriend do it?"

Vika, the light witch who was currently mixing drinks for what had become a party of many, gave Valor a curious wink. She'd asked if Kelyn would donate a bit of faery dust for the drinks. Because with a little magic and dust she could make an out-of-this-world drink.

"Faery dust will get you high, but you won't have a hangover," she added. "I've only had it once before. CJ would love it."

"He will if I ask him sweetly," Valor said, because this was a fun challenge. And while she wasn't into recreational drugs, what could a little faery dust hurt anyone? Wasn't as if she were a vampire who could become addicted to the stuff. "What do you have in those drinks?"

The mason jars Vika used for drinking glasses sparkled under the many chandeliers lined above the kitchen area of the vast loft. The whole place was open with only a few walls for semiprivacy, such as the ones sectioning off the bedrooms and the one backing up Vika and CJ's spell area. The twins had been tucked away in their cribs before Valor and Kelyn arrived, and Vika had checked on them briefly before gathering the drink supplies.

A boisterous redhead laughed over near the gray sofa where she and her boyfriend, a former angel/soul bringer, stood chatting with Kelyn. She was Vika's sister, Libby, and her boyfriend was Reichardt. They had stopped in on the way home from a day at the park, and when they saw the party starting they had jumped right in. Valor secretly wondered if Reichardt could still produce angel dust. She was running low on that particular ingredient, thanks to her failed attempt at—argh. No, she wasn't going to land on that depressing thought. Her love life was actually looking up. Dwelling on her flaws would never move her forward. *Onward!*

"Cherry juice, vodka, cardamom and salt," Vika said as she mixed a shaker full of said ingredients. "Ice, of course, and a touch of dragon's blood."

"For a fiery taste," Valor added.

"You know it. And now we need the secret ingredient." The witch glanced through elegant kohl-lined green eyes over to Kelyn, who was laughing along with the others over Libby's gyrations that detailed trying to actually fly a broomstick.

CJ's brother, Thoroughly Jones—also called TJ— had arrived with his wife, Star, a cat shifter. The man was CJ's twin, and together they put out some awesomely dark, sexy vibes that Valor hadn't realized could attract her until she saw them in double. What had become of her preference for the big, beefy bad boys?

The dark witches were bad personified. Some Lynyrd Skynyrd blasted, and one of the twin witches was currently drawing a chalk circle on the floor while explaining to the menfolk how to catch a war demon in three easy steps.

"Kelyn!" Valor gestured for him to come over. Nursing the whiskey CJ had poured him, he wandered toward them, barefoot. When had the man abandoned his footwear? Actually, all the men, save Reichardt, were barefoot.

She made a show of glancing at his feet, and Kelyn shrugged and offered, "The floor is heated. Can you feel it? It's awesome." He kissed her on the cheek. "What's up? You ladies making drinks?"

Valor glided her palm up his chest and kissed him. "We are, and I have a big favor to ask. Sort of a fun one, actually."

"Anything for you, lover."

Valor tapped his chest and worked her best pouty lips with lash flutter on him. She'd once practiced before a mirror.

"You got something stuck in your eye?" he asked with concern.

"Seriously? I work my one and only sexy move on you and you think I've got a condition?"

He laughed. "Just teasing. What's up?"

"Could we borrow a sprinkle of your dust? Vika says when added to the drinks it'll get us high."

"Is that so? And what about the faery in the room who doesn't want to drink his own dust?"

"I have an angel dust elixir for you," Vika said, pointing to the vial of iridescent liquid that sat next to a canning jar half-filled with a green drink.

"Angel dust, eh?" Kelyn shrugged. "I've never been much for alcohol." He waggled the whiskey glass that could only be minus a few sips. "But I've been doing a lot of new things lately. I'm intrigued. I'm in!" With a snap of his fingers, his dust sprinkled over the jars that Vika had been mixing, settling onto the surface with a glint.

Vika met Valor's wink with her own. "Dust Bombs for all!"

An hour later everyone was dancing around the chalk circle drawn on the hardwood, in which stood a war demon, who also nursed one of the Dust Bombs. Built like a block with obscene muscles, the visitor from Daemonia had black skin with a distinctive sheen. His horns glowed crimson, and he couldn't stop giggling.

TJ was currently arm wrestling with Kelyn, and Kelyn was holding his own simply because the dark witch, who had removed his shirt to expose tight muscles, was so high on the Dust Bombs he could barely see straight.

Libby was dancing with Valor, and every time she hip bumped her, Valor went flying into Star's arms. The women laughed and Valor's snorts always brought up Kelyn's head in search of her. The room sparkled with dust, and yet Kelyn hadn't imbibed any more of the whiskey. Vika had made him something special that contained pomegranate seeds and angel dust. His grin had grown unstoppable.

Certainly and Vika danced slowly before a window, and every so often he'd spin her and he'd put up his arms and shout, "Witch of My Heart!" Apparently the man had a thing for bestowing titles of affection upon his lover.

The arm wrestling match suddenly ended in a tie and the war demon challenged Kelyn with drunken taunts. "Come on, step inside the circle, my faery boy!"

As Kelyn wobbled toward the circle, CJ made a quick detour and shoved the faery away. Kelyn landed on the sofa, sprawled, his grin growing crooked. "Careful, faery. He'll take you to Daemonia."

"You're no fun!" The war demon pouted, then tilted back his jar, which was empty. He lashed out a long black tongue, mining the bottom of the glass, but couldn't get any more out. "Aggh! I want me some more faery dust!"

At that outburst, Kelyn shuddered and called out, "Leave the faery alone!" which then segued into drunken laughter.

This time a hip bump set Valor on a trajectory toward the sofa. Kelyn saw her coming and held out his arms to catch her—but she missed and landed on the opposite end. The faery hugged his empty arms across his chest. And Valor snorted out peals of laughter.

"I'd come after you and kiss you," Kelyn managed, "but I can't even see straight!"

"Ha!" Valor rolled off the couch and landed hard on the floor. Turning onto her back and gazing up into the constellation of chandeliers that blurred and turned into a massive cloud of muted light because of her inebriation, she decided that the witches in Paris knew how to party. Big time.

The music switched to something sensual, and CJ called out, "Lover, oh, Mistress of the Faery Dust Bomb!"

Vika popped her head up from the kitchen fridge, where she'd been looking for more ice. A snap of her fingers spun a flame into the air and it floated toward CJ, who caught the amber ball on his palm and then, with a sip from his glass, blew the alcohol through the flame, creating a magnificent burst of blue sparkly flames that alighted into the air.

"Don't burn the place down!" Vika called. "I don't have enough ice for that!"

Kelyn reached out to catch a falling blue flame, and as it lit onto his fingers it alchemized into liquid and glided along his skin, finding the silvery scars at his wrist and, for a moment, lighting up the sigils that had once been there. "Sweet. Whoever said dark witches were evil?"

Meow!

Valor lifted her head from the floor and spied the black cat with the white star on her chest chase the blue flames rolling across the floor as if they were marbles.

"CJ," Vika called admonishingly. She tried to look stern, but she wobbled drunkenly, too.

CJ called out a Latin word and all the flames fizzled.

"Aww..." The war demon pouted. "They were so pretty."

"Who's up for naked limbo?" someone shouted.

The airplane hadn't even left the tarmac at Charles de Gaulle, but both Kelyn and Valor sat in first class with heads bowed toward each other, snoring. Still on a high from the Dust Bombs, Valor had glided onto the plane, arms held out and making noises like a kid would were she playing at flying. She'd been hyped with exhilaration and when Kelyn had followed with a staggering gait—yet he'd managed a perfectly sober stride through customs—she hadn't felt an ounce of the usual nervous anxiety.

Once seated in the confining tin can, Valor had yawned and whispered a spell for sleep. It might have been the faery dust coursing through her system, or it could have been a lucky magical moment, but the spell actually worked.

It had been a long adventure, and but one ingredient remained. And then to Faery.

Nine hours later, Kelyn sat in the back of a cab with Valor, cruising from the Minneapolis airport to the northern suburb of Tangle Lake. Both were still a little drowsy, but whether it was jet lag or dust lag they couldn't be sure. They didn't need to talk now. Holding hands? That was some kind of awesome.

They'd come down from the high and he was thinking he should have gotten a drink recipe from Vika. Angel dust? That had been some good shit. He'd seen in a range of colors he'd not even imagined before. And while his senses had seemed to increase to what they had once been, it had all been a crazy rushed blur of dancing, laughing, avoiding the war demon's challenging taunts, chandeliers—and, yes, naked limbo.

Chandeliers? He still didn't get it, but he didn't care. They'd had a great night to say goodbye to Paris.

Now he could feel Valor's energy flowing into him and it didn't so much invigorate him as exude through his body with a reassurance that she was the right woman for him. He'd not felt this way with a person before. So trusting. Completely at ease. Relaxed.

Was he too relaxed? Should he be more cautious of her magic and the forthcoming spell? A spell that could change his life. Would she perform the spell right? What if it failed? He needed to get to Faery and find his wings.

But even more? He wanted to finally set foot in Faery. It was a home that had always called to him, a place where he belonged. Growing up, he'd felt as if he lived in the wrong world. Sure, his family and home felt right. And the forest surrounding his home, along with the Darkwood, were what he imagined freedom must feel like. But they could never be Faery. Right?

So when finally he did make it to Faery, and found his wings, would he then be able to turn away from all that it offered and return to the mortal realm?

Why would any man do such a thing if given the opportunity to stay?

Kelyn walked Valor up to her building door, but she noted he'd told the cab to wait for him. Back here in the United States it was midafternoon, and she was no longer tired or high, though she couldn't promise her aching bones she wouldn't crash the minute she saw the bed. Travel had whipped her good. And even though Vika had said there'd be no hangover from the Dust Bombs, she wasn't so sure the throbbing in her temple wasn't just that.

Yeah, a few winks of rest felt necessary. But she wanted to crash with Kelyn by her side. Didn't he want to come in and stay with her? They could make love until they fell asleep together from jet lag and adventure withdrawal.

She opened the door to the building, and Kelyn put a palm up on the door frame and leaned in to kiss her. She grasped at his shirt, pulling him closer, wanting to feel his body heat against her breasts, wanting to jump inside him. To make him stay. He couldn't leave her now.

How could he leave?

"I've got some things to check on," he said as he broke the kiss. "Call you soon?"

"Sure. Uh…"

He lifted a brow, waiting for her to say something.

"It's good," she decided. "Right. Uh, back to business. I'll talk to you soon and we'll make plans for stage two of the operation."

"Awesome." He kissed her again. It was too quick. Not even long enough for her to kiss him back. "Thank you, Valor. This adventure has meant a lot to me." He clasped her hand and kissed her knuckles. And with a squeeze of her hand, he strode down the sidewalk to the waiting cab.

As if he'd said goodbye for the last time.

Fingers clutching at the door pull, Valor stood in the doorway, watching the cab drive off down the street until it turned the corner at the end of the block.

Gone without a care? Her heart pulsed. It felt as if she'd received a blow to all the feels. She gasped as sudden tears spilled from her eyes.

She missed the man already. And it felt as though he'd taken a piece of her heart along with him. He hadn't looked at her as the cab rolled away. Not even a goodbye wave.

Why hadn't he looked at her?

Touching the tears on her cheeks, Valor had a sudden, devastating realization.

"Seriously? Oh, my goddess! By all the television doctors!"

She slammed the door shut and dashed up three flights. Once inside her loft, she aimed for her spell room and found an empty vial.

Chapter 20

Kelyn waited for his brother Trouble to open the front door, and before his oldest sibling could manage a grin, Kelyn swung up his fist and laid his brother out with a right uppercut.

Mostly.

Trouble wobbled, stepped backward, put out his arms to balance, then landed on the easy chair behind him with a grunt. "What the…?" He rubbed his jaw. "Dude, you really have lost your strength. That punch should have knocked me flat. Good try, though." He smirked.

Kelyn strode inside and closed the door. He had gotten that out of his system, but he still felt dissatisfied. As if his lady's honor required defending. So he bent before his brother. "That was for making me think you and Valor had something going on."

"Me and the witch? Of course we did. We used to get together for Netflix and chill all the time."

"You made me believe you'd slept with her."

Trouble shrugged. "A guy can't have too many notches, can he?"

"But you didn't earn a notch from her."

Another shrug. Yeah, so Trouble had a habit of boasting about his conquests. Real and, apparently, imagined. Kelyn had always figured his brother padded the number and the experiences with his own ideas on what that total should be. But Kelyn had always believed he and Valor had had sex. It was the very reason he'd not pursued her and had such a tough time initially trusting her.

"So what's the deal?" Trouble shoved Kelyn backward. "You and the witch getting it on now? She's the one who stole your wings, man!"

"For the last time, she did not steal my wings. And yes." Kelyn fiercely stabbed his brother's chest. "She. Is. Mine. Got that?"

Trouble put up placating hands. His smirk was a constant. But for once could the guy move beyond the childish teasing and boisterous grandstanding and attempt to show some understanding?

"She means something to me," Kelyn insisted, "so you stay the hell away from her."

"I have been walking a wide circle around that witch. As you should be. What happened on your trip that changed your mind about hating her?"

"I've never hated her. You know I don't hate on women. I sacrificed my wings for her, Trouble. She had nothing to do with that decision. It was all my doing."

"You sacrificed your wings because you are a good man and you could never let a woman suffer or die.

Which would have happened had you not made such a selfless sacrifice. But she meant nothing to you at the time. You meant nothing to her. She played you, man. You were a sucker!"

Another punch was due. This time Kelyn managed to clock Trouble up under the jaw, shifting his skull on his spine. That knocked him out.

"She's always meant something to me. It just took me a while to figure out what it was, exactly."

Standing over his silent brother, Kelyn heaved out a frustrated sigh. This was not his way. He didn't beat on his brothers. Not unless it was a friendly fight. And such scuffles had happened often growing up in the Saint-Pierre household.

Why now was he so defensive over what he had with Valor? He knew he didn't have to protect her from Trouble. To defend her honor. A simple *stay away* would have sufficed.

He rubbed his fist, coming down from the anger.

What an asshole to come here and do such a thing. He turned and opened the front door.

Behind him, Trouble roused and muttered, "My little brother is in love."

Fingers clenching the door frame, Kelyn tightened his jaw. Was that it? Was he in love?

Maybe he was.

Yet the witch gave no clue that she felt the same way. So what was he going to do about that?

An hour after Kelyn had left Valor alone at her loft, her door buzzer rang. Tossing aside the towel with which she'd been scrub-drying her hair after a long shower to erase the travel from her skin, she checked her reflec-

tion. The soft pink velvet sundress she'd slipped on because it had been conveniently hanging on the back of
the bathroom door hung to her thighs. She slept in it, but
it was a dress, so she could answer the door in it, as well.
Wasn't like she had abundant cleavage to worry about
flaunting. She was flat chested, but never too pissed over
that. Especially since lying on her stomach was the only
way to sleep. *Suck it, big-busted women.*

Dodging Mooshi, who was sprawled on the floor beside the sofa, belly up, she glided up and slid the massive rolling door open. Kelyn stepped over the threshold,
cupped her head with both hands and gave her the most
sudden and delicious kiss she'd ever gotten. It stole her
words. And it erased her anxiety over his earlier abrupt
departure.

Wrapping her legs about his hips, she tasted mint
on his tongue as it danced with hers. He clasped her
thighs, kicked the door shut and carried her in toward
the kitchen and beyond, not breaking the kiss.

"Watch out for the—"

Mooshi meowed angrily and scampered off while
Kelyn managed to double-step to avoid a stumble. And
then he resumed the kiss, which was so greedy and demanding it felt as though he was begging for her without words.

Just when she'd been bumming that he'd walked away
from her without wanting to stay, he returned. And without a word he was proving how much he wanted to be
here now.

Setting her on the big round table before the windows, which she generally used for cleaning auto parts,
Kelyn moved the kiss from her lips to her jaw. A few
hungry nibbles with his teeth and lashes with his tongue

had her cooing and squirming upon the table. He glided those teasing kisses up to her earlobe, which he suckled. Drawing his teeth along the shell curve, he tickled the top inner cove of her ear. That was a new erotic spot.

"Mmm, I was hoping to see you again. I didn't think it would be tonight."

"Need you," he muttered and pushed up her dress. "Right now. Wait—a dress?"

"Don't read too much into it."

"Not a problem." He unzipped and shuffled down his pants. Commando was his style and his cock sprang up at attention. "Yes?"

So he was a man of few words? Worked for her.

Bracketing his hips with her legs, she turned her feet inward, pushing him toward her with her toes. He bowed over her, one hand guiding his hard-on into her while the other gripped her wet hair as he kissed her breast none too gently. The hot, searing heat of his entrance granted Valor a rush of giddy pleasure. She gasped and pulled at his hair and then pushed up his T-shirt so their bodies could be skin on skin.

His intensity was off the scale. He thrust roughly inside her as if he were trying to pin her to the table. This pinning she could handle. Digging her fingers in at his shoulders, she moaned and whispered, "Yes."

A nip to her breast deepened her pleasure and then she muttered an actual swear word. He pinched her other breast, and the shock of it increased the high of this wild and wicked coupling.

When dust exuded from his skin, it put off a sweet, tantalizing scent. And maybe she got a little high from it, too. Not as high as she had been at the dark witch's home in Paris. But it added another element to their coupling that pushed all sensation high up the charts.

Licking his shoulder, Valor bit him, testing his reaction.

"Oh, yeah?" He bit her breast but kept his lips over his teeth, and then toyed with her nipple until she pumped her hips roughly against his, demanding, seeking, wanting.

And when his body began to tremor above hers, Valor reached down to tighten her fingers about the base of his cock. But he thrust too rapidly for her to keep a good hold, so she let him come inside her. His loud, short shout sounded like a yes mixed with a sigh.

He hilted himself within her, pushing up and lifting her derriere from the table, the fingers of one hand still at her breast as he tilted back his head and rode the orgasm. "Dr. House!"

Valor laughed and snorted, which sent him into a delicious growl. With a slip of his finger over her clitoris, and as she ground her mons up against Kelyn's torso, she, too, reached orgasm and shuddered beneath him, her elbows knocking the table. She almost slid off until he caught her and bowed over her, laying his head against her chest.

Somewhere in the loft a cat meowed, with judgment.

"Just needed to be inside you," he said. A jerk of his hips tightened his erection within her. He groaned and rocked his hips, the move further rubbing him against her clitoris, which prolonged the exquisite aching giddiness. "Feels right here."

Gasping and breathing heavily, she clasped her hands over his head, holding him there as they experienced a long and delicious gaze into each other's soul. Their sweat-sticky bodies melded skin against skin. So much in his violet eyes. Could it all be hers?

With a kiss to her breast, Kelyn collapsed on top of her and they lay there for long minutes in a silence that harmonized with their breaths and sighs.

Valor sat on Kelyn's lap, and he sat in the big wicker chair placed before one of the tall windows overlooking the street below. This end of town was mostly residential apartment complexes and some old factory buildings that housed hip restaurants and coffee shops as well as a quilting store and a couple art shops.

She licked the cherry Popsicle she had suggested they share to cool them down. She hadn't pulled up her dress, and her tiny breasts hugged his bare chest. With a bite of the Popsicle, Valor pulled away from Kelyn as she giggled and teased him with the red frozen treat.

He bit off a big chunk and let it melt in his mouth. Then, before the juice was completely swallowed, he kissed her, dashing his cherry-sweetened tongue with hers. She curled into him, and he cupped her ass to hold her tighter to him. He'd pulled off his pants, and his cock was hard. Valor's foot toyed with it absently, but when she noticed, she turned her attention to stroking the side of it with her toes.

"So we have all the ingredients, then?" he asked. "You got the fifth and final?"

"Yep. I had it in stock like I thought I would."

"So that was tears of love or something?"

"True love's first tears. Silly stuff."

"Right. And tell me why or how a witch keeps something like that in stock?"

"I had it right next to my frog's bellow and banshee's scream."

"Of course. How stupid of me not to know that is standard witch's gear. So, when are we going to do this?"

"We have one more thing we need." She hooked a thumb over her shoulder, pointing to the paper lying on the kitchen counter under a yellow highlighter. "I had a chance to read over the whole spell that Certainly copied for me, and it looks like I'll need a familiar."

"You mean like a cat shifter?"

"They come in all breeds, but yes, cat shifters are the most common familiars. My best friend Sunday is a familiar."

"Dean Maverick's wife?"

"Right. Dean was promoted to principal of the Northern pack because Ridge Addison has retired. But I'm not sure I should ask Sunday to do such a thing for me. The familiar needs to lead us through the portal into Faery. Could be risky. And I don't want to endanger Sunday."

"You don't have to. I think I have something better than a familiar."

"What's that?"

"Matilda."

"Should I ask?"

"Matilda is my kestrel falcon. Well, I don't own her, but she is my friend and we've been together since I was little. I don't keep her in a mews, though. She lives free in the Darkwood. Whenever I visit the woods she finds me. She can cross over to Faery."

"Really? Wow."

"She's gone into Faery many times. Likes to bring me back things. Like these." He held up the mouse alicorn and the tourmaline cipher. "She could guide us through the portal. And it would mean a lot to me to finally get to Faery accompanied by the one friend I've had for so long."

"I think that'll work. It's only nine. We could head there tonight, if you want to."

A huge red drip from the Popsicle splattered Kelyn's abs, and Valor bowed to clean it with a lash of her tongue.

"That," he said on a low growl. "Or we could have sex again?"

"I vote for the sex. The spell didn't specify a time of day, only during the waning moon, which it is, so I think we can do night or day. And if I have to return to that place, I'd prefer day."

"Are you okay with going back into the Darkwood?"

"Honestly?" She curled up against his chest and met his gaze. "I'm a little scared. Hell, I'm freaked. What if that tree comes after me again?"

"I'll protect you."

"You will. But you've nothing left to sacrifice this time."

"I would give everything I have for you, Valor."

"You already have." She caught a breath in her throat, feeling it tickle and threaten at tears. "We make a good team, yes?"

"That we do."

She kissed him and he made a grab for her breast while he was still holding the melting Popsicle. Valor jumped at the cold touch against her nipple. The soft treat crushed into her skin, and the stick fell to the floor. "You going to take care of this mess?" she asked her lover.

"I thought you'd never ask."

* * *

After sex, and a shower to wash off the faery dust and Popsicle juice, Kelyn suggested they head out on the town for a little celebration. He wanted to take Valor out, treat her special.

"You could wear the dress you had on before our wild table sex," he said. "Never thought I'd see you in a dress."

"I do dresses. When I feel like it." She was still naked and combing her fingers through her hair at the end of the bed. "But you know, I'm not actually a real girl, Kelyn. In case you hadn't noticed."

"What in the world does that mean?" He pulled up his pants but didn't zip and leaned over her to kiss the crown of her head. "You're real."

"Yeah, but not in the girlie sense. I don't do pink or ruffles or makeup. It's just not me. So if we go out…"

"You can wear whatever you like. It doesn't have to be a dress. And I think you're a girl no matter what you say. A girl who rocks combat boots."

She smirked, but he sensed her reluctance. So she was a tomboy. Didn't bother him. Valor was the first woman he actually felt comfortable around. No need to worry what the chick would think of him if getting on his horny exploded dust all over her skin. And, seriously, what man liked sorting through ruffles and tons of makeup to get to the real woman beneath?

"Where did you plan to take me?"

He figured someplace too upscale might freak her out. Much as he wanted to treat her and show her a good time, they could do that anywhere, really. Didn't have to be a four-star restaurant or a fancy ballroom. Of which Minneapolis didn't have a lot to offer.

"How about the Blue Room?"

"The nightclub in St. Paul?" She shrugged, indifferent. "That's cool. Maybe I could manage a little makeup for that place."

"The whole place is blue, including the lights. Makeup will make you look weird. Go natural, the way I like you."

She nodded. "Okay, but let me find something to wear. I can be ready in ten."

"I'm going to head down to the car and give Blade a call. Ask him about entering the Darkwood by his place tomorrow. I'll wait for you outside?"

"Yep."

Chapter 21

She was stunning. But Kelyn didn't tell her that. The
first time he'd given her a compliment, she punched him
in the biceps and sneered. So he kept it to himself as he
admired Valor wandering to the bar to get a drink. She
wore a silky number. Violet. It was cut high to expose
one thigh. And her combat boots were like her trade-
mark. He loved the look so much he wanted to shout it
for everyone to hear. He loved the tomboy with the purple hair and an affinity for invoking television doctors'
names when she was pissed—or well sexed—and who
could kiss him so silly he forgot about his woes.

She tossed back a shot of vodka at the bar, then turned
and gestured with a kink of her finger for him to join her
on the dance floor. Some kind of erratic, bouncy tech
music rocked the blue-lit bar. It shimmied through his

veins. Always one for some let-loose dancing, Kelyn joined his lover in the middle of the dance floor.

Having a mom and dad who loved to dance to any music that was on the radio when he was growing up had encouraged Kelyn to dance right along. And he had some moves, if he did say so himself. Hands above his head, he bounced to the beat along with the dance floor crowd. This was freedom. This was also connection.

"I love that you love to dance!" Valor shouted above the music.

He pulled her against his body and licked the sparkling skin below her earlobe. "I could dance with you all night."

"Then let's do it!"

And so they did. Basked in the blue glow, their teeth and the whites of their eyes glowed under the black lights, revealing laughter, smiles and a sexy wink every now and then. They closed down the bar, dancing nearly every dance, save for a few drink breaks.

At two in the morning, the pair wandered down the tree-shaded sidewalk toward the parking lot, hands clasped and Valor's head tilted onto Kelyn's shoulder.

"I've never known a man who likes dancing so much," she said and hugged him tightly. "You rock in so many ways I can't even begin!"

"Makes me feel alive." He kissed the crown of her head as they arrived at the Firebird. "It's like flying."

"Oh." She sobered quickly, and only then did Kelyn realize what he'd said.

"Well, it is. I can't deny it." He leaned against the car door, crossing his arms. "So the wings made me... me. And I'm eager to get them back. Is that what you need to hear?"

"Yes. And we're going to make that happen tomorrow. Then you can fly all day and never touch down."

"I'll have to if I want a kiss from you. I could take you flying over the treetops."

"Would you? That would rock." She pumped a fist. "Is what I've heard about faeries and their wings and, uh…sex, for real?"

That when someone stroked a faery's wings it was a sexual touch and produced the same sensations as if more intimate parts of them were being touched? Hell, yes. And with sigils activated? Beyond words. But he'd not had an opportunity to experience such. He'd actually never slept with another faery. And wings out with a human woman? Wasn't going to happen.

"You'll have to wait to find out." He winked at her and she plunged into his arms and kissed him. "First thing I'm going to do after I get my wings is make love to you."

"That could be awkward if we're still in Faery and, I don't know, there's a defeated and pouting demon standing nearby."

"You have a point. I'll save it for when we get back home. I expect I may have to do some demon fighting to get back my wings. But I can take the guy. This time he won't have a helpless witch to hold over me."

"I'm so—"

He kissed her quickly so she couldn't apologize again. "Let's go to my place."

"Your place?"

"What?"

"I've never been there. Yes! I finally get to see my man's place."

"Nothing to get excited about. It's a place out in the country. Pretty simple."

* * *

It was simple, and gorgeously stark. Kelyn lived about five miles west of his parents' home in Forest Lake. The road to his home wound through thick spruce trees and white paper birch. Even when they'd arrived, Valor wasn't sure they had because she didn't see the house until they stood on the doorstep and he invited her in.

The small, one-level house sat over a stream. Yes, a narrow stream actually flowed beneath the framework and parallel to the footings. Inside, it was decorated with what Valor decided was a Japanese aesthetic. Simple rice paper walls slid noiselessly aside to reveal the tiny kitchen done in unvarnished blond pine. The living room offered low gray seating cushions set on a long bamboo mat. No other furniture beyond a small wood altar placed before a window that made up an entire wall.

She bowed to study the altar and found a piece of quartz, tourmaline, a raven's feather and a small copper bowl on it. Understated and, apparently, the man was not a collector of things. She could dig it.

"Please tell me you have a bed?"

His kiss to her neck sent shivers directly to her nipples, which tightened in anticipation. Clasping her hand, he tugged her toward another rice paper wall, which he pushed open to reveal a mattress set on a low pine base. The white sheets were pulled taut, making her want to jump on it and mess it up. Again, another wall was completely a window, and it revealed the dark woods outside.

"I'm in love," she said as she bowed and landed on the bed, stretching her arms across the sheets that smelled like cedar. "I wasn't sure what to expect of your place, but this is you. Simple and spare."

"Are you calling me simple?" He landed on the bed, on top of her, and nuzzled a snuffling kiss between her breasts.

"No!" She laughed and kicked her feet. "Kelyn! No tickling! Please?"

"Fine." He rolled off her and splayed out his arms. Tilting his head backward, he managed to reach a little remote at the head of the bed and push the button.

Faint white light illuminated the forest outside the window, and Valor turned in time to see a doe dart away. Another pair of eyes glowed from within a grassy crop at the base of a tree. "A possum! Wow, it's so beautiful out here. You must hate going into town."

"I do spend a lot of time out here by myself. I could spend all day flying through the trees."

She clasped his hand and kissed it, but it didn't feel right to bring up the wing thing again. Tomorrow was the day. "Is this woods a thin place?"

"Parts of it are, but it's not like the Darkwood. You are welcome in this forest whenever you wish to roam. And you can pick mushrooms to your heart's content and collect whatever it is you witches use in your spells."

"So why even go to the Darkwood?"

"Because it feels different there. I sense the connection to that place I want to touch."

"I get that. It's sacred to you."

"It is."

"Then why not live there?"

"No one lives in the Darkwood. Blade lives as close as any would dare."

"I was a fool to go in the Darkwood. I knew the warnings."

Valor sighed and felt the emotions that had preceded her stupid venture well up in her heart and threaten tears. She'd thought she'd gotten over that. But really? She was a woman who had needs. She'd never get over it.

"Why *did* you go in there?" he asked. "You said it was for a spell, but you never told me what spell you were casting. Was it as dark and dangerous as I've teased at?"

She rolled onto her stomach and he did, too, so they both looked toward the window. A squirrel crept close to the cabin, digging in the soil on a quest for nuts. Kelyn brushed the hair from the side of her face and kissed her cheek softly.

The idea of confessing to him both encouraged and frightened her. The weird gulping feeling in her throat, which could result in tears, cautioned her. And yet her heart leaped. She needed him to know her completely. For good or for ill.

"It was a personal spell," she said, eyes straight forward, peering through the window. Her heartbeat thundered and she tucked her fingers over the edge of the mattress to hide that they were shaking. "I had recently broken it off with a man I really thought I loved."

Kelyn rolled to his side and looked up at her. Yeah, so she had had a boyfriend and, believe it or not, that did sometimes happen in her world.

"Actually, he was the breaker upper. I didn't want to break it off. But it was the classic reason."

"The classic reason?"

"Yes. None of my boyfriends or lovers over the years ever said it so plainly as he did. But…he did."

She bowed her head against the sheet for a moment. Not crying, but trying to summon the courage to spill. The room was so still. She thought perhaps even the creatures outside had suddenly paused to listen to what she had to say.

"So, he told me," she said, lifting her head, "I wasn't the kind of girl men considered for marriage and having babies and happily-ever-afters. Because, you know, I *know* I'm not a real girl. And apparently all men do, too. But no one had ever said it to me like that. Just straight-out calling a fish a fish. He actually shrugged, kissed me on the head and said goodbye. Then he calmly stated that he'd been dating another woman at the same time and he intended to ask her to marry him. Can you believe that?"

Kelyn shook his head. "Asshole."

"Right? So, anyway, I think I'd finally had enough. I mean, I've lived a long time. I'm heading toward my eighth decade. And I've had a great life. I love my life. But you know? I felt like he could have been the one. That maybe we could have had something. Together."

"I'm sorry," Kelyn offered. "Breakups are tough. But what he said to you? It wasn't true."

Valor smirked. "Yes, it was. I know that. I like being one of the boys. Except when I don't want to be." She tilted her head to look into his violet irises, feeling as if he would never be so cruel to her. And she knew that with a certainty that made her smile.

"So, did you intend to cast a love spell in the Darkwood that night? Bring your true love to you?"

"Love spells can be messy, and you've got to really want the intended one because you could be stuck with him for-freaking-ever. Actually, I was going to cast a spell on myself to make me more lovable."

"Valor, you are so lovable. Combat boots and all."

"Yeah, well, you're Mr. Nice Guy. You have to say stuff like that."

"I think the spell worked." He teased at the ends of her hair. "But not the spell you wanted to cast."

"What do you mean?"

He kissed her then and pulled her into a hug. "Just think about it for a while. I'm not going to point out the obvious. In fact, I have something more interesting in mind."

"Such as?"

"I've never had sex with a woman on this bed."

"What? I don't believe that."

"I've told you, I have to pick up club girls who are all sparkly and then go home with them. I wake in the mornings amid pink frills and so much freaking glitter it's like I landed in a fun house. The only advantage was that the woman was never the wiser that I put off faery dust while we were getting it on."

"That is…quite the problem to have. So…" She spread her hand across the white sheets. "Virgin sheets?"

He nodded. His grin teased at her like no tickle ever could.

"But first." She pressed a hand to his chest to stop his approach for a kiss. "Tell me what worked when I was supposed to speak the spell in the Darkwood. I don't get it."

"Valor." He tugged her against his chest and pushed the hair from her face, staring into her eyes as if to seek her soul. "I'm not telling!"

And with that, he landed a tickle right at her waist that had her flinching out of his grasp and squirming across the sheets.

"Cheater!" she managed. Snagging the end of his shirt, she pushed it up over his head and forced him back onto the bed, his head landing on the pillow. His hands and lower arms were still tangled in the shirt, so she had him in an effective pin. "My turn to tease you."

Kelyn tossed aside his shirt but then put his arms up above his head and clasped his hands together. "Okay." He rocked his hips under her. "Go for it."

Valor waggled her brows at him. Time to tease the faery.

Bowing to his chest, she kissed him at the base of his neck, then lashed out her tongue to taste his skin. He didn't have the salty taste she would expect, but rather something a person could not describe with taste words, so she settled on wild green forest freshness. It had become her favorite flavor.

Dragging her tongue down the defined indent between his rock-hard abs, she twirled it around his belly button, then ventured lower to explore the angled cut muscles that V'd into his jeans.

"You men are so interesting," she said. "What do you call these muscles here? I mean, they're like the sexiest thing ever."

"I'm not—oh, yeah." A nip of her teeth to the skin above his jeans' fly dissuaded any discussion.

She unbuttoned and unzipped him, being careful because the guy did not wear underwear. His soft blond curls sprang out behind the unzipped metal teeth and then his erection rose like the mighty totem it was, demanding worship.

"Dr. Who," Valor muttered in appreciation.

"I don't think he was an actual doctor."

She gripped his cock firmly. "You want to argue semantics or are you going to lie back and take it, faery?"

"I'm cool. I'm sure he was a doctor. Somehow. Maybe?" He pushed his palms over his face and as she touched the tip of his cock with her tongue, his groan bellowed out from his chest. "Oh, yes, a doctor for sure."

Bowing to the lush, bulging head of him, Valor took it in her mouth and sucked it like the Popsicle they'd shared earlier. While she stroked her curled fingers up and down the shaft, she used her tongue to tease, prod, circle and dance over the swollen smooth helmet until his hips were pumping in demand.

So she answered his unspoken plea by taking him deeply into her mouth, up and down, sucking and squeezing. Feeding his wanton moans. At his sides, his fingers clenched at the bedsheets. Beneath her breasts, his thighs tightened. And with one hand she cupped his testicles, which were tight and so hot. That touch set him off. His shivering muscles suddenly pulsed and he came into her, spilling down her throat. The faery shouted, "Yes!" and his hips bucked a few times before he relaxed with a heavy exhale.

Valor kissed his thigh and gave his softening erection a squeeze. Her fingers sparkled with faery dust, and she tasted a familiar sweetness that reminded her of the Dust Bombs she'd drunk in Paris.

The sheet glittered with fine dust. And a glance out the window spied a pair of curious glowing raccoon eyes. Valor's laughter echoed out into the night and was joined by her faery lover's laugh as he flipped her onto her back and made love to her until morning glinted on the horizon.

Chapter 22

Kelyn leaned over and kissed Valor, who sat in the passenger seat of his car. He'd parked on the loose gravel drive, which circled before his brother Blade's barn. The big red barn served as a garage slash home and also sat a hundred yards away from the Darkwood.

"You want to come in and meet my brother?"

"I met Blade once. I know his woman, Zen." She tucked her hands between her legs and shrugged. "Right now I'd rather sit here and concentrate on not being so nervous."

He knew she was crazy afraid to go back in the woods again. Witches and the Darkwood? Not cool. And she'd only gone there because she'd wanted to speak a spell to make her lovable. His heart had broken to hear that.

"You know I'll protect you, Valor."

"I know that. You go tell your brother what we're up

to. While I wait, I'll check through the spell stuff and make sure I've got the incantation down."

"Sounds like a plan."

He left her in the car because he didn't want to push, and he had felt her anxiety radiate out from her in a distinct quaver. He was nervous, too. But it was an opposite feeling to Valor's, which had her all pent up and closed off. While him? He felt like stretching his arms wide and opening himself to the universe.

Striding across the gravel that fronted the property, Kelyn ran a hand across his hair. The sun was high and his body jittered with anticipation. This could be it! If Valor's spell went as it should, a portal to Faery would be opened. And he could step through.

Yet his excitement tangled with dread. Kelyn had always dreamed of Faery. But no detail from his mother's tales had ever been enough to satiate his imagination or longing. And once finally there? Would he want to return to the family and friends who meant so much to him? To Valor?

"Hey, bro!"

Blade stepped up to the opening of the garage that spread across the entire lower area of the massive barn. He used it to work on cars and had a shop fully stocked with every tool imaginable toward the back. The upper level was where he lived with Zen, his girlfriend who had once been part faery, part angel *and* part demon, and yet was now merely faery. Long story.

Blade hooked a thumb at the hip of his black leather pants. His bare abs were as cut as Kelyn's, yet his shoulders were broader and his long, straight black hair dusted at his elbows. "Where's the witch?"

"She's waiting in the car." Kelyn thumbed a gesture over his shoulder. "A little nervous."

Kelyn stepped into the garage's cool shade. The scent of motor oil mixed with sawdust wafted in the air. His brother, who stood shoulder to shoulder with him, waved toward a half-assembled '57 Ford F-100. A pair of legs stuck out from under the low front end. Stryke rolled out on a creeper and winked at Kelyn, then stood and slapped his greasy hands together.

"You guys should have Beck over here helping you," Kelyn commented. Beck was their brother-in-law, who actually owned an auto body shop. Valor and Sunday worked there on occasion on their own projects, which was how Kelyn had originally heard about Valor.

"Beck and Daisy Blu are on vacation in Greece. Didn't you know that?" Stryke asked. Tall and brunette, he smiled and punched Kelyn's shoulder gently. Of all the brothers he was the calm, wise one whom everyone else went to with their problems. "Or you been too busy with your own woman to care?"

"Maybe." Kelyn set back his shoulders.

"So the witch is your woman?" Blade whistled. Kelyn did not miss his side-eye, a warning yet discerning look. Of course, none of them could ever avoid the family assessment of dates, lovers and otherwise. "Trouble said she's bad news."

"Trouble is a jerk-off who let me believe he fucked her when he had not. He's trying to steal the spotlight like he always does."

"Sounds like Trouble," Blade muttered, a common assessment oft issued by any and all family members.

"Valor is cool. And yes, she's my woman."

"Well, then." Stryke wiped his greasy hands across

the thighs of his jeans. "Best I meet her." And he strode off toward the Firebird.

Blade put a hand on Kelyn's shoulder when he turned to follow Stryke. "Witches can be bad news. You sure about her, bro?"

"Positive. She's a witch of the light. Doesn't work dark magic. And she saved my life. If it hadn't been for her air magic, I would have drowned in the ocean when we were in Wales. I trust her."

"Wales? And you? Going near large bodies of water? You have been on a trip. Is this spell going to work?"

"Hey, boys!"

"It will." Kelyn's eyes followed the stairway up to see Zen, clad in jean cutoffs and a white tank top, skipping down the steps from the upper loft. "Zen." He gave her a kiss on the cheek when she tilted up on her tiptoes to seek the acknowledgment. Her soft copper dreads batted his shoulder and she smelled like maple syrup.

The threesome watched as Stryke offered a handshake to Valor, who now stood outside by the hood of Kelyn's car. The twosome exchanged words.

"Valor is cool," Zen said. "Why didn't you bring her in?"

"She's nervous for today's adventure. I'll bring her around, official-like, when all this is done."

"So you're going to venture into the woods with a witch?" Zen mocked a shiver. "I know you go into that Faery woods all the time, Kelyn. It's like your second home. But with a witch? I mean, for as much as I like her, you know about witches and the Darkwood."

Stryke wandered back in while Valor remained by the car, arms crossed and her sight fixed on the forest.

"She's anxious," Stryke commented as he joined the

threesome. "But pretty. Who would have thought my little brother would hook up with a witch?"

"Right?" Blade put an arm around Zen and kissed her on the brow.

"Would you guys get off the witch thing?" Kelyn said. "She's no different from the rest of us, and we're all a bunch of misfits trying to fit into this crazy mortal realm. So back off."

"Officially backing off," Stryke said with a salute and a curt but mocking bow.

"I'm going in." Kelyn turned and backed toward the drive, pausing in the open entrance. "Shouldn't take us too long. But, uh…well, you know."

Blade nodded. Stryke gave him a thumbs-up.

Kelyn turned and strode off.

Arms akimbo, Zen stepped forward, her eyes tracking her brother-in-law. "You boys going to keep an eye on them?"

"Fuck, yeah." As Kelyn and Valor strode toward the forest edge, Blade released his wings in all their gothic glory. The black-and-silver appendages that resembled large bat wings flapped once and he folded them up against his shoulders.

At his side, Stryke shifted to four-legged wolf shape and stepped out of the pile of clothing that had dropped off during the transformation. The two brothers waited at the garage door opening, keenly aware of the risk Kelyn was stepping toward.

Kelyn and Valor paused before a maple tree that soared thirty feet high at the edge of the forest. It was massive and the red leaves shivered with the breeze.

It didn't appear menacing, but one never knew in this crazy woods.

He clasped Valor's hand and looked down at her. "I know you're worried." He hooked his other fingers in the quiver strapped over his left shoulder. It contained his arrows; the bow he held at his side. He'd claimed them from the trunk before walking out here.

"It's cool," she said.

"No, it's not. You're scared, and I get that. We can go elsewhere. Find another thin place."

"No. I had a good think before your brother came out to say hi to me. This trip back to where it all started is kind of full circle for me. And you. Us." She squeezed his hand. "Besides, Matilda is here and I want you to be comfortable with everything."

"I'm as nervous as you are, lover."

He felt her relax against his arm. With a brave inhale, Valor nodded decisively. "Then let's rally all that nervous energy and do this."

The rambling forest floor was carpeted with moss, tree roots, branches and mushrooms, flowers, seedlings, anything and everything. The trees grew thick in some spots, almost as if hugging together in a family photo. Scents of life, both plant and animal, perfumed the air with a sweet summer fragrance that made Valor smile.

Kelyn had said he knew of a clearing that he would take them to, and he assumed the lead, bow held in one hand, eyes taking in all surroundings as he deftly navigated the uneven ground with sure steps. He must know the forest well enough that he needn't rely on his wonky ley line navigational skills. No matter. The man exuded a virile confidence and sex appeal that hit her right in the heart. He'd said he was nervous too? He certainly did not show it. And that went a long way in alleviating some of her anxiety.

Valor hadn't put a protection ward over herself before entering the dusky emerald woods because she needed to be clean to pass through the portal, and CJ had said it was a necessity to maintain the dark blessing on the lake water.

She kept an eye peeled about her periphery. And she walked as far from tree roots as she could manage. Though that was virtually impossible, for in some spots the roots crissed and crossed like a loomed rug. She had to be prepared for any surprise attacks. Of course, calmness was key. Kelyn's fate relied on her performing the spell accurately and without fail.

"Where's Matilda?" she asked as they strode deeper into the woods where the shadows deepened and the air thickened with humid soil and pollen. A dragonfly flittered close, then darted off with a silent flutter of wings.

"She'll find me. How you feeling?" Kelyn clasped her hand. Concern beamed from his violet eyes.

Valor nudged up beside him and they walked a little slower, shoulders hugging. "When I'm with you I don't fear a thing."

"You should never fear when I'm with you, Valor. I'd do anything to protect you."

"I know that." Which was the reason they were here, wasn't it? He'd sacrificed so much. Could she ever repay him? Today, she would.

"Can I tell you something?" he asked.

"Always."

His eyes glittered, even in the darkening shadows.

Somehow, the thin strands of moonlight squeezing through the treetops managed to land right in his irises.

"I've dreamed about Faery all my life and have longed to go there. I've always felt it was missing from my very soul. So now? *Excited* is putting my feelings lightly. But I'm also worried."

"Why? You're going to finally visit Faery."

"Yeah. *Visit*."

They tromped over a fallen log coated with moss and lichen, and he tugged her to a stop, gesturing for her to sit on the log beside him. She first checked the nearby roots—they seemed thin and weren't close to the base of any wicked-looking trees—so she sat. He nuzzled his cheek against hers and kissed the edge of her jaw. She could sense his tension despite his seeming eagerness for everything to happen.

"What if, when I get to Faery, I don't want to leave?" he asked.

Valor's heart dropped in her chest to consider she might never see him again after today, but she coached her face to remain neutral, to not wince and show him how such information devastated her. "But your family is here in the mortal realm."

"Right. But...Faery," he said in such an awe-filled tone Valor felt his awe shiver over her skin as if falling faery dust. "It could be the place where I belong."

"Do you feel like you don't belong here?"

"Sometimes. Don't get me wrong, I love my family. They are everything to me. But with three older brothers, two who've worked the alpha-wolf thing all my life and the other a vamp with wings even bigger than mine, I've tended to stand to the side, never confident of my place in *this* world." He glanced at her, his eyes dancing between hers. Pulling her hand up to kiss, he offered a wink. "Though lately, I've felt more settled. This might sound forward, but…I can't imagine leaving you, Valor."

"Then don't," she said too quickly. It took all her inner strength to fight tears. Because only real girls cried, and she would use her tomboy for all it was worth right now. "But, I mean, if you want to take a look around while you're there…"

He bowed his forehead to her hand. To have won his respect and know how he felt about her went a long way in kicking the door shut on that silly witch who'd once thought she wasn't lovable. But he struggled with a choice that hadn't even been presented to him yet. And that worried her.

"You wouldn't *not* come back, would you, Kelyn?"

"I honestly can't say."

"Oh."

"I'm sorry, Valor."

"Don't be. It's your right." She tilted her head against his, and this time the shiver was impossible to staunch. Her heart hurt. After her confession to him last night, she'd actually begun to feel lovable. If he left her, it would devastate her and prove, once and for all, that Valor Hearst would always be one of the guys. "If you feel such a strong calling to Faery, then you should stay there. Or maybe visit and then come back here to see me? I…I don't want you to stay."

He wrapped an arm around her shoulder and hugged her close. "I needed to hear that from you. I don't *intend* to stay, but when I'm there, I'm not sure how I'll feel, so I wanted to tell you. To warn you, I guess."

"Duly warned. Just, uh… Kelyn?"

"Yeah?"

She should do it. Tell him she loved him right now. But that wasn't going to change things. And—

"Ah!" He stood and pointed high. "There's Matilda."

A piercing cry from the kestrel sounded overhead. Kelyn rushed ahead into the clearing.

"Right," Valor muttered as she followed him. "The silly girl stuff can wait for later."

The bird landed on Kelyn's shoulder. He pulled something out of his pocket and fed it to her. She was beautiful. Wings of brown, gray-blue and black folded over her back as she perched on her owner's—make that faery friend's—shoulder. She was small, but her big black eyes seemed soul filled and she looked at Valor as if she were assessing her. With a tilt of her head, she rubbed it against Kelyn's jaw.

Wow. Now, that was trust.

"Matilda, this is Valor. She's my friend," Kelyn said. "Matilda and I have been together since I was a teenager. I guess that makes her my longest and most trusted girlfriend, eh, sweetie?"

"I'm honored to meet you, Matilda," Valor said. "You hang with a very esteemed kind."

The bird actually bobbed her head, as if in a bow. Then she bent forward and plucked at the leather straps around Kelyn's neck, briefly lifting the one that held the cipher Never had explained could only be used by the Wicked.

"She likes that one," he said. "It's our bond."

"Cool. She brought you that from Faery?"

"Yep. Matilda is always bringing me presents. She's my girl."

"I'm a little jealous of a bird, and not afraid to admit

it." She winked at him. "So, is this the place you want to work the spell in?"

"Yes."

The clearing they'd wandered into was deceptively beautiful. It was similar to the clearing Valor had found when *that thing* happened. Looking about, she felt the hairs at the back of her neck prickle. Sunlight beamed through the leaf canopy, lighting the mossy clearing like a stage. Scattered branches and a massive fallen oak were frosted in green moss and tiny yellow wildflowers. Yet beneath the beauty lay a sense of unease and rot. Valor felt it as a shiver over her arms.

But they were here. And she had a job to do. The oak log would make a perfect altar to set up the spell, yet the exposed roots were thick and gnarled and seemed to creep toward her.

Valor took a step back. "Nope."

She scanned about and spied another fallen log, also coated in moss. It was not still attached to roots. Probably it had fallen decades earlier. It would serve for an altar. Setting her leather spell bag down, Valor began to sort through the items while Kelyn chattered with the bird.

"She'll guide us through the portal," he said after a round of chitters shared by both of them.

"You speak falcon?"

"Yes. Don't you?"

Valor smirked. He could probably speak to all the animals. "Well, if a tree comes after me, would you have a few words with it, please?"

"Will do. You need my help?"

"No. I'm going to draw a casting circle and I should be the one in it. You and Matilda stand over there by the

maple sapling. I'll focus the direction for the portal..."
She turned and faced two parallel birch trees sporting
peeling white paper bark. "There. Between those trees.
Sound good?"

"Better than good."

"All right. Stand back. I'm going to sprinkle some
ash for the circle." She tugged out the bag of ash taken
from a fallen rowan tree.

"Kiss me first," Kelyn said.

Dropping the supplies at her feet, Valor rushed to
Kelyn and plunged into his arms. She lost all fear of
crazy trees as Matilda flew up from his shoulder and
cawed.

The kiss dazzled her senses. Dragonflies fluttered
in her heart. Kelyn's arms were kind tree roots that
wrapped about her body and comforted her soul. And her
core tingled with the promise of intense sexual energy
between the two of them. She could rip away his clothing right now and take him on the mossy forest floor.

Maybe she should? If there was the chance he'd not
return from Faery?

Tickling the tip of her tongue with his, Kelyn ended
the kiss and gave a quick kiss to one of her eyelids and
then the other. He bracketed her head between his hands
and bowed to meet her gaze.

"Let's do this," he said. "For good or for ill, I've got
your back."

She bumped fists with him. "Here's to you getting
your wings back, and…the two of us having wild faery-
wing sex later tonight."

Chapter 23

The witch knelt in the center of an ash circle before the altar placed on a mossy oak log. Matilda perched on Kelyn's shoulder, her head cocked forward, wings back, fiercely intent on the witch's actions and her mesmerizing intonations that echoed up from the circle and bewitched the forest into a humble calm.

Sunlight melted over Valor's violet hair, gilding her a Wicked enchantress who moved her hands slowly, ritualistically, as she took up the first item and held it before her to bless it. The werewolf claw stolen from a time traveler. It glinted once, betaken by her magic. She placed it on the moss and swept her fingers over it as she spoke words in a language that must have been created and brewed by witches throughout the centuries.

Second, the vial of unruly lake water the shade of chewed bubble gum that the dark witch had blessed.

Valor had specifically put up no protection spell of her own because of that ingredient.

Kelyn glanced high toward the tree canopy. He knew others watched. They would not interfere unless necessary. And he trusted them.

She poured the water over the claw and it emitted a pink smoke reminiscent of the lake's color that lingered before her. The mermaid's kiss she held above the smoke so it infused the paper and then seemed to peel the kiss off so it dropped onto the claw. Valor's fingers curled and her shoulders swayed as her intonations grew more rhythmic, like a song that only monks could chant. She sprinkled the skull dust stolen from an eclectic archive over the concoction on the moss. A sudden flare ignited the claw and burned blue in thin flame.

And, finally, the last ingredient. True love's first teardrop. How did a person come by such a thing? Sure, witchy spell stuff was all odd and rare and mysterious, but...

It struck Kelyn at that moment that it might, indeed, have been something she stocked for her witchy trade, or, on the other hand... Had she obtained it recently? Because it was...hers?

The realization made him crouch and bow his head. He touched his heart, sending out all that he felt for her toward the witch. Respect, admiration and love. And in that instant she lifted her head and turned to look at him. Matilda cawed. Kelyn nodded, confirming something neither had dared speak out loud to each other. She loved him?

And he had fallen in love with her. Wow. This was immense. He wanted to pull her into his arms and kiss her silly, then—

A banshee's cry erupted in the sky, startling Kelyn upright. He gripped an arrow from his sheath and notched it on the bow. Matilda veered, aiming at the dryad that stalked toward Valor. And as the arrow missed the vile creature, another winged being swooped down and delivered a shoulder punch at the dryad's chest, sending it off course and reeling in the air.

"Thanks, Blade!" Another arrow notched onto the bow, Kelyn tracked the dryad who had come from a nearby oak while shouting to Valor, "Don't stop!"

Valor spread out her arms. With a few more incantation words, the blue flame, emitting pink smoke, rose above her and soared toward the birch trees she had designated as a portal.

Kelyn followed the returning dryad. His brother, who had unfurled his black-and-silver wings, followed it, but the creature was small and swift, and blended with the tree bark, so one moment it was visible, the next, not. Just as it tracked overhead, and Kelyn's arrow once again missed the target—curse his lacking faery skills!—the dryad dodged low and was met by Stryke's wolf, who snatched it by the throat with his powerful maw.

"It's ready!" Valor announced. She gestured to Kelyn. "Where's Matilda?"

Kelyn searched the sky but didn't sight the kestrel falcon. He caught Valor's hand with his and now he saw the portal that gleamed before them. An oblong oval centered between the two birch trees like a liquid skein of ocean water. He hoped there weren't mermaids on the other side.

"Are those your brothers?" Valor asked as they rushed toward the portal.

"Yes, they'll keep the dryad at bay."

"You ready for this?"

"All my life! Matilda!"

The kestrel dived from the tree canopy and swooped over their heads. She glided toward the portal and, with a flap of wings, broke the skein into myriad glitters of wavering sky.

"Now!" Kelyn pulled Valor after him. They both leaped through the portal and landed...

...in thick emerald grass dotted with red mushrooms. Their bodies rolled and they sprawled amid a dusting of blue-and-violet flower pollen.

Kelyn stood and brushed the violet pollen from his forearms. He helped Valor to stand and before he could hug her, she pointed behind him and shouted in surprise. He swung around quickly, but when reaching for his bow, realized he'd left it behind in the mortal realm.

He didn't see anything wild or vicious headed toward them. "What is it?"

"The sky is freaking azure and that tree bark is actually yellow."

He chuckled at her marvel. And then took a moment to look about. Indeed, the deep blue sky bejeweled the air. The yellow tree resembled most trees, only the bark was golden and the leaves were also a shiny yellow gold. The grass at their feet was green. Looked like normal grass. And the mushrooms dotted about also looked normal.

And there in the sky, far yet large, loomed a green moon, and beside it hung a pearl moon.

"Is that for real?" Valor asked as she noted the same thing.

"Most definitely."

Kelyn rubbed his fingers together and sniffed at the violet pollen. "Whew! That's potent." Like the lushest flower he'd ever smelled. And yet a darkness permeated that scent and he wanted to get it off his fingers. But rubbing frantically against his thigh did nothing more than further imbue it into the whorls.

Insect sounds chirped, buzzed and chirred about them. Nothing too unfamiliar, but the noise seemed to rise and fall in sync, almost like a symphony. Cool.

They stood in a field that edged an extremely dark forest. Kelyn couldn't see past the tightly spaced trees any farther than about ten feet. He highly expected to see eyes flashing at them from within.

"I wonder if these are the same as in the mortal realm." Valor squatted to inspect the mushrooms.

"Uh, sweetie?"

She looked up at him in inquiry, her violet hair spilling over the grass tips.

"Remember what happened last time you tried to take something from Faery?"

She quickly dropped the mushroom and stood. "Right. Just here for your wings. So, where do you think we should go? I vote no on the creepy forest."

"Two votes against the forest. So maybe..." Kelyn swung in the opposite direction. Gray boulders serrated by glistening violet crystals sat on a low hill and were frilled with trimmed shrubbery.

That was odd. Who trimmed the shrubs way out here? Or *were* they way out anywhere? They could have landed in someone's backyard for all Kelyn knew.

Much as he'd like to wander about and admire the scenery and take in the scents that at first smelled familiar, but then changed to something slightly sinister, he had come here with a job to do. Get in, get out.

In theory.

After he had his wings, could he not spend some time wandering about as he wished?

"I think that's them!" Valor rushed across the grassy field toward the forest.

"I thought we voted against that way." But when Kelyn saw what she headed toward, he took off, as well.

The *them* she'd shouted about was what looked like his wings. And two of them were not attached to a body, because the demon who had taken them was cutting them off his back at the edge of the forest.

As they neared, the demon snapped upright, one wing in hand, the place where it had been severed leaking thick black blood. The other wings, tattered and almost beyond Kelyn's recognition, lay on the ground in a pool of demon blood.

"Ah! So you've come for your wings, eh?"

"Looks like they are not serving you well."

The demon clutched the severed wing to his chest and gave them both an imperious lift of chin. "They're mine. You gave them to me." Then he eyeballed Kelyn, at right about neck level. His eyes glowed brightly.

Kelyn touched the cipher hanging from his neck. "Do you see something you'd rather have much more than my useless wings?"

The demon's lower lip quivered.

"I can make a trade. Of course, this is merely a trinket. And those…"

"These are worthless!" The demon thrust one wing at Kelyn and he caught it. "You can have them for the cipher. Awful bit of goodness and nice. I should have taken the cipher from the start. I knew I could use it, but I'd always wanted wings."

The wing in Kelyn's grasp shivered. He clasped it to his chest, feeling as if a part of him had been returned, and yet that part was now tainted and worn. "What have you done to them?"

"Not a bloody thing. I've worn them since you gave them to me. Thought they'd get me entrance back into the Unseelie court's good graces, me being Wicked and all. Those unspeakably *pleasant* things!" He kicked at the wings on the ground. "I cannot raise my fist at an attacker to save my life! Awful bit of niceness and honor running through those ugly wings. Do you know I helped a crippled sprite across a stream? What was that about?"

Valor cast Kelyn a knowing grin. So his kindness had paid off. But how, exactly? Sticky demon blood smeared across Kelyn's arm and wrist. It smelled rotten, while the sheer fabric of his precious wing had tears in it and the edges were frayed.

"Give me the cipher!"

Kelyn tugged the leather cord from around his neck but clasped the circle tightly. The demon made a gimme gesture with his hand. As Valor bent to touch one of the severed wings, the demon slapped a foot onto it and *tched* at her. "Not until he hands over the cipher."

Kelyn rubbed his thumb around the cool, hard surface of the thing. He'd never known what it was, beyond that it had sort of sealed his friendship with Matilda because it was the first gift she'd brought him from Faery. He swallowed and searched the sky. Matilda flew overhead. It was a nervous flight in a tight circle that made him second-guess giving the thing away. "I'm not sure."

"Kelyn, your wings?" Valor nudged.

Matilda cawed once. The stark cry pleaded with him. But it wasn't the same plea Valor had made. The bird had issued a confirmation of alliance. He could feel her heartbeat in his chest. The flap of her wings beat the air, holding her aloft. She didn't want him to hand over the cipher?

But he'd come all this way. He held his reason for being in hand.

"I'm waiting, faery." The demon stepped forward, crushing one of the wings under his foot. "It's a bit of stone that'll allow me to navigate to my people. You know they hide us here in Faery. Cast us out to a place at the edge where no others can be bothered by us, the half-breeds who are so hideous."

"You're not hideous," Kelyn said. And he meant it. The demon had helped him and Valor when they were desperate. And he had chosen freely how to pay the demon for such help. "But I'm not sure…"

He looked to Valor, who shrugged. She could never understand all the complicated consequences that ran through his brain right now. If he handed over the cipher, would Matilda…? What would become of his and Matilda's bond?

And yet with his other hand he clutched the tattered wing against his chest. He could not survive with but the one wing. He needed all four. And his soul screamed for him to fit those missing pieces back into his life.

"Very well." Kelyn thrust the cipher forward. It dangled from the leather cord. "It's yours." He flipped his hand, and the necklace soared toward the black-skinned demon, who caught it with a gnash of his fangs.

"And these are yours." The dark thing kicked the remaining wings across the grass toward them.

Overhead, Matilda keeled out a warning caw. It was so piercing Kelyn winced.

"I'm out of here." The demon stepped backward into the forest and became one with the blackness, red eyes flashing twice in blinks before dissolving to nothing.

Valor picked up a wing and inspected it. She turned a beaming smile at him. "That was easy. Who'da thought, eh?"

Right. But what had he sacrificed in turn this time?

"Never look gift wings in the mouth. You did say the spell would take us directly to my wings." Kelyn traced the serrated end that yet bled black demon blood. "Good job, witch."

"You don't look happy. I know this looks bad, but they'll clean up."

"They're tattered," he said on a breath that caught at the back of his throat. "Used and damaged."

"It was the demon that made them this way. Once you have them back on, they'll be good as new. I'm sure of it."

"Sure." His eyes searched the azure sky. No Matilda anywhere. Had the moons darkened?

Valor stepped up to him. "Let's put them back on, yes?"

He nodded and with one last search of the sky, bowed his head and fell to his knees before her. With a reluctance that felt as heavy as grief, Kelyn pulled off his shirt and then handed her the wing he'd held.

"How do I do this?" she asked.

"Just put them where they belong. Right over the scars. They should heal to me. I hope. Valor."

She paused before walking around behind him.

"Thank you," he said. "For everything. I know how you got the final ingredient."

"Y-you do? Right. I told you, I had it in stock."

"Valor." On his knees before her felt right because she stood a goddess before him, and he her lucky consort. "You are a real, exquisitely lovable woman. I love you."

"Oh. I, uh… Jeez. Are we going to do this right now?" She sniffled and a teardrop spilled down her cheek.

He hadn't expected that reaction. And he wasn't sure what to do now. Miss Tomboy was going all tears on him?

"Yeah, so maybe I did get that last ingredient right after you left me at home the other day. I was hoping you might have stayed the night with me. But you walked away. And I, uh…you know."

She couldn't say it. But he didn't need her to say it. He felt the love emanate from her.

"Sorry I left you hanging like that. I had to go to my brother's house and straighten something out between us."

"Oh. And did you?"

"Yes. Trouble and I are good now."

"I'm glad. I sure hope he can be good with me, too. I hate having lost him as a friend."

"Give him some time. I have a feeling he misses pizza night with you."

Valor shrugged. "It's fun, but if I'm going to share my pizza with anyone now, I'd prefer it be you."

"No pepperoni?"

"How about veggies on half?"

"Deal."

The moment demanded a fist bump, but Kelyn instead pressed his cheek to her stomach and hugged her. The witch was his. He was no longer threatened by her friendship with his brother. And his wings had been found. And even as the insect song seemed to rise in warning about them, he could only be thankful.

Rocking back onto his toes and looking up to her, he winked. The witch actually blushed. Yep, he loved her.

"So," he said with a splay of a hand, "you going to stand there with my wings or will you put them on and let me see if I can get them to work again?"

"Yes, of course!" She scampered around beside him, and then she backtracked and leaned down to kiss him. "I love you, too. Thank you, for not giving up and for letting me help you get to this moment."

"I couldn't have done it with anyone else. Now…" He shrugged, feeling itchy to return to normal. Tugging off his T-shirt, he tossed that aside. "Let's do this!"

"All right!" She went around behind him and he thought he heard her brushing something across the grass.

"What are you doing?"

"I'm trying to get as much of the demon blood off as I can."

"Good call." Kelyn leaned forward, catching his hands in the thick grass.

A sprite buzzed nearby. The creature was no larger than a bumblebee, but she was as perfectly formed as most humans, with wings, and wore tiny pink petals as a dress. She buzzed back and forth before his nose until he had to swat at her to make her stop. But he did so carefully.

"Do you notice the insect buzzing is getting louder?" Valor asked.

"Maybe they're upset about us being in their territory." He shrugged again. "Do it now, please?"

At first touch of the wet, sticky base of a wing to his back, Kelyn felt the sensation vibrate through his being as a weird electric current that touched all nerve endings beneath his skin. He flinched, but Valor held the wing in place. And when she immediately placed another wing on his back, heat rushed through at the point of connection. The last two she set against his skin at the same time, doubling the strange jolt of vita that at once hurt, but then seemed to cool and glow all over his skin.

At his wrists another cool burn revitalized the violet sigils. He felt the same icy cut as they drew in curves and mandalas into his chest.

He gasped and his body seized up, his back arching. The wings were fusing to him and it was more painful than the phantom pains he'd experienced. Yet he smiled through it all. They were back. And soon he would be the man he once was.

"Whoa!" Valor stumbled and fell into the grass beside him.

"What happened?"

"I think some of your faery vita repulsed me. It's powerful stuff. Yikes!" She shook her hand. Kelyn noticed a pale blue vine shooting up from the grass that attempted to twine about her wrist, but she managed to unloose it. And when she stood, she gasped with awe. "Wow, your wings are… Oh, Kelyn, can you feel them?"

"Yes, they're almost completely restored. How do they look?"

He tried flapping them and was able to move each independently and then all four in tandem. The sweep of air against his face from the movement felt great. Familiar.

"Oh…" Valor's utterance felt unfinished. Like it should have ended with the invocation of a TV doctor's name.

"What? Valor, tell me. Did something go wrong? It doesn't hurt anymore. I think I should give flight a try."

"Oh, Kelyn."

He stood, feeling his old and familiar strength surge through his system like blood rushing back to an unused limb. Mighty and renewed, he spread out his arms and looked to Valor, who sat on the ground, hands supporting her and mouth open in a horrified gape.

"What?" he asked.

"Your wings," she said. "They're black."

Chapter 24

Her gorgeous lover, the man with whom she had fallen desperately in love, stood before her renewed and strong. His fists were tight and veined, wrapped with fierce power. His abs and chest, ornamented with the violet sigil markings, were like steel. Broad shoulders stretched proudly back. And behind him, his wings gleamed... black.

When once his wings had been violet and silver, shimmery with life and boldness, now they swept out behind him, tattered and the blackest black. More so than his brother Blade's gothic wings. Yet Kelyn wielded them as if he knew nothing else and they hadn't changed.

Perhaps they had not changed? Was it merely the demon's blood that had altered their appearance but not their original goodness?

"Black?" Kelyn looked over a shoulder and preened one wing forward with a hand. "Huh. Yep. They're black. I'll survive."

"You'll..." He was being obnoxiously dismissive about what she felt had to be a horrible change. Maybe the wings needed a little time to readjust to Kelyn's body and reacclimate? "Right. You will survive. We should probably get the heck out of here while the getting is good. Where's Matilda?"

"There!" He pointed overhead and Valor spied the kestrel soaring toward the silver portal. "Run!" he shouted. "We haven't much time!"

Valor took off after the kestrel, combat boots crushing the long grasses, and stirring up the blue-violet pollen in her wake. The insect chirring sounded like a tornado engine. That couldn't be good.

Everything would be all right. They'd return to the mortal realm and Kelyn's wings would return to violet and silver. He'd be as he once had been. Life would move forward. Together.

Pumping her arms, Valor was thankful her boots were worn and comfortable. She wasn't much for running, but when survival was at stake? She could manage.

The portal loomed close ahead. Matilda banked to the left, aiming for the gateway—

The insect noises had ceased. The only thing Valor heard was her own huffing breaths and the blood pounding through her veins. A split second of wondering if she should stop and look around surfaced. Dread surged to Valor's throat as she realized the world had gone so still. And she slowed but didn't stop.

Something hissed, like a massive snake.

Turning, even as she kept moving across the grass,

she caught a glimpse of the threat. The creature rose from the long grasses in a slithering, sinuous glide. Narrow, pointed wings flapped, pulling it off from the ground. Blue and violet scales covered it from its long head, all down its snaking length, to the tail. A freaking snake with wings? Oh, man, she did not like Faery one bit.

"Dr. Doug Ross!"

The creature cawed like an entire unkindness of ravens, then violet flames whipped out of its fanged mouth and snapped up toward Matilda. The flames lashed at the bird's tail feathers as she banked in the azure sky. But she could not avoid the attack. The kestrel screeched and went down like a cannonball, landing in the grass before the undulating portal.

Valor screamed and the sound alerted the creature. A monster snake? She turned completely and picked up her speed toward the portal, seeing a smoking mist rising from Matilda. Behind her the flapping wings drew closer. The thump of something beating the ground intermittently made her decide it must be hitting the ground with its tail. And the smell of smoke rose as she realized a new sound filled the air.

That of flames.

With one glance over her shoulder to see the trail of flame following her in the grass, Valor used her last burst of energy to leap and dive for Matilda. She landed over the bird on all fours, pressing her body down but not completely touching the bird, enough so that she could protect her as a wild path of flame ate through the grass and...

Valor closed her eyes, muttering a witchy prayer for safety and wishing like hell she had water magic to put out the flames. When finally she lifted her head, the world had again quieted. And…she wasn't on fire. Yet.

Still huddling over Matilda, she looked around behind her. The flames had fizzled to smoke. And the only reason they hadn't gone after her was that she was lying in the cool shadow of the liquid portal. Burned grass smoked all around the oval on which she lay. The shadow had saved her from a burned ass. And death.

"Blessings," she whispered.

Glancing about, she didn't spy the snake creature. It was gone. Maybe. She'd keep an eye out. It couldn't have hidden in the grass. It had been so large.

A snake. A freakin' snake, of all things!

Setting her repulsion aside, Valor turned back to the ground. Nestled in the grass lay Matilda. She wasn't dead, but a few tail feathers smoked from the fire attack that had knocked her out of the sky. Valor wasn't sure how to handle a bird without causing it further harm. Kelyn could do it. He had an affinity with all animals.

She scanned the meadow. Where was Kelyn? Hadn't he been behind her? He must have taken off after the snake thing. She called out to him. He'd been right there behind her, telling her to run for it—

Her heart dropped to her gut. Realization cut her to the bone.

"John Carter," she swore. "He's staying. He knew exactly what he was doing by telling me to run. He knew if I ran through the portal without him… Oh, Kelyn."

She bowed her head over Matilda, and the tears rushed up so quickly she couldn't think to fight them or consider that girls like her didn't cry. Because she was a real girl. Kelyn had made her realize that. And yet. He'd sent her away. Without him.

Had he been lying to her all this time? Had he never seen her as she'd only dreamed he could? Had her stupid hopes for a hero been quashed by the man's blind desires to return to his homeland?

It hurt to know she'd been used. Had he done that to her? She didn't want to believe it, but all the past hurts and rejections now came rushing back to plunder her soul. No man would ever have a care for her beyond what she could do for him. Like gaining him access to Faery.

"I've been such a fool!" She beat her thighs, kneeling there beside the inanimate bird. "Why do I let men treat me like this?"

A chitter of insects stirred nearby. She didn't care who heard her rant. She needed to shout and scream and...

Why couldn't she keep a man interested in her? Did she have to do the skirts-and-heels thing? Kelyn hadn't seemed concerned about the way she dressed. Maybe it was her stupid, idiotic laugh? But that had seemed to actually turn him on.

Was it that she was too alpha, always trying to be the one in charge? She had let him take the lead. Hadn't she?

Catching her forehead in her palms, she growled in frustration. And yet the portal behind her reminded that she hadn't the leisure for this ridiculous pouting. Her time to escape this horrid realm could be coming to an end.

"Right. Suck it up, witch."

Something she'd said to herself many times before. And the last time she tried to suck it up, she'd wandered into the Darkwood, to devastating results.

"Not going to be a fool anymore." She turned on her

knees and looked up at the portal. "I will get out of here. Leave him behind. And never look back."

Because Kelyn was doing his own thing now. In... Faery. Exploring. Or whatever it was he felt he had to do in a place he'd always longed to go to. Hell, he'd tossed over the cipher, knowing it somehow connected him and Matilda. Was that why the bird had been struck down? She'd been weakened when Kelyn severed their bond? The man *should* run off. He had no right to claim friendship with such a majestic creature.

Valor hoped he flew off forever. With wings that had been tainted by evil.

"No," she whispered in protest to her foolish anger.

Were the tainted wings the reason he'd pushed her away so easily? Given up on Matilda, as well? She wanted to cling to that, but a new resolve tugged her away from the stupid reaction. The man wasn't interested in her anymore.

Time to move on.

The portal undulated, a liquid, silvery oval. Valor had no idea how long it would remain there; it was her escape to the mortal realm. Yet she needed a guide through, and that was Matilda.

She stroked the bird's wing and cooed softly. Injured, but how so? Spreading out her hands over the bird, Valor focused her vita downward and whispered a healing charm that would transfer her life force into the bird. She'd never tried it on an animal before, only bees, and even then her healing powers had been minimal. Yet with a touch of vita, a bee could flutter back to the hive to restore its energy on the honey.

She could heal a boo-boo, ease Kelyn's aches and

pains, but beyond that? "I won't let you die, Matilda. I've got to try this."

Something swooped overhead. Still holding her palms to infuse Matilda with her vita, Valor glanced upward. It wasn't a faery man with black wings. Nor was it the snake creature. Just a bird? Nerves rose to prickle her skin with a fear she hadn't wanted to acknowledge.

She did not like being abandoned in a foreign land. How could he have been so cruel?

"It's the wings," she muttered, and pulled back her hands to her hips. "They've changed him." Just as Never and CJ had warned would happen.

But that didn't mean she wasn't walking away from him when she got the chance. He'd made his choice. Now she had to make hers.

She inspected Matilda. Eyes closed, the bird seemed to be sleeping, so Valor would allow her to rest and let her magic do what healing work it could.

Standing, she pressed a hand against her forehead to shield her eyes from the brilliance, even though she saw only the two moons. The vibrant sky had grown almost white. It seemed to reflect up from the emerald grass, making her wish she had a pair of sunglasses.

How to track Kelyn? Did she want to find him? She'd decided to walk away from him. He could do what he wanted now.

"Unless he was attacked by the snake thing before it went after Matilda?"

Much as she knew he had not been, a small part of her still wanted to make sure the man was, at the very least, safe. He could stay. That was what he wanted. But she couldn't leave until she saw him alive.

Yeah, that was her story, and she was sticking to it.

She could use her air magic to summon creatures of air and wing, but that might bring back the thing that had attacked Matilda. The other option was to go on a search, which would involve entering the dark forest. And she wasn't keen on entering any forest in Faery.

"Summoning spell it is."

She clapped her hands decisively and stepped away from Matilda to plant her feet squarely yet still remained within the portal shadow. No telling what the smoking grass might do if she touched that. It could have vicious monster spume in it that would melt her boots. Focusing her energies to her fourth chakra—the air chakra—she spread wide her arms to open her diaphragm. She wasn't sure her mortal-realm magic would work here in Faery—in proof, Matilda had not remarkably come to from her healing magic—but she had no other option than to try.

Chanting an invocation to bring forth the creatures of air, she kept one eye peeled for the snake and was prepared to halt the chant if she spied it. Her body hummed as her chant grew faster and deeper and seemed to birth from her lungs and permeate her chest in vibrations that imbued the universe with her will. Forming mudras with forefingers touching her thumbs, she focused the energies to draw what she could toward her.

And when something landed beside her, and she sensed it was another person—not a snake—Valor opened her eyes to look upon a man who was not Kelyn.

Tall and lithe, his dark hair listed in the breeze. Silver-eyed, he wore rich, bejeweled clothing that reminded her of something from the nineteenth-century Bohemian times. A violet frock coat hemmed in jewel-glittered lace served as a backdrop for the sparkling rings on his long fingers. A matching glitter twinkled in his eyes. Behind him, magnificent silver wings folded down neatly as he assumed a haughty pose.

"Who are you?" she asked.

He quirked an annoyed brow above his silver gaze, as if she was an idiot for not knowing the answer to that one. Propping a hand on a crystal staff that suddenly appeared at his side, he announced, "I am Malrick. King of the Unseelies."

Kelyn had raced into the dark woods after sending Valor off toward the portal. It had been a cruel trick, but he knew she wouldn't have left without him.

And now that he was here in Faery, he didn't want to leave. Nor would he. This was his homeland. He belonged here.

Whistling a few times did not summon Matilda to his side. The kestrel must have led Valor through the portal and could not hear him from the mortal realm. Just as well.

Maybe. Kelyn brushed his shoulder, wishing his sidekick were there, along with him. Matilda was his connection to...not home. This place was his real home. It had to be. He felt the call of its earth, sky and vital beings in his wings.

And he could taste the awesome adventure waiting him on the air.

Marching forward, he ventured deeper into the woods but found the brambles tugged at his ankles, so he lifted up a few feet to fly slowly between the trees. Man, it felt great to fly again! Black or otherwise, his wings were back. Sprites and birds littered the dark confines of the woods, and creatures with eyes of violet, gold and blue watched him from the inky shadows.

Scents of musty rot, fruiting lushness and a liquid crispness combined in a heady perfume. His sensory skills had returned to their usual übersensitivity. Thank the gods for that. Now he could find his way with his eyes closed, or smell when predators approached before they got too near. He could even draw in Valor's innate womanly perfume and get lost in it...

No, he'd sent her away for her own good. She didn't belong in Faery. And as much as he'd enjoyed her company these past days, she would only hold him back now. Because a witch *in* Faery? That couldn't be good for the witch.

He winced as his thoughts settled. She could never hold him back. But he didn't want to acknowledge how much he'd like to have her along with him on this venture. He couldn't. What had been done was done.

Compelled, Kelyn followed a curiously exotic scent that curled into him and softened his determination. It coaxed with a hint of juicy citrus and led him onward with a hearty splash of warmth and suede. Spices he could not name alchemized with the earthy scents below his feet. He wanted to know the source of the perfume so desperately that his heartbeat sped up, as did his wings. He glided forward, deeper into the black woods.

The sprites darting in and out of his path seemed to screech at him, but he couldn't understand what they were trying to convey. If they were warning him back, he didn't need a tiny creature telling him what to do. With a snap of his fingers, he sent one of the diminutive things reeling into the shadows.

A crimson haze wove betwixt and between the obsidian tree trunks. Kelyn inhaled the mist like a dark witch's drugged cocktail. And he landed on his feet in a clearing lighted by thousands of fluttering lampbugs. There, before him, loomed a void in the darkness in a form about as high as he was and no wider. Reaching forward, he touched the void. It was cold, and it actually flinched as his fingers barely skimmed the fabric. It was something…

A woman spun about and he stepped back with a gasp. Adorned in floaty red fabric that barely covered her breasts and mons, her pale violet skin glinted. Her violet eyes beamed brightly, and her lavender lips curled into a wet, sensuous entreaty.

Kelyn drew her in and sighed at her utter loveliness. He could taste her already and wanted to feel the skim of her bright skin over his.

"You desire me, visitor?"

Her voice slipped over his skin as if slickened with exotic oil and followed by what he imagined were greedy kisses.

Entranced, Kelyn nodded. "I do."

The red fabric or dress—whatever it was she wore—seemed more a part of the misty haze and moved over her, caressing and always barely concealing. And that weird mist wove within her hair, which was so black it truly did appear a void set against the backdrop of dark trees.

She opened her lush mouth and Kelyn saw the fangs, which glinted like diamonds. With a lift of her chin and a lowering of her lashes, she sniffed once and said, "You've the stink of witch on you, my faery warrior."

He liked being called such and took a step closer. Shaking his head, he couldn't find words to argue or defend. All he desired was to be closer to her, to feel her, to be inside her...

"She doesn't love you." Red sparkles dazzled the air as she spoke, seeming to form words in puffs before her. "She is a witch. Most wicked and vile."

Kelyn smiled drunkenly as the sparkles floated onto his face and tickled his eyelashes.

"She uses her wiles as magic. A magic that destroyed you once and will do so again."

He followed the seductress's hand, which swept gracefully before her, stirring the bewitching dust that had emanated with her words. One finger crooked and her coo of welcome splashed against him with roses and earth and all the scents of desire.

With a purse of her lips, she teased him to kiss her. And he wanted to taste that luscious mouth.

Stepping closer, he found himself surrounded by the curling ruby mist. It embraced and caressed, and everywhere it touched him he felt her lips on his bare skin. A man could close his eyes and get lost, never desiring to return.

She hummed what sounded like an angel's song, yet it was tinted with something deep and longing. Something illicit.

Kelyn leaned closer, his feet planted on the ground and his wings fluttering to hold his body at an extreme forward angle. Tendrils of the woman's hair wrapped across his shoulders, luring him into her sweet yet slippery seduction. He closed his eyes, ready to fall into the kiss...

"Kelyn!"

Snapped out of the enchantment, he hitched a look

over his shoulder in the direction from which he'd heard Valor's scream. She was still in Faery?

The seductress grasped him by the neck, her thumb squeezing his windpipe and a long, sharp nail cutting his skin. "You are mine!"

He felt his tongue rising, stretching as if she were trying to pull it out through his teeth. His jawbone cracked. Kelyn kicked at the woman, but his foot only plunged through red mist.

Grasping at his back, he cursed that he'd left his bow and arrows in the mortal realm. A swing of his hand forward cut through the red mist, yet landed on no solid body. Briefly, he felt the thumb release from his neck, but as he gasped in a breath the squeeze of her fingers resumed.

Again, his name carried through the dark woods, perhaps on a whisper of Valor's air magic. It sounded sweeter than this bitch's seductive mist. How had he managed to walk right up to her and not be suspicious?

Grasping at the arm and hand that held him, his feet now off the ground, Kelyn dug in his fingers, but she didn't flinch. The woman's mouth snarled, and her fangs grew longer, stretching below her chin.

"I will eat your tongue, wrong one," she said on a growl.

And he expected it to go down that way if he didn't get out of this horrible vise clench quickly. In his periphery he saw the flashing illumination of hundreds of sprites buzzing about their struggle. Choking from the tug on his tongue, Kelyn swung out a hand and grasped madly. The burn of sprite fire pierced his fingers and palm, yet he clutched a few of the creatures. Not having a plan, and acting purely on instinct, Kelyn crammed the sprites into the seductress's mouth as she lunged for him.

Sprites squealed, and the bitch's mouth sparked as if she'd swallowed fireworks. The red haze whipped about Kelyn's body, squeezing his arms tight against his sides. But his tongue had been released and he was able to yell as the pain of having his organs compressed could not be squelched.

And then, with a sudden hiss, the haze slipped away from him like a dead snake falling to the ground. The red mist spumed in a great mushroom cloud before him, covering the black void. Kelyn stumbled backward, his heel hooking on a tree root.

When the mist dissipated it revealed the tree trunks and a few sprite corpses sprawled on the dense forest floor. No more red seductress.

"Kelyn!"

"Valor." Energized by the call for help, Kelyn turned to sprint out of the forest, taking to the air with a flap of his wings and a surge of determination.

Chapter 25

Kelyn swooped down to land in the tall field grass before the violet-haired witch. He folded down his wings and rubbed his throat where ichor had dried from the cuts. He made a quick summation of the scene around him.

The portal had not been breached. It still undulated, set within the sky and riding low over the meadow. Why hadn't Valor left Faery? But more important, who was the faery standing beside her now? Didn't the man know Valor was *his* woman? And no faery seductress would make him believe otherwise. He'd been close to dying in that seductress's hands. Or, at the least, losing his tongue. *Fool!*

But he wouldn't stand powerless now.

Kelyn grabbed the man by the throat and lifted him from the ground. In reaction, his captive repulsed Kelyn with but a nod of his head, lifting him from the ground and sending him backward to land against the portal's base. Kelyn felt the weird liquid vibrations surround him, but he would not be sucked through. A familiar was necessary...

He noted the kestrel falcon lying on the ground. Still. Dead? Had the witch done something to her?

"What is going on?" Kelyn demanded. "What did you do to Matilda?"

"Me?" Valor stabbed her chest in question. "You're the one that severed your connection with her. You hurt her!"

The mysterious man stepped up beside Valor. "This fool is the one you are so worried about missing?" the silver-eyed faery commented snidely. "He stinks of the Wicked."

"I am not. I sent the demon off after he left me with tattered wings!"

"Yes, you gave him a cipher." The stranger clucked his tongue accusingly. "Poor move. You and the bird were connected through that talisman. She'll not listen to you again unless you get it back. But the stink that clings to you is very much demon. You've been kissing a Wicked One in the Wilds."

The faery served Valor a side glance and she, in turn, crossing her arms tightly, cast an accusing glare at Kelyn.

Kelyn stood with a proud thrust of his shoulders and flapped his wings once, drawing them tight together and straight out behind him in warning. "I am Kelyn Saint-Pierre, and I am faery."

"Saint-Pierre?" The man narrowed his gaze on Kelyn. Adorned in clothing that looked as if it had been stolen from a museum featuring aristocratic court costumes, the pompous bit of pouf and jewelry had the audacity to challenge him with his sneering smirk. Who *was* he? "Do you know Rissa?"

Startled to hear that name from the stranger, Kelyn could but speak the truth. "She's my mother. And who are you?"

"He's King of the Unseelies," Valor interrupted. "Where were you? Is he telling the truth? Were you kissing another woman? I thought we were going back to the mortal realm together. And Matilda! Some snake creature shot flames at her and took her out."

"A wyvern," the Unseelie king said. "Malicious bits of fire and scale, but they are not carnivores. I sense the falcon is still alive, if wounded. Let me hold her. I'll give her back the vita she has lost. Not that it'll help your return journey home."

Kelyn stepped before the fallen bird. "No, she's mine. And I don't care what you're king of, you can step away from Valor right now. She's mine."

Valor bristled at that announcement.

"You certainly claim a lot while standing in a land that isn't your own," Malrick said.

"Faery *is* my home."

"Not at all," Malrick proclaimed. "You, boy, belong where you were born. There is a reason we are come into this world in the realm in which we are placed. No one is misplaced. Ever." The king twisted his beringed fingers about the crystal staff. "Rissa's son, eh? A sylph with soft pink curls and a ruby-rose mouth? I loved her once."

Kelyn gaped at the man. His mother had never told him about an Unseelie king. Or had she mentioned him in her faery tales? He couldn't believe him—Malrick.

Didn't want to. It didn't matter anyway. He would not allow the man to dissuade him from his explorations.

"That was a long time ago," Malrick added.

"My mother was born in Faery. Are you telling me she was not misplaced to the mortal realm and should still be here?"

"No. She was called to the mortal realm, as some are. She belongs there now, but she is always welcome in her homeland. And in my…well…" Malrick let that one hang.

And rightfully so. The creep.

"Ah." Malrick walked around before Kelyn. "Your wings are tainted with blood from the Wicked. That's what's making you so obstinate. They can be cleansed and you'll be in your right mind again. He's changed, yes?" He turned a look to Valor. "Not who he once was?"

"You're telling me. The Kelyn I know would never have left me to return to the mortal realm alone. Though he did warn me before we came here that very thing might happen."

"Exactly," Kelyn snapped at her. "So get yourself back to where you belong and leave me here where I belong. Let the Unseelie heal Matilda, and then she can guide you back." He picked up the bird and handed her over to the king, who carefully took the bird, but also gripped Kelyn's wrist. The sigils burned brightly on Kelyn's skin, searing painfully, and it took all his strength to rip away from the grasp. "What in Beneath?"

"Not Beneath, boy. This is Faery. And it is not your home. Nor will it ever be. You seek to find your roots? They are buried deep and sure within your family, which resides in the mortal realm."

"I'll be the judge of that. You spout nonsense to confuse me."

Malrick gently caressed the bird at his chest. "I never speak nonsense. And I would never lie to Rissa's son."

The king bowed his head over Matilda and kissed her soft, feathered crown. Whispering words Kelyn did not recognize, but that he felt in his veins, the man tended the bird carefully. Silver static sparkled over Matilda's body, flashing in reds, violets and gold.

Kelyn glanced to Valor. She wouldn't meet his gaze. Instead, she shoved her hands in her back pockets and toed the grass with a boot. He'd almost kissed the Wicked red seductress. Almost. But obviously Valor believed otherwise.

Every moment he stood defiant before the Unseelie king and the witch, he betrayed the woman he loved. But...he was home. And it felt right. Maybe?

He didn't belong? Then where *did* he belong?

Malrick released Matilda, who flew up into the sky with a joyful peal and began to circle their trio, waiting for her cue to lead them back through the portal.

But Kelyn wasn't about to leave. And nothing could make him. Not a Faery king. Not even a guilty conscience.

Lifting his palm, he touched a sigil on his chest and repulsed the king with a blast of focused faery energy.

Malrick stumbled backward, and only by stabbing his staff into the ground did he prevent himself from falling.

Valor cast him an accusing glare. Why hadn't she left when he'd been determined to stay? He didn't want to hurt her, but he didn't want her around him now. Because, indeed, he'd been tainted by the demon's blood coursing through his wings. And yet that taint felt powerful and he could use it to survive in this land so unknown to him.

It was for Valor's sake that he must be cruel to be kind.

Malrick approached and Kelyn unfurled his wings to their full expansion, displaying them in all their glory. "You stay back. This is what I choose. The witch can leave. She'll be much better off without me."

"No, Kelyn, I won't be," Valor said. She sniffed back tears.

Really? Again with the tears? Since when had Valor become such an emotional, pouty...woman? Well, he wasn't going to let the ridiculous display affect him. And the tug of remorse in his chest was a fluke. The result of testing his newly returned magic.

"I love you!" Valor suddenly shouted.

Malrick lifted a brow, silently imploring with a *don't you want that?*

"You love me, too," Valor insisted. "I know you do. So does your family. You've no family here in Faery."

"I belong here!"

"You do not," Malrick insisted.

With a splay of his hands, Kelyn announced, "Then I belong nowhere."

"You belong here." Valor thumped her chest, right over her heart. "Don't stay, Kelyn. You have nothing here! You won't even have the cooperation of the Unseelie king. That's got to warn you."

Malrick shrugged and with a flick of his beringed fingers, he offered, "I can be what the mortals deem an asshole at times."

"Yeah? Well, so can I."

Kelyn charged the king, slamming into his chest. Intense magic clashed with his own. He felt it in every pore, vein and bone. Shoving off from the ground, the twosome soared through the faded azure sky. Flapping their wings, they traveled higher, struggling with both fists and wings. The king was more powerful; Kelyn knew that. But he wasn't about to give up so easily.

"How could I even return now?" he asked as he deflected a kick from Malrick. "If what you said about my connection to Matilda being severed is true."

"She trusted you once. But you gave away that trust. It will have to be re-earned."

"I had no idea the cipher bonded us!"

"Oh, yes, you did!"

Malrick swung up his staff, catching Kelyn in the gut. Intense electricity shot through him. His wings ceased flapping and he dropped. As he fell, he saw Matilda fly low, aiming for the portal. The time to enter must be drawing to a close. The kestrel could sense it; he knew that. He needed Valor to go through.

Suddenly Malrick twisted in the air and, from behind, he clasped Kelyn across the chest. He tried to beat his wings, but the Unseelie king held tight. The king chanted foreign words that felt ancient and sacred. Faery language? They seeped into Kelyn's thoughts, softening and...oh, the ache for acceptance. Then, all of a sudden, Malrick released him with a push that sent Kelyn soaring toward the portal.

Malrick called from the sky, "You may return for a visit, son of Rissa! That is all you are welcome to do here in Faery. Be kind to the kestrel. But be patient. She does not trust you now. Begone, the both of you!"

Try as he could to flap his wings, Kelyn couldn't halt his trajectory. Below him Valor raced toward the portal.

Matilda pierced the skein and flew through, followed by the witch, and—it was as if he were being sucked into a vortex.

Kelyn yelled as he was forced from Faery.

Chapter 26

He had to be alive.

After all they had been through, Valor was not going to let it come down to Kelyn dying after he'd finally gotten back the one thing that meant more to him than even her.

Palms pressed to his chest, she couldn't feel it rise and fall. He lay sprawled across the loamy forest floor. Tree roots cradled him on either side. Matilda circled above. Valor sensed the bird's nervous energy. Matilda knew something was wrong with her friend. Or was she still Kelyn's friend? The things Malrick had said about the bird no longer trusting Kelyn were horrible. A simple talisman had bonded the two of them?

Since walking into Faery, Kelyn had betrayed both of their trusts.

Glancing at the wings spread across the ground, Valor

couldn't find excitement for the fact that the darkness had left them. Now violet and silver, they'd returned to their original condition and were no longer tattered. Malrick had done that for Kelyn. The Unseelie king had also been responsible for forcing Kelyn back into this realm.

But to his detriment?

"You are not dead," she stated as a confirmation to the universe. "I will not allow it! You survived nearly drowning. You can survive this! Come back to me, Kelyn."

She laid her ear on his chest and listened and…she heard a heartbeat. Faint and slow, yet it seemed to increase by the second. Spreading her fingers over his bare chest, she closed her eyes and focused her vita toward him. Her palms heated over the violet sigils that tickled at her touch and then they grabbed her and held her there as if by force.

It didn't frighten her. In fact, Valor felt as though Kelyn were drawing on her energy through his sigils. If he could heal himself through her, then more power to him.

Matilda cawed and swooped low, brushing Valor's hair with a wing tip. It hadn't been a warning, but rather a touch of reassurance, so she persisted. Kelyn drew from her in increasing intensity. Her vita flowed out in vibrant violet energy gleaming with iridescent sparkles, and it flowed in through Kelyn's pores, brightening his skin and causing his sigils to glow.

Fingers growing stiff above her lover's chest, Valor's breaths segued to gasps. A moan preceded her dropping beside him onto the forest floor.

Eyes closed, Kelyn came to, knowing that, once again, Valor had brought him back to life. Perhaps this time he wouldn't have died. He'd been knocked unconscious by the shove through the portal and landing on some particularly hard tree roots.

He'd been shoved. Back to a realm...that he could no longer deny was his home.

He'd acted terribly toward Valor in Faery! Tricking her into running off without him. Sacrificing his bond to Matilda. But it had been the wings. They'd been tainted by the demon's blood. A Wicked One. And the seductress. She had been another Wicked One according to Malrick.

He'd had the audacity to defy the Unseelie king. And now he felt regret for all of it. He had been out of his mind, acting like someone else. So he'd deserved that shove. And he was thankful for it now.

But could Valor forgive him? And Matilda? Where was the kestrel? And the witch? He'd drawn on Valor's vita, the rich, warm energy of her being, to surface to consciousness.

Kelyn pushed himself up and away from the tree root. Looking to the side, he found Valor collapsed next to him. He carefully tugged the hair away from her face and bent to press his mouth to her forehead. She was warm and he felt her pulse at her temple. Alive, but weakened by him?

He gently shook her shoulder. "Valor!"

"Huh?"

"Blessed Herne." He bowed his forehead to hers. "I think I took too much from you. I'm sorry."

"No problem." She shook her head, weak, but alive. "You can always take what you need from me. Whew! That did take a lot out of me, though. Might need to sit here a bit and catch my breath." She looked him over, from his face to his chest to his wrists.

All his sigils glowed brightly, at his chest and about his wrists. His wings even sparkled, and he pulled one forward to stroke it and see that the ichor flowed through his veins circulating through the shimmery fabric.

"They're good as new," he offered. "The Unseelie king did this for me. And that would have never happened without you."

She smiled up at him. "You mean so much to me. I know you wanted to stay in Faery, but so many people need you here in this realm."

Kelyn nodded and whispered, "I know that, lover."

"But you were forced back here. You're not here because you want to be."

"I'm going to be okay," he said, hugging her as tightly as she hugged him. "That was the tainted wings talking when we were in Faery. I promise that I want to be here. With you. No one else but you." He tilted down his head to kiss her forehead. "I'm sorry for how I treated you in Faery, Valor. It was…"

"The wings. They were blackened with evil magic. We both know that. But, uh, what's up with kissing some Wicked chick?"

"I chanced across her in the Wilds. I didn't kiss her. I mean, I wanted to. I think she was working some kind of enchantment on me."

Valor shrugged. "It's cool."

"No, it's not. And I didn't kiss her. In fact, she tried to rip out my tongue."

"Probably what I would have done if you had kissed her," she offered nonchalantly.

"I'll never kiss another."

"Really?"

He knelt before her and kissed her, there beneath a beam of perfect moonlight that highlighted them upon the stage of lush moss and loam. Curling his fingers into her hair, Kelyn pulled her closer, wanting to never lose grasp of her again. Or to even think he could survive in a world where she did not exist.

Not only had she helped restore his wings, she had given him back that wild crush for the woman who had fascinated from afar. And now he had her. No woman had ever felt so right in his arms. Or at his mouth. Her soft, lush lips were meant for his. Her breaths bled life into him, and her heartbeat kept his racing.

"Mmm…" She broke the kiss, bowing her forehead to his. "I'd love to continue this, maybe even have sex with you. Right here. Right now."

"Sounds like a plan to me," he said. "We did have plans, if you remember."

"I do. But besides feeling like I've run a marathon, there's the thing about me—a witch—being in this forest."

"Forgot about that."

"I will never forget." She glanced aside to the massive tree trunk, which appeared firmly rooted into the ground, but one never knew. "I think I should skedaddle while the skedaddling is good. But where's Matilda?"

"I…I don't know. I think I've lost her." Kelyn pressed a hand over his chest where it ached to even consider the friendship he had so callously handed over in a greedy grab for his wings.

"You didn't know the cipher connected the two of you like that. Did you?"

"I knew it was a bond between us. It was the first

thing she ever brought me from Faery. I shouldn't have been so stupid."

"You would never have gotten back your wings."

He bowed his head.

"You'll have to earn back her trust. Give it time. You are a kind man, Kelyn. Matilda knows that. And I have to believe you had no other choice to get back your wings."

"Maybe," he whispered.

He felt Valor shiver mightily and remembered her urgent need to get out of the Darkwood.

"Right. Matilda, I honor you!" he called out. "And I will do everything in my power to win back your trust. Good friend, I thank you for your guidance into Faery. Please feel my love!"

Somewhere, high above, Matilda cawed. And Kelyn smiled. She wasn't swooping down for a greeting, but she had replied. It was a start.

"We'd better leave," he said.

"Sure. But you might have to help me walk out of here."

"Say no more." Kelyn stood and, still holding her about the waist, flapped his wings. "You ready for this?"

She laughed and hugged him. "Oh, yeah!"

They soared through the forest and up through a clearing in the leafy canopy. Clutched against Kelyn's body, Valor couldn't be afraid of this flight. Instead, she spread out her arms and laughed with joy as they crested the treetops and took to the open air. His wings carried them swiftly through the sky. She'd never once considered flight in anything other than a dreadful airplane.

Why had she waited so long?

"This. Is. Awesome!" she yelled.

Kelyn joined in her joyous laughter and swooped low over the treetops so she could touch the leaves as they passed over. The air brushed her skin and left behind a wondrous shiver, and she left all her worries behind in the Darkwood below.

"Can we do this more often?" she asked as her lover veered toward the big barn in the distance.

"As often as you like. You're the first woman I've ever taken on a flight. You're the only one I've trusted. I love you, Valor."

"I love you!" she shouted.

Clasping her firmly, he rolled them so Valor felt the leaves brush her hips and shoulders, and then they spun upright again, taking the air like birds. Or faeries.

Matilda whisked by them, teasing with a caw that she was faster, and Kelyn laughed and shouted thanks to his friend.

"I'm going to have to start incorporating flight into my air magic," Valor said. "This is amazing!"

"Hold on! We're heading in for a landing."

Banking to the left, Kelyn descended lower and swept down toward the gravel drive. They landed before Blade's barn. The brothers, in their human forms, stood waiting to greet them. They were thrilled to see Kelyn had gotten his wings back.

"That didn't take long at all," Blade commented as Kelyn tucked down his wings. "Less than an hour."

"Less than an hour?" Valor shook her head. "It was more like half a day."

"Faery time," Kelyn said. "You gotta love it. Hey, do either of you guys know anything about Mom and the Unseelie king?"

Stryke whistled and searched the ground as if something near his boots suddenly fascinated him. Blade crossed his arms high over his chest and shrugged.

"You both know something. That's crazy." Kelyn shook his head. "I met him. If he and Mom had a thing..." He didn't want to think about it now. And besides, that had been *before* their dad met Rissa. He hoped.

Valor yawned and Kelyn got the hint. Much as he'd love to tell his brothers about the short but wondrous time he'd had in Faery, he could save it for another day.

"We should go," he said, putting an arm around Valor's shoulders. "We have things to, uh..."

"No explanation necessary," Blade said quickly.

"Yep." Stryke kicked at the stones on the gravel drive. "See you two another day."

Furling his wings back and tucking them away, Kelyn grabbed Valor's hand and they strode to the car.

Chapter 27

Kelyn strolled through the forest behind his house. Valor skipped ahead, dazzled by the moonbeams that seemed to light her path. She didn't even notice the hand-size night moths that flittered by or that the underbrush harbored curious hares, ferrets and smaller animals.

Everything he had lost was now back! He took in the world like a blind and deaf man who had regained those missing senses. He could read the air and earth as he had done since he could remember. It would rain tomorrow, for the humidity combined with the color of the sky told him so. The oak tree to his right had lived for seventy-five years and had many more years ahead. And he knew the elk family that often lingered outside his home was grazing about a quarter mile away, closer to his father's land. The earth seemed to rise beneath him and welcome his every footstep, marking each step he took as familiar.

As well, he felt the ley-line energy. Two such lines crossed ahead at the clearing. Ancient and ever sending out vibrations, the lines hummed in the sigils at his wrists, veering him slightly to the right until he stood directly on top.

Tapping a fingertip against the violet sigil below his left pec, he turned his finger around the circle design, testing his magic. Ahead, the fallen branch that blocked Valor's path lifted into the air and landed in a crop of thick brush.

Valor glanced back at him. He gave her a thumbs-up. Yeah, he had his magic back, too.

The witch turned and raced toward the clearing he'd told her about. No witches disallowed here in this woods; she was as welcome as she was in Kelyn's heart. And, actually, this forest was his heart. Why had he believed that Faery would welcome him with open arms and that he actually belonged there?

Here was home. Standing alongside the most amazing woman he had ever known.

With her long brown-and-violet hair streaming behind her, Valor shouted in awe as the mossy clearing opened before her as if stage curtains were being pulled back to reveal the glorious set. She bent to tug off her boots and tossed them aside, then wandered across the moss as if testing new carpeting.

An emerald hummingbird buzzed up to Kelyn. He nodded. "She's cool. Just excited." The bird fluttered off. He'd sensed its uncertainty, but as quickly as it had left, it returned and hovered around Valor as she stood in the center of the clearing and gazed up toward the tree canopy. Moonlight sparkled on her face, hands and bare feet.

"This rocks," she said as he gained her side. "That bird is so cute! I never see hummingbirds. Wow."

Orbiting her a few times, the bird then zipped away toward the tree canopy, its wings flashing in emerald winks.

Each footstep across the moss released fresh and verdant perfume. Combined with the dry oak and pine resin, and the subtle sage that wisped in Valor's hair, the night smelled abundant and welcoming. Kelyn bracketed his lover's face. Excitement lived in her deep brown irises. And trust. Yes, he was thankful that the Unseelie king had forced him back here to the mortal realm. How he would have missed staring into her eyes had he remained in Faery.

"You are so beautiful, Valor. Breathtaking," he said. "I'm glad I gave my wings away for you. And I'm glad I trusted you enough to work with you to get the spell ingredients. And I'm glad that you fell in love with me. I love you."

He kissed her, deeply, abidingly. Every sigh, laugh and tear she put out he wanted to be there to receive it, enjoy it, wrap his arms around her and be the man she needed him to be. A man who did, indeed, see her as a real woman, not one of the guys.

Her fingers glided down his bare chest to his waistband. She unbuttoned his jeans, which alleviated the pressure on his erection. They both knew the reason for coming out here tonight. There was nothing more either wanted right now than to make love. Faery-style.

He pulled off her T-shirt and bent to kiss each breast. How her body undulated to meet his kisses, to show him how good his touches felt to her. And her moans spoke a language of passion.

"This moss is cushy and thick," she said. "Almost like a bed, if you get my hint. Oh, don't stop that. I like it when you do that."

He put an arm behind her back and pulled her close as he sucked in her nipple through tight lips. She squirmed sweetly. Using his free hand, he pushed down her leggings and she wiggled them off. She attempted to push down his jeans, but his hard-on prevented it from being a smooth action, so he stopped what he was doing and shoved them down.

"Wait!" Valor said as he aimed for her breasts again.

He stepped back, spreading out his hands in question. How the moonlight danced over her pale skin! It was almost as if she were coated with faery dust, it was so soft and magical.

"Wings out, lover boy. I came here for the big reveal."

"This isn't big enough for you?" He shook his hips to waggle his cock.

"Oh, it is. I'm talking wings, faery."

"You've already seen them."

"Oh." She crossed her arms over those delicious breasts. "Fine. I guess you don't want me to touch them. You don't want me to run my tongue all over them, either? Suit yourself."

The witch didn't actually think she could stand there, naked, and expect him to pass on such an intriguing challenge?

"I'll bring them out for a kiss," he coaxed, wanting to play the teasing moment out longer.

She shrugged. "Seems like me touching your wings

is an advantage for you. So I should be the one getting something for that. Yes?"

Her logic was…almost there. And the little quirk of smile at the end of her statement made him wish it had ended with her snorting laughter. Man, he loved her laugh. He'd get it out of her before the night was through.

Bending and falling to his knees on the soft moss, Kelyn kissed her belly and glided his fingers over her skin. Up, toward her breasts, where he lightly brushed her nipples and stirred a wanting gasp from her. Her long hair swung over his knuckles and he swept it purposely across her breast.

Then he kissed her mons, tickling his tongue within the soft nest that topped her sex. She wobbled a bit, but he caught her hip with a sure hand.

"You want to stand for this?" he asked and gave her hip a little shove with two fingers.

She toppled backward, and as her feet gave out, he tapped the sigil at his hip, which activated his air magic. A sweep of wind caught Valor and gently cradled her to lay her on the moss.

"You trying to show me up?" she asked.

"Admit it. That was impressive."

"Eh."

He blew out a mock-frustrated breath. "You are one hard woman to please. Guess I'll have to go deeper."

He bowed over her and moved his tongue along her sage-scented folds, and with his fingers traced her salty wetness. She spread her legs, inviting him in. With a leisurely sigh, she splayed her arms up over her head and wiggled her hips. Settling in.

He knew she loved it when he tongued her clit quickly, so this time he worked slowly, tasting all of her in long sweeps, then using more abbreviated yet intense pressure, memorizing her tiny whimpers and noting each specific tilt of hip or tense of thigh muscle as his tongue mastered her breaths.

If all he had to do for the rest of his life was make Valor happy, sign him up for the long haul. He'd never tire of her moans, her giggles and that awful yet strangely sexy snorting laughter.

"I love you," he said. A kiss to her thigh and then a deep tongue kiss to her clit. Pushing two fingers inside her, he curled them forward.

"Oh, yes," she growled.

A good clue she was ready to come. He made all his touches more focused, intense and so slow...

With a shout and a clutch at the moss by her hip, Valor orgasmed, her mons thrusting against his hand until she shivered and settled into the wild carpet with a gasp and a sigh.

Overhead the hummingbird flittered. And a family of chipmunks watched from within a fallen log. Kelyn smirked at that. They had an audience.

"Again?" he asked and licked her swollen clit.

"Give me a few minutes to catch my breath. And quit stalling! Let out your wings, lover. I want to see them." She sat up, tugging up his head by his hair as she did so. "Time for me to show you how much I love you."

He was good with that. "You ready for this?"

She nodded, her grin curling into a wickedly gleeful giggle.

Kelyn stood, pulling her up with him. He stepped back and tilted his head to catch the moonlight on his eyelids, cheeks and mouth. He could feel *la luna*'s cool presence shimmer in his veins. And his sigils hummed with recognition of the immense power he gained standing there. Spreading out his arms, he took a moment to honor the moon and this forest and his home. This was the only place he'd ever existed and held in his heart.

And now his heart had made room for the witch.

As he willed his wings out, they materialized in a sparkle of dust and unfurled behind him. He extended them as if stretching his arms, and it felt so good. The air whispered across the satiny-sheer wing fabric, and the bone-like cartilage that stretched along the tops of the four sections tightened until the wings were taut and at their full spread.

Valor whispered a soft, "Wow. I like those much better when they are not black. They fit you so well. You are like a regal forest prince. Goddess, you're my hero."

The admiration that seemed to surprise her rippled over his skin like a warm tongue teasing up his pleasure. He held out a hand to her and she took it, but didn't step before him. Instead, she dropped his hand and walked around behind him. He had never allowed a woman to touch his wings. Never had had the reason or chance to reveal himself so completely until now. So he was as curious and excited as Valor seemed to be.

"I wish you could see how the moonlight looks on them," she said. "It's like liquid stardust. I think I can even see the ichor moving through the veins. So cool!"

She hadn't touched them yet, and Kelyn shrugged. He never felt his wings at his back, just as a man did not feel his arms on his body. They were appendages that worked without needing command and were as airy and light as his very bones.

He would allow Valor her curious fascination. He trusted her completely. With her, all his secrets were safe. And even the not-so-secret stuff he wanted to share with her. Always.

The first touch of her finger to the top of one of his uppermost wings sent a shiver through that wing and tingled at the point where it met his back. Kind of like wind brushing his nipples. She trailed her palm along the top of it, drawing it to the curved end, which was at least five or six feet long. Between both hands she pressed the end of his wing, and then he felt her lips against the sheer, delicate fabric.

Kelyn shivered. Now, that felt amazing. Almost as if she had touched her mouth to his cock. Wow! He'd never anticipated that such a simple touch could make him feel that sensation. As he felt her fingers move inward toward his spine, he curled back his wings, for he could move them much like arms, and touched the ends of them over her hair and arms and legs. His wings were so sensitive he could determine where and what on her he touched. Even a flutter of her eyelashes!

"That tickles a little," she whispered, then blew on one of his lower wings. "How do you like that?"

"Oh, yeah." That breath moved over all his skin and landed right at his core. And with each breath that followed, he moved closer to the edge. His toes dug into the moss. His hands, he didn't know what to do with, so he put them at his hips, then, no—that didn't feel right, so he... Ah, hell. He stretched out his arms, grasping nothing but air. This was awesome.

He wasn't sure what she was doing, but now it seemed as if more of her body touched his wings. So he curled them back and wrapped them about her waist and chest, and she moaned as he knew that sensation was her nipples gliding across the sheerness.

But when she turned and pressed a palm against the base where his four wings met his body, perhaps to steady herself, Kelyn lost it. The pressure building in his cock released and he came. Just like that. Body shuddering, and muscles tensing and relaxing, he grasped at the air and hissed a sweet cry. Dust sprinkled out from his pores, falling gently to the moss.

Valor twisted under his wings and walked around before him. Her eyelids glittered with dust and some glinted on her lips. She kissed him even as he gasped in elation. Crushing his body against hers, he drew his wings forward and around his shoulders to wrap her tightly against him. She wrapped her legs about his hips. And the kiss did not end, nor did the second orgasm that swiftly followed.

And not wanting her to miss out on all the fun, he found her wet clitoris with his fingers, gently easing over the sensitive flesh. But a few dashes coaxed her to surrender.

There beneath the moonlight, the two of them had wing sex. The night air coruscated with dust. And all the creatures hidden in the shadows chirped or cawed or even bellowed in an approving chorus. And Valor and Kelyn would never again be the same.

Later, they both lay on the moss, bodies panting and skin glinting. Kelyn spied the shadow fly overhead and followed it as Matilda circled.

"See?" he asked quietly, and sensed Valor stir from what had been a reverie.

"Matilda. Oh, she dropped something—I caught it!" Valor lifted her hand, which held a leather strap, and turned to her side to show Kelyn.

It was the cipher that had bonded them. Matilda had

dropped it to land specifically on Valor's hand. Had she returned to Faery to steal it back from the demon?

"It's yours," she said, offering it to him.

"No, you keep it for now. She wanted you to have it. She approves of you. I want to deserve her trust. And I will. String it next to the moonstone so every time I see you I'll know Matilda is not far away."

Valor kissed him and tucked her head against his shoulder.

When they returned to Kelyn's cabin, Valor suggested they drive to her place. She wanted to shower, change clothes and check on Mooshi. Twenty minutes later, he joined her in the shower at her place. Mooshi sat on the closed toilet seat waiting for them to come out.

"That cat doesn't like me very much," Kelyn said as he dried himself off.

"He is cautiously optimistic of you."

Kelyn lifted a brow at that one. "Sure. Whatever you say." He glanced at the cat, who eyed him and revealed a fang with a lift of its furry lip. So much judgment in that tiny movement. "It's still early," he said, leaving the bathroom as quickly as he could to avoid a possible cat attack. "Only eleven. You want to do something?"

"Like what?" Valor teased at his nipple with her fingernail. "More sex?"

"I actually don't want to do anything that will make Mooshi uncomfortable. I was thinking...dancing."

"Yeah?" She kissed him quickly. "Yes! Let's do it."

"There's this place I want to take you to." He raked his fingers through his hair. "It's a faery nightclub Up North."

"Really? Cool. But Up North? That's like a three- or

four-hour drive. The place will be closed by the time we get there."

He waggled his brows. "Not if we fly."

She thought about it a few seconds, then thrust a victorious fist above her head. "Let's go dance our booties off! But I can't wear that." She glanced to the piled heap of clothes that she'd worn to venture into Faery.

"Find something that makes you happy. I'm good with jeans and a shirt."

Valor sorted through her clothes rack with the glee of a girl who had gotten invited to the prom by her secret crush. Only it wasn't a secret anymore. And the guy had told her he loved her. And he meant it. She knew that he meant it because he loved her stupid laugh and he'd showed her himself with his wings out and had allowed her to touch them. Never had she felt more like a woman in those moments when they made love on the moss beneath the moonlight.

Kelyn saw her for the woman she was. The man was her hero.

She pulled out a particularly bright blue spangled minidress that she had borrowed from Mireio years ago and hugged it to her chest. She could do the sexy when she wanted to. And her man deserved it. But would it look as good during flight?

She thought about soaring over the treetops for miles, hundreds of miles, in the spangled dress. "Yeah, it'll rock."

Five minutes later she wobbled into the kitchen and Kelyn turned with a big smile on his face. The guy looked amazing, his hair always tousled and emphasizing his gorgeous bone structure. He wore the same T-shirt he'd

worn into the forest, but it was still clean and the dark
jeans hung low on his hips. Sex personified.

"You look…" His eyes dropped to her feet, and she
turned out one foot in display. "Uncomfortable. Amazing.
But…not right."

"Ah, come on. I actually like this dress. Makes me
feel sexy."

"The dress is dazzling. I love it on you. Goes with the
faery dust sparkling in your hair. And these are the best
of both of us." He tapped the moonstone and cipher that
dangled before her breasts. "But the shoes?"

"I'm trying to do the sexy."

"And you do it well. But five-inch heels are not *my*
kind of sexy. I prefer the combat boots."

"You do?" Her heart thudded in relief as she clasped
her hands before her and spread her legs to manage her
balance. "You're saying that because you don't want me
to fall and break my neck in these things."

"There is that." He glided his hand up along her neck,
sending delicious shivers over her skin. "I like the boots.
Valor, you were right. You're not a real girl."

She wasn't sure where he was headed with that statement, but her giddy heartbeat took pause.

"You are a strong, confident, gorgeous, real—" he
kissed her "—woman. And you're mine."

"You mean it?"

"That you're a woman or that you're mine? Both.
Now get rid of the stupid shoes and put on some dancing gear."

The flight Up North was a dream. The night was
warm and the sky fluffed with clouds, which they flew
well below. They remained as close to the treetops as

possible to avoid a late-night driver picking out the large unknown flying object in the sky.

Valor kept her arms spread out most of the journey, eyes to the moon and cheeks kissed by the brisk sky. Kelyn held her firmly against his chest, but when at one point he grasped only her hand and flew out at her side, she couldn't believe it was actually happening. She was flying! With the man she loved.

It took less than an hour of flight to land before the secret club plopped in the center of a dense forest. Pine sap and cicada song filled the night. Kelyn said it was another thin place, but not specifically Faery—it also served Daemonia—so she would be welcome there, as were any and all. So long as they were not human.

The three-story gray brick mansion sported black-tiled turrets at two corners. Light from inside flashed out from the high turrets, turning them into neon light-houses. Entry was gained with a fist bump from Kelyn to the slender bouncer with long pink hair, green eyes and six arms. Fortunately, she only lifted one fist so Kelyn didn't have to figure which to meet with his knuckles.

Valor followed eagerly, taking in the bright walls, which seemed to undulate and glow in neon. The floor beneath her boots was lit in squares of pink and violet, and littered with faery dust, confetti and spills of iridescent drinks. Scents of alcohol, candy, earth and the ocean filled the gigantic ballroom. Splashed in neon and dazzled with faery dust, the people undulating, bouncing and dancing were stunning.

The faeries were an easy call for Valor. Most had violet eyes, wild hair colors and clothing that barely covered their skin. Their multishaded—and colored—skin glittered with dust. Demons sported red eyes and dressed a little darker, though not all of them. A horned woman with an undulating spotted tail had a reason to show off her steel abs and high breasts. Valor had never seen blue areolae on a woman before. Fascinating.

A few sets of eyes glowed as Kelyn led her through the melee and toward the center of the dance floor. A sniff of faery dust signaled to Valor that she'd probably get high from this experience. Awesome!

Her lover danced away from her, but not too far, finding the beat in his bones and swaying his hips in time with another dancer who Valor wasn't sure was male, or female, or perhaps both. Chrome scales moist with perspiration grew along the dancer's hairline, and down its neck and most of the exposed skin that was covered by a simple black sheath.

It was a different crowd from the folks the Decadent Dames served. And standing amid the crazy wildness made Valor shout in joy and end with snorting laughter.

"This rocks so hard!" she shouted over the noise.

Kelyn's wings swayed in time with the beat as he bounced up to her and, taking her by the fingers, twirled her like a ballet dancer. He spun her up to him and grasped her tightly across the back, bowing to kiss her even as he dipped her beneath a fall of iridescent faery dust.

"I love you, witch!"

"I love you, wings and all!"

Wings, witchery…and combat boots. It would keep them together for a long and wondrous time.

* * * * *

I hope you enjoyed Kelyn and Valor's story.
I write most of my paranormal stories in a world I
call Beautiful Creatures. All the stories should stand
alone, and you don't have to read one before another
to understand what is happening from story to story.
If you are interested in reading more about some of
the secondary characters mentioned in this book, you
can find their stories at your favorite online retailer.

Stryke's story is MOONLIGHT AND DIAMONDS.
Blade and Zen's story is THE VAMPIRE'S FALL.
Daisy Blu's story is GHOST WOLF
(Denton Marx was also in it).
Eryss's story is TAMING THE HUNTER.
Johnny and Kam's story is THE DARK'S MISTRESS.
Sunday and Dean's story is RACING THE MOON.
Tamatha's story is CAPTIVATING THE WITCH.
CJ and Vika's story is THIS WICKED MAGIC.
Libby and Reichardt's story is THIS SOUL MAGIC.
Malrick pops up for a scene or two in MOONSPUN,
MALAKAI and ENCHANTED BY THE WOLF.
Never has a couple scenes in
THE VAMPIRE HUNTER.
And I couldn't resist mentioning Annja Creed, who
has her own series, ROGUE ANGEL,
written under the Alex Archer pseudonym.
In this series, I wrote THE BONE CONJURER,
which explains how she found the Skull of Sidon.

MILLS & BOON®

n o c t u r n e™

AN EXHILARATING UNDERWORLD OF DARK DESIRES

A sneak peek at next month's titles...

In stores from 19th October 2017:

- **The Witch and the Werewolf** – Michele Hauf
- **Vampire Undone** – Shannon Curtis

MILLS & BOON®

Why shop at millsandboon.co.uk?

Each year, thousands of romance readers
find their perfect read at millsandboon.co.uk.
That's because we're passionate about
bringing you the very best romantic fiction.
Here are some of the advantages of
shopping at www.millsandboon.co.uk:

* **Get new books first**—you'll be able to buy
  your favourite books one month before they
  hit the shops

* **Get exclusive discounts**—you'll also be
  able to buy our specially created monthly
  collections, with up to 50% off the RRP

* **Find your favourite authors**—latest news,
  interviews and new releases for all your
  favourite authors and series on our website,
  plus ideas for what to try next

* **Join in**—once you've bought your favourite
  books, don't forget to register with us to rate,
  review and join in the discussions

Visit **www.millsandboon.co.uk**
for all this and more today!